BOOKS BY STUART WOODS

FICTION

Kisser[†]

Hothouse Orchid[*]

Loitering with Intent[†]

Mounting Fears

Hot Mahogany[†]

Santa Fe Dead[§]

Beverly Hills Dead

Shoot Him If He Runs[†]

Fresh Disasters[†]

Short Straw[§]

Dark Harbor[†]

Iron Orchid[*]

Two-Dollar Bill[†]

The Prince of Beverly Hills

Reckless Abandon[†]

Capital Crimes[‡]

Dirty Work[†]

Blood Orchid[*]

The Short Forever[†]

Orchid Blues[*]

Cold Paradise[†]

L.A. Dead[†]

The Run[‡]

Worst Fears Realized[†]

Orchid Beach[*]

Swimming to Catalina[†]

Dead in the Water[†]

Dirt[†]

Choke

Imperfect Strangers

Heat

Dead Eyes

L.A. Times

Santa Fe Rules[§]

New York Dead[†]

Palindrome

Grass Roots[‡]

White Cargo

Deep Lie[‡]

Under the Lake

Run Before the Wind[‡]

Chiefs[‡]

TRAVEL

A Romantic's Guide to the Country Inns of Britain and Ireland (1979)

MEMOIR

Blue Water, Green Skipper (1977)

[*]A Holly Barker Novel [†]A Stone Barrington Novel

[‡]A Will Lee Novel [§]An Ed Eagle Novel

LUCID INTERVALS

STUART WOODS

G. P. PUTNAM'S SONS
New York

PUTNAM

G. P. PUTNAM'S SONS
Publishers Since 1838
Published by the Penguin Group
Penguin Group (USA) Inc., 375 Hudson Street, New York, New York 10014, USA • Penguin Group
(Canada), 90 Eglinton Avenue East, Suite 700, Toronto, Ontario M4P 2Y3, Canada (a division of Pearson
Penguin Canada Inc.) • Penguin Books Ltd, 80 Strand, London WC2R 0RL, England • Penguin
Ireland, 25 St Stephen's Green, Dublin 2, Ireland (a division of Penguin Books Ltd) • Penguin Group
(Australia), 250 Camberwell Road, Camberwell, Victoria 3124, Australia (a division of Pearson Australia
Group Pty Ltd) • Penguin Books India Pvt Ltd, 11 Community Centre, Panchsheel Park, New
Delhi–110 017, India • Penguin Group (NZ), 67 Apollo Drive, Rosedale, North Shore 0632,
New Zealand (a division of Pearson New Zealand Ltd) • Penguin Books (South Africa)
(Pty) Ltd, 24 Sturdee Avenue, Rosebank, Johannesburg 2196, South Africa

Penguin Books Ltd, Registered Offices: 80 Strand, London WC2R 0RL, England

Library of Congress Cataloging-in-Publication Data

Lucid intervals / Stuart Woods.
p.   cm.
ISBN 978-0-399-15644-1
1. Barrington, Stone (Fictitious character)—Fiction.   2. Attorney and client—Fiction.
3. Private investigators—Fiction.   4. Lottery winners—Fiction.   I. Title.
PS3573.O642L83   2010   2010000527
813'.54—dc22

Printed in the United States of America
1   3   5   7   9   10   8   6   4   2

BOOK DESIGN BY NICOLE LAROCHE

This is a work of fiction. Names, characters, places, and incidents either are the product of the author's
imagination or are used fictitiously, and any resemblance to actual persons, living or dead, businesses,
companies, events, or locales is entirely coincidental.

While the author has made every effort to provide accurate telephone numbers and Internet addresses at
the time of publication, neither the publisher nor the author assumes any responsibility for errors, or for
changes that occur after publication. Further, the publisher does not have any control over and does not
assume any responsibility for author or third-party websites or their content.

This book is for Ted and Barbara Flicker.

LUCID
INTERVALS

1

Elaine's, late.

Stone Barrington and Dino Bacchetti were sitting at their usual table, eating penne with shrimp and vodka sauce, when a young man named Herbert Fisher walked in with a tall young woman.

Stone ignored him. Herbie Fisher was the nephew of Bob Cantor, a retired cop with whom Stone had worked many times. Bob Cantor was Herbie's only connection with reality. Herbie Fisher, in Stone's experience, was a walking catastrophe.

Herbie seated his girl at a table to the rear, then walked back and took a chair at Stone's table. "Hi, Stone," he said. "Hi, Dino."

"Dino," Stone said, "you are a police officer, are you not?"

"I am," said Dino, spearing a shrimp.

"I wish to make a complaint."

"Go right ahead," Dino said.

"What's going on, Stone?" Herbie asked.

Stone ignored him. "There is an intruder at my table; I wish to have him removed."

"Remove him yourself," Dino said. "I'm eating penne with shrimp and vodka sauce."

"You are a duly constituted officer of the law, are you not?" Stone asked.

"Once again, I am."

"Then it is your duty to respond to the complaint of an upstand-ing citizen."

"What kind of citizen?"

"Upstanding."

"I'm not at all sure that the word describes you, Stone."

Herbie, whose head was following the conversation as if he were seated in the first row at Wimbledon, said, "No kidding, Stone, what's going on?"

Stone continued to ignore him. "Dino, am I to understand that you are ignoring a citizen's complaint?"

"You are to understand that," Dino said, mopping up some vodka sauce with a slice of bread. "Do your own dirty work."

"Stone," Herbie said, "I'm rich."

"That's rich," Dino replied.

"No kidding, I'm rich. I won the lottery."

"How much?" Dino asked.

"Don't encourage him," Stone said.

"Thirty million dollars," Herbie replied.

"How much you got left after taxes and paying off your bookie and your loan shark?" Dino asked.

"I'm warning you," Stone said. "Don't encourage him, he's dangerous."

"Approximately fourteen million, two," Herbie replied. "I want to hire you as my lawyer, Stone," he continued.

"Why do you need a lawyer?" Dino asked.

"All rich people need lawyers," Herbie said.

"Could you be more specific?" Dino asked.

"Dino," Stone said, "stop this, stop it right now. He's sucking you in."

"Prove you're rich, Herbie," Dino said.

"I'll be right back," Herbie said. He got up, walked back to where the girl sat, picked up her large handbag, came back to Stone's table and sat down. He lifted up the handbag and opened it wide, displaying the contents to Stone and Dino. "What do you think that is?" he asked.

"Well," Dino said, gazing into the purse, "that would appear to be approximately twenty bundles of one-hundred-dollar bills each, or two million dollars."

"Absolutely correct," Herbie said.

"Do you always walk around with that much money, Herbie?" Dino asked.

"Only since I got rich."

"Oh."

"Stone, I want to retain you as my lawyer. I'll pay you a one-million-dollar retainer in cash, right now."

Stone stopped eating. "Dino, have you had any recent training at recognizing counterfeit bills?"

"Funny you should mention that," Dino said. "We had a guy in from Treasury the day before yesterday who gave us a slide-show presentation on that very subject."

"Would you examine the bills in the bag, please?"

Dino dipped into the bag and came out with a hundred-dollar bill. He held it up to the light, snapped it a couple of times and laid it on the table. "Entirely genuine," Dino said, then he turned to Herbie. "They don't hand out millions in cash at the lottery office, you know. Where did you get it?"

"I cashed a check," Herbie replied.

Stone flagged down a passing waiter. "David," he said, "would you please go and find me a good-sized paper bag?"

"Sure," David replied. He went into the kitchen and came back with a plastic shopping bag. "No paper bags. Will this do?"

"Yes," Stone said, accepting the bag and handing it to Dino. "Will you please put one million dollars of Herbie's money into this bag, Dino?"

"That okay with you, Herbie?"

"Sure, go ahead," Herbie replied.

Dino held the plastic bag close to the purse and counted out ten of the bundles. He handed the bag to Stone. "There you go."

"Just put it on the floor beside me," Stone said, and Dino did so. Stone looked at Herbie for the first time. "All right, you've got my attention; I'll listen for one minute."

"They're trying to kill me," Herbie said.

"Who is trying to kill you?"

"People who want my money."

"Are these people aware that you walk around with two million dollars of it in a woman's handbag?"

Herbie shrugged. "Maybe."

"Herbie, you've been flashing this money around, haven't you?"

"Well, sort of."

"The hooker must know about the money, since it's in her handbag."

"What hooker?"

"The one you walked in here with."

"She's not a hooker."

"Herbie, she's with you; she is, ipso facto, a hooker."

"Part-time, maybe," Herbie admitted.

"Who do hookers work for, Herbie?"

"Me?"

"Besides you?"

"Madams? Pimps?"

"And who do madams and pimps work for, Herbie?"

"They're self-employed, aren't they?"

"They work for or associate with bad people, Herbie. If a hooker knows you've got two million dollars in her handbag, then her madam and her pimp know it too, and if they've had a moment, they've already sold that information to someone who wants to take it from you."

"Sheila wouldn't do that," Herbie said. "She loves me."

At that moment, as if for punctuation at the end of Herbie's sentence, a fist-sized hole appeared in the front window of Elaine's, and a loud report rent the air. This was quickly followed by two more shots.

Everybody hit the floor.

Stone raised his head an inch. "Are you *sure* Sheila loves you, Herbie?"

2

Dino was up and running at the door, clawing at the gun on his belt. He disappeared into the street.

People began cautiously to pick themselves up, look around and brush themselves off. Elaine sat two tables down, unmoving, looking unperturbed. The door opened, and a tall woman of Stone's acquaintance, though not recent, walked in carrying a very feminine attaché case.

Her name was Felicity Devonshire, though she was not called that by anyone who worked with her. She was, in fact, a high official of British intelligence who had formerly been called Carpenter but more recently, after a big promotion, had been dubbed Architect. A man had preceded her into the restaurant, and another followed her. They stationed themselves at the end of the bar, near the door, and watched the room.

Stone got up from the floor, dusted himself off, spotted Felicity and waved her over. They embraced casually. He could feel her ample breasts through her coat and his.

"Stone," she said, "what is going on? Dino is out in the street waving a gun around and shouting into a cell phone, and this place is a mess."

"Just a little after-dinner entertainment," Stone said, taking her coat and holding a chair for her, not missing the sight of her cleavage as she sat down. He took his seat, picked up the plastic bag with the million dollars in it and stuffed it into the hooker's handbag. Shoving the bag at Herbie, he said, "Go away."

Herbie began to protest, but Stone held up a hand like a traffic cop and then waved him back to his own table and the clutches of the perfidious Sheila.

Felicity watched him go. "Isn't that the awful little twit who gave you so much trouble a couple of years ago?"

"I'm afraid so."

"What was in the carrier bag?"

"A million dollars in cash."

"Oh." There were sounds of the sweeping up of glass from the front of the room, and a waiter appeared.

"Would the lady like a drink?" he asked.

"Thank you," Felicity said. "The lady would like a Rob Roy with ice."

Dino came back through the front door, holstering his weapon. "Felicity!" he said. "I thought that was you getting out of the Rolls."

"Hello, Dino," Felicity said warmly, for a member of the British upper class. She allowed herself to be pecked on the cheek. "How are you?"

"Pretty good," Dino said. "Sorry about the excitement; somebody put a couple rounds through the front window."

"Of course," Felicity replied.

Elaine came and stood by the table. "So," she said, "who's paying for the window?"

Stone jerked a thumb toward the rear of the room. "Herbie Fisher, and he's got the cash on him."

Elaine walked back to Herbie's table and slapped him on the back of the head. Stone could not hear what she was saying to him, but Herbie dipped into Sheila's handbag and came up with a thick slice of hundreds. Elaine tucked the money into her bosom without a word and moved on to the table of another regular.

"This has always been such an interesting place," Felicity said, sipping her Rob Roy.

Stone gazed with heartfelt lust at her pale red hair, her unblemished skin, and her very English but nevertheless sexy clothes. "You make it even more interesting," he said.

Felicity patted him on the cheek. "Aren't you sweet."

"See anything outside, Dino?" Stone asked.

"A van, headed downtown," Dino replied. "I didn't have a shot. I called it in." He looked at the floor beside the table. "Where's the million bucks?"

Felicity spoke up. "Do you mean that there was *actually* a million dollars in that carrier bag?"

"It was Stone's retainer," Dino explained. "Herbie Fisher wanted legal representation."

Felicity regarded Stone with a curious glance. "And you declined? This is not the Stone I know."

"So," Stone said, changing the subject, "what brings you to town, Felicity?"

"Her Majesty's service," she replied.

"Oh, come on," Stone said. "Give us a hint."

"We are not in the 'hint' business," she said.

"Of course you are," Stone said. "Hints are what you do. I mean, you never come right out and say anything; you just hint."

"You may have noticed that I have not hinted. What on earth do you mean by refusing a fee of a million dollars?"

"You do remember Herbie, don't you?"

"How could I forget him?" she asked. "Asked to take a photograph of an assignation from a rooftop, he fell through a skylight and broke both of one my colleague's legs, as I recall. Of course, my colleague was already dead, but that hardly matters in the circumstances, does it?"

"It does not," Stone said, "but you have just illustrated why I didn't take Herbie's money. It would have bought me ten million dollars' worth of trouble."

"Quite."

"Would you like some dinner?"

"Yes, please. I couldn't eat what they gave me at the Saudi UN embassy. I believe it was goat or something very like it."

Stone signaled for a menu, and she glanced at it.

"Order for me, would you?"

"You're starved?"

"Ravenous."

Stone turned to the waiter. "Bring her the *osso buco* with polenta and a bottle of the Chianti Classico," Stone said to the waiter.

"That's goat, isn't it?" Felicity asked. "Or something very like it?"

"You know very well that it's veal," Stone said.

"If you say so."

"Excuse me a minute," Dino said, and then headed for the men's room.

"He's being discreet," Stone said. "He knows you want to talk to me about something."

Felicity polished off her Rob Roy. "I wish to engage you," she said.

"I'd be delighted," Stone said.

"Not in *that* capacity," she said.

"In my capacity as an attorney?"

"In one or more of your capacities," she replied, "although Her Majesty can't compete with Mr. Fisher's generosity."

"What did you have in mind?"

"Well, we can do this one of two ways," she replied. "At your hourly rate—two hundred dollars, isn't it?"

"Five hundred," Stone replied.

Felicity blinked.

"Everything has gone up," Stone said.

"Apparently."

"What was the other way we could do this?"

"I had in mind a more result-oriented arrangement," Felicity said.

"What sort of result, and what sort of arrangement?"

"The result would be complete success, and the arrangement would be a payment of one hundred thousand dollars upon achieving it—to include all your expenses and any subcontractors you may require."

"And what is the assignment?"

"The location and disposition of a weasel," Felicity said.

"Have you tried the pet shops?"

"A weasel in the person of a disloyal former employee."

"More information, please. What do you mean by 'disposition'?"

"I mean putting him into my hands or those I may designate. You don't have to kill him. I'm afraid that is all I can tell you until you have signed this," she replied, removing a document from her briefcase.

Stone looked at the title. "The Official Secrets Act?"

"You read well."

"Doesn't this apply only to British subjects?"

"It applies to anyone who signs it," she replied.

"Pounds," Stone said. "Not dollars."

Felicity uncapped a large fountain pen and handed it to Stone.

"I assume this is filled with blood," Stone said.

"Yes, but not yours. Pounds, it is."

Stone signed the document. "All right, tell me about it."

Felicity's *osso buco* arrived. "In the morning," Felicity said, attacking the veal shank.

3

Felicity put down her fork, having demolished her *osso buco* and most of the bottle of Chianti. "That was superb," she said. "Now let's go to your house."

"Delighted," Stone replied. He had forgotten how blunt she could be.

"Would you be delighted to have me as your guest for an indeterminate period?" she asked. "I'm not speaking of years or even months, perhaps a week or two."

"Absolutely delighted," Stone said.

"Then let's be off," Felicity said.

As it turned out, "off" didn't mean in a cab but in a large, somewhat elderly Rolls-Royce.

"Nice ride," Stone said when they were settled into the leather rear compartment and on the way downtown to his home in Turtle Bay.

"That sounds like something one would say about a hunter," Felicity replied, "meaning a horse."

"I know what a hunter is," Stone replied. "How did you acquire this transport?"

"It belongs to the British ambassador to the United Nations, who is, at the moment, in London being instructed. He has placed it at my disposal while he is away, and I represented him at the dinner earlier this evening."

"When did you arrive in New York?"

"About an hour before the dinner," she replied, "and I am quite shattered. I've been traveling since dawn this morning, London time."

"Then we must put you right to bed," Stone said.

She placed a hand on the inside of his thigh and squeezed lightly. "I should bloody well hope so."

THE DRIVER UNLOADED her bags and, at Stone's instruction, took them to the third floor in the elevator. A man emerged from a car behind them. "What are your instructions, ma'am?" he asked.

"Stone, this is Mr. Pickles, one of my security detail. He or one of his colleagues will be required to be in the house when I am here. Don't worry—he will be quite invisible."

"As you wish," Stone said. He showed the man how the security system operated and where the kitchen was. "There's an entrance to the common garden from the kitchen," he said.

"I know," the man replied. They were the only words he spoke.

Stone put Felicity's cases in the dressing room opposite his, then went to his own. There was a note from his secretary, Joan Robertson, on his dresser.

Stone, you really must put your hands on some money if you are going to preserve your credit rating. The bills are piled high.

Stone hated getting notes from Joan, but he knew she was right. He wondered how long it would take him to pry Felicity's hundred thousand pounds from Her Majesty's grasp.

The bedroom was dark when he emerged from his dressing room, with only a shaft of moonlight through a window to light his way. Felicity was already in bed and, as he discovered, already naked.

She drew him to her. "I want to sleep until noon," she said. "Make me even more tired than I am."

Stone did his very best.

THE FOLLOWING MORNING Stone awoke early, snuck out of bed and left a message on Joan's phone not to buzz him during the morning. Then he returned to bed to be there when Felicity awoke. He was sound asleep when he felt a hand run down his belly.

Stone opened an eye. "Did you sleep well?"

"Extremely well," she replied, rolling on top of him and giving him a wet kiss.

"It's not noon yet," he said.

"Then let's use our remaining time well," she said, straddling him and helping him inside her.

AT NOON, STONE'S housekeeper, a Greek woman named Helene, sent up breakfast for two in the dumbwaiter. She must have had a conversation with Mr. Pickles, he thought.

They sat up in bed and ate the large English breakfast off trays.

"Now," Stone said, when they were on coffee, "just what is it you want done?"

Felicity took a dainty sip of her coffee and set the cup down. "There is a person called Stanley Whitestone," she said, "or at least that's what he used to be called back when he worked for us."

"What is he called now?" Stone asked.

"I haven't a clue," she replied.

"Do you have a photograph of him?"

Felicity reached for her briefcase on the bedside table, opened it, produced an envelope and handed it to Stone.

Stone opened the envelope and extracted a photograph—two photographs, actually, a head-on shot and a profile—of a man, apparently in his thirties, with short, dark hair and an aquiline nose. "He's pretty nondescript, isn't he?"

"My service has always preferred nondescript types," Felicity replied. "Perhaps that is why I haven't married."

"Are you required to marry someone in your service?"

"No, but that is the preferred arrangement. It makes security so much simpler if both spouses are employed; then they can tell the same lies about their work to their acquaintances."

"How old is this photograph?" Stone asked.

"Twelve years," she said.

"So he could look quite different now?"

"I would be very surprised if he didn't," she said. "It was one of his gifts to look different when required."

"And what did Mr. Whitestone do to make you willing to pay a hundred thousand pounds to get your hands on him?"

"Quite simply, he betrayed us," she said. "Oh, not to the Soviet Union or the People's Republic of China but to Mammon."

"So he liked money. What else is new?"

"What's new is that he did not retire from our service to make a fortune in the City," she said, referring to London's financial district. "Instead he remained in the service for years while selling information that made him very wealthy."

"To whom?"

"To whomever would pay him for it, presumably."

"I see. And why didn't you have him arrested and tried?"

"He vanished a moment before we knew what he had done,"

she said, "and, in any case, a trial would have been out of the question."

"A great embarrassment?"

"A great humiliation," she replied. "He had risen to near the top. A public recounting of his sins might have destroyed the service."

"Destroyed it? How could that happen?"

"Believe me, it could have happened. Actually, it still could."

"What other information do you have about this man?" Stone asked.

"He has been seen twice only a few blocks from here: in the lobby of the Seagram Building, at Park Avenue and Fifty-second Street," she said.

Stone was well acquainted with the building, since the law firm for which he was of counsel was housed there, as was one of his favorite restaurants, the Four Seasons.

"What does he do there?" Stone asked.

"I've no idea," she said. "He could work there, he could have been visiting someone who worked there—we just don't know."

"Who saw him?"

"A member of Parliament who once worked for our service."

"And what description did he give you?"

"None," she replied.

"I don't understand. If he saw the man, why didn't he describe him?"

"He called our firm and reported the sighting but didn't wish to discuss it on the phone. He made an appointment to meet with a member of my service who works in our UN delegation, but he didn't keep it."

"You make that sound sinister," Stone said.

"It *is* sinister," she replied. "The MP has not been seen again by anyone."

"You're right," Stone said. "That *is* sinister."

"I am happy you perceive it as such," Felicity said, "because I am fond of you, and I would not wish you to suffer for a lack of caution."

"So, let's summarize," Stone said. "Stanley Whitestone is smart, wily, nondescript in appearance and inclined to kill rather than be discovered."

"That is correct."

"Surely there is something else you can tell me about him," Stone said.

Felicity looked thoughtful. "He is fond of women, fine dining and most of the arts—the opera in particular."

"Is there anyone in your service in New York who might recognize him on sight?"

"I might; I knew him as a young agent. He had a peculiar way of walking, as if he had had some childhood disease that slightly crippled him."

"A limp. That could help."

"Not a limp, exactly, just an odd gait. He could walk normally for short periods, if he concentrated, but he always reverted to the gait."

"I'll add an odd gait to his list of traits," Stone said. "You haven't told me what to do with him if I find him."

"Invite him to this house," she said, "then sit on him until I can get here."

"In this country, we call that kidnapping."

"Well, yeessss," Felicity drawled, "there is that. Try not to get caught doing it, or I will have to deny all knowledge of your activities."

"I see," Stone replied, and he did.

4

Felicity dressed and departed in her borrowed Rolls, and Stone dressed and went down to his office. There was little on his desk to demand his attention. He began thinking about where he might borrow a couple of hundred thousand dollars to square his more pressing debts.

The law firm of Woodman & Weld, which employed him to handle cases they did not wish to be seen to handle, came to mind, but Bill Eggers, his law school friend and the managing partner of the firm, was not a ready lender, and it would be humiliating for Stone to beg.

His banker liked him, but Stone had already, with great reluctance, taken out a large loan secured by his house. He could pay some of the bills with his credit cards, but that would buy him less than a month.

There was a knock at the door, and Joan stood there, smiling. "Good morning!" she said cheerfully.

Stone looked at her suspiciously. "What's so good about it? I read your note."

"You'll be happy to know that the money arrived, and I've paid all the bills, including the loan on the house."

Stone stared at her, stupefied. "Have you started drinking in the mornings?"

"Of course not, silly."

"What money are you talking about?"

"The money you were expecting."

"Have *I* started drinking in the mornings?"

"Well, I don't know. Have you?"

"Joan, I am completely baffled. Please explain this to me."

She looked at him as if he were simple. "That nice young man said that he had retained you, and he handed me a million dollars in cash. I couldn't get to the bank fast enough."

"Was that nice young man named Herbie Fisher?"

"Yes, that's the one."

"You give that money back immediately," Stone said sternly. "I have no wish to have anything to do with Herbie Fisher."

"Get it back? Are you insane? This is a gift from God."

"It's a gift from hell," Stone said. "Send it back to him."

"Stone, this is how it works," Joan said, as if to a child. "I get money, I deposit it in your bank account, I send a check to the IRS for the taxes, I pay off the bank loan, I write checks to everyone we owe, and I mail them immediately. How do you expect me to get the money back?"

"Stop payment on the checks."

"You want me to stop payment on a check to the IRS? They'll come and get you."

"Well, stop the others, then."

"The bank has already debited your account to pay off the loan. I can't stop that, either. And those two payments took most of the money."

Stone put his face in his hands and tried not to sob.

"I don't understand," Joan said. "All you have to do now is represent Fisher."

"No, you don't understand," Stone said. "You've sold my soul to the Devil."

"No, I've just paid your bills with money you earned or are going to earn."

"I dread to think of what I'm going to have to do to earn it," Stone said.

"Well, just chip away at the retainer with little jobs for Herbie."

"A little job for Herbie has a way of becoming a minefield."

"Well, then, tread carefully," Joan said. She turned and flounced back down the hallway to her office. Then she stopped and came back. "I forgot to tell you that that woman was back yesterday."

"What woman?"

"The one who stands across the street with that big man and just stares at the house. She's been there for three of the past five days."

"Dolce," Stone said tonelessly.

"Eduardo Bianchi's daughter?"

"What, didn't you know that?"

"I've never seen her before," Joan replied. "I thought she was locked in a rubber room in her father's house. What is it with you and that woman, anyway?"

"You wouldn't believe me if I told you," Stone said wearily.

"Try me."

"All right, Dolce and I once had a . . . thing."

"A thing?"

"We were very, very briefly married."

"You? Married?" she began laughing.

"It's not funny."

"It's funnier than you know. I can't imagine such a thing."

"Neither can I," Stone replied. "It seemed like a good idea at the time. Until she started shooting at me."

"*That's* who shot you that time, right before I came to work for you?"

"That's who shot me."

"It was just a flesh wound, right?"

"It hurt a lot."

"And after that, the old man locked her up?"

"If he hadn't, the District Attorney would have locked her up in a much less welcoming place. I think Eduardo may have bought himself a judge to keep her out of the slammer. Come to think of it, he may have already owned a judge or two."

"How does one *own* a judge?" Joan asked.

"Don't be naïve. One *buys* a judge. With money."

"Oh. I didn't know that sort of thing still goes on."

"It has never stopped. Only the price has changed."

"I've still got that gun you gave me in my desk drawer," Joan said. "If she crosses to this side of the street, I'm going to shoot her."

"Joan, do not shoot her unless she shows you a gun. *Then* shoot her. I'll get you off, I promise."

"Well!" Joan said, then flounced off again.

"Get me Bob Cantor!" Stone shouted after her. He had found, over the years, that one got more respect if someone else placed one's phone calls.

Seconds later his phone buzzed. "Cantor on line one," Joan said.

Stone picked up the instrument. "Morning, Bob," he said.

"To the rest of the world, it's afternoon," Bob replied.

"Oh, sorry. I had a late breakfast meeting."

"I'll *bet* you did," Bob said. "What's up?"

"Work," Stone said. "How soon can you round up Willie and Peter Leahy and get to my office?"

"Hang on." Bob put him on hold, and then he came back. "Half an hour. Willie and Peter are here now."

"Half an hour is good," Stone said.

"How long is this going to take?"

"It depends on how lucky we get," Stone said.

"Oh, one of those."

"Yeah, one of those," Stone said. "See you in half an hour."

5

Bob Cantor and the Leahy brothers arranged themselves in chairs around the coffee table in Stone's office. Cantor had been a detective in the 19th Precinct squad when Stone had been on the force; the Leahys were of a later vintage, but Bob trusted them, so Stone did, too.

"What we've got here . . ." Stone began, then stopped. "No, that's not it. I was going to say a missing person, but it's more than that."

"A missing person who doesn't want to be found?" Bob asked.

"That's a lot closer, but there's more," Stone said. "All I can do is tell you everything the client has told me."

"Who's the client?" Bob asked.

"I'm afraid I've signed a document that prevents me from answering your question," Stone said. "Let's just say it's somebody from overseas."

"Okay, let's say that," Bob replied, and the Leahys nodded as one man, as they did almost everything. The brothers were not twins but very close.

Stone handed each of the three men a copy of the photograph Felicity had given Stone. "This man used to be employed by an intelligence agency. His name used to be Stanley Whitestone."

"How old is the photo?" Cantor asked.

"Twelve years. It was, apparently, the last picture anyone ever took of him."

"Was he a spy?"

"I'm not sure what his duties were, but let's assume he was. It will make it easier to understand how hard it is going to be to find him."

Cantor shrugged. The Leahys looked sleepy.

Stone buzzed Joan. "Could you bring us a pot of coffee, please?"

Stone continued. "Mr. Whitestone left his employers under very suspicious circumstances, only a day before their suspicions were confirmed. His crime was selling information to people who used it to make money."

"Did his employers turn over his finances?"

"I haven't been told, but it is what they would do."

"Did they come up with anything that might give us a lead?"

"I can inquire about that, but if such information existed, I expect I would already have it."

"So, exactly what do we have to go on?" Cantor asked.

"Three things," Stone said. "One: the photograph. Two: the fact that someone who once knew him saw him twice in the lobby of the Seagram Building during the past few weeks. And three: the person who saw him, who was, incidentally, a member of the legislature of his country, has not been heard from again."

"Somebody offed him?" Willie Leahy asked, coming to life.

"That is the assumption," Stone said, "so watch your ass."

Joan came in with a coffee tray. "Did you say something about Willie watching my ass?" she asked.

"No," Stone said.

"I was, though," Willie added. "Nice."

"You're sweet," Joan said, flouncing out of the office.

"So," Peter Leahy said, "we stake out the Seagram Building?"

"No," Cantor said. "First, we find out on what days Whitestone was spotted. Then we review the security tapes. I can get hold of those."

"Good idea," Stone said. "Excuse me a minute." He went to his desk, picked up his phone and dialed Felicity's cell number, which was on a card she had given him.

"Yeesss?" she drawled.

"Can you give me the dates on which Whitestone was seen in the Seagram Building?" he asked.

"One moment," she said. He heard high heels on a marble floor, then a door closing. "To the best of my recollection, one of the dates was near the end of last month. The other was a couple of weeks before, but that's the best I can do."

"Thank you. Have you, in the light of day, remembered anything else at all that might help me?"

"I'm afraid not. See you in the early evening." She hung up.

Stone walked back to the sofa and sat down. "Both sightings were last month: one near the end of the month, one a couple of weeks earlier. The client couldn't be more specific."

"Anything about personal habits?" Cantor asked.

"Women, fine restaurants, and fine arts, especially the opera."

"We're not going to have to go to the opera, are we?" Willie Leahy asked.

"You are, unless the Seagram tapes pan out," Stone said.

Willie made a disgruntled noise.

"I like the opera," Peter said.

Stone was surprised that he liked something his brother didn't. "Okay, you can volunteer for the opera house."

Cantor was looking at the photograph. "If a guy wants to get lost, he has to do one of two things: he has to go somewhere nobody would think to look for him, or he has to change his appearance, or both."

"He's not a Nazi war criminal," Stone said. "It's unlikely that he would have a network of supporters; he'd have to disappear on his own. Of course, he probably had time to set up an identity, and he probably was acquainted with people who could supply documents."

"What country are we talking about, Stone?" Cantor asked.

"Why do you want to know?"

"Because I want to know fucking everything you can tell me and because it might matter."

"Britain."

"Then he'd lose his accent for starters. A Brit accent is too easy to remember."

Peter Leahy was looking at the photo. "He might have lost some hair, too. He's got kind of a high forehead, and the hair in front of his sideburns is thin."

"He's had twelve years to go gray, too," Willie said. "And most guys gain some weight in early middle age."

Cantor spoke up. "British guys love their tailors; I'll bet he's still wearing Savile Row suits but not from whoever made his clothes in the old days. That's one of the things the tracers would check first. Let's find out what English tailors are working in town."

"Good idea," Stone said, "and I'm sure you'll have some others. But right now the Seagram Building security tapes are our best bet."

"I agree," Bob said, standing up. The Leahys stood up with him.

"Let's talk in the morning," Stone said. "Things will come to you in your sleep."

The three men filed out, and Joan appeared at the door. "Herbie Fisher is here to see you," she said, then raised a hand to stop his response. "He knows you're here, because he just saw his uncle Bob come out of your office, and he's paid for your time in advance."

Stone sighed. "All right, send him in, but interrupt me after five minutes. Make up a meeting or something." He sat down and awaited his fate.

6

Herbie Fisher walked into Stone's office wearing a surprisingly good suit. "Hey, Stone," he said. "Thanks for taking my case."

"What case?" Stone asked.

"*My* case," Herbie said plaintively. "I told you last night."

"You told me somebody was trying to kill you."

"Right," Herbie said. "That's my case."

"Herbie," Stone said with as much patience as he could muster. "You are an attorney, are you not?" Herbie had gotten some sort of degree from an Internet diploma mill and had actually passed the bar exam—or, more likely, had paid someone to take it for him.

"Yeah, sure," Herbie said, "I'm a bona fide lawyer."

"Well, you're a member of the bar," Stone said. He had seen evidence of the fact in a list of those passing the exam in a legal newspaper. "And as such, you should know that people trying to kill you is not a legal case."

"Sure, it is," Herbie replied, with the confidence of a newly minted pseudo-attorney.

"How is it a case?" Stone asked. "Are you suing somebody? Is somebody suing you?"

"Not yet," Herbie said, failing to choose an option. "But I'll sue, if I can find out who's trying to kill me."

"Well, Herbie, you let me know when you find out, and I'll sue them for you."

"Great!" Herbie said, as if his prayers had been answered.

"Anything else?" Stone asked, looking at his watch.

"That's a nice watch," Herbie said. "What kind is it?"

"It's a Cartier," Stone said.

Herbie produced a small notebook and took a pen from his pocket. "How do you spell that?"

"T-H-A-T."

"No, that Cardeay name."

Stone spelled it for him.

"Where did you buy it?"

"From Cartier," Stone replied. "They have a big store on Fifth Avenue and Fifty-seventh Street."

Herbie wrote that down, too.

"Is that an English suit you're wearing?" Stone asked.

"Yeah, do you like it?" Herbie replied.

"It's very becoming. Who made it for you?"

"An English tailor."

"What's his name?"

"Sam Leung," Herbie replied.

"Leung is a Chinese name," Stone pointed out.

"Yeah, but he makes English suits. He makes any kind of suit you want."

Stone jotted down the name. "Where is he?"

"Lex and about Sixty-fourth, upstairs."

"Thank you," Stone said. "Anything else?" Why the hell hadn't Joan interrupted him?

"Gee, I don't know. Why don't we just talk?"

"Talk about what?" Stone asked, intrigued by this turn in the conversation.

"I don't know," Herbie said, shrugging. "What do lawyers and clients talk about?"

"Legal problems," Stone said.

"Like wills?"

"Sometimes." Stone looked at his watch again.

"You gotta be somewhere?"

"I have another meeting," Stone said.

"With who?"

"With a client." Stone's phone buzzed, and he picked it up. "Yes?"

"You said to interrupt you after five minutes."

"It's been at least half an hour," Stone replied.

"No, it just seems that way when you're with Herbie."

"You have a point. Send him right in as soon as he arrives."

"Herbie?"

"No, my other client."

"Oh, *that* client," Joan said, then hung up.

"You'll have to excuse me, Herbie," Stone said, looking at his watch again.

"Why? What did you do?"

This was turning into an Abbott & Costello routine. "Another client is due here right now, and I have to see him."

"Can't I stay until he arrives?" Herbie asked.

"No, he wouldn't like that. It's a client confidentiality thing."

"Can't I just wait outside until he's gone?"

"I'm afraid not, Herbie. Good day."

"Good day," Herbie repeated. "I like that—'Good day.'"

"Good day," Stone said again. "It means you're leaving."

"Oh, okay," Herbie said, as if the thought had just occurred to him.

Stone stood up and offered his hand. "Good day. I'll see you when you have a legal problem to discuss."

Herbie shook his hand. "Good day, Stone."

"Good day and good-bye," Stone said. He pointed at the door. "That's the way out."

"Won't I run into your client if I go out that way? That would be a breach of confidentiality, wouldn't it?"

"I'll just have to risk it," Stone said. "Joan!" he shouted. "Show Mr. Fisher out!"

Joan emerged from her office. "This way, Mr. Fisher," she said, and Herbie followed her to the door like a puppy.

Stone picked up the phone and dialed Bob Cantor.

"Cantor."

"Bob," he said, "do you have some special technique for getting rid of your nephew?"

"I just tell him to get the fuck out," Cantor replied.

"I don't know why I didn't think of that," Stone said. "Herbie was wearing a very nice suit."

"Yeah, he's dressing better since he got rich."

"He said his suit was made by a tailor named Sam Leung at Lexington and Sixty-fourth. You might show Mr. Leung the photo of Stanley Whitestone."

"Yeah, okay. I'll call Willie. He and Peter are canvassing tailor shops right now."

"Any luck with the Seagram Building security tapes?"

"I got somebody running them down right now."

"Let me know if you come up with anything."

"Well, yeah, Stone. What else did you expect?"

"Bob, was Herbie dropped on his head as a baby?"

"I've often wondered that myself," Cantor replied. "See ya."

Stone hung up. Then Joan came in again.

"I've got news," she said.

"What news?'

"Dolce is hanging out across the street again. You want me to shoot her?"

Stone thought for a moment. "No, but call Eduardo Bianchi's secretary and find out if he'll see me for lunch tomorrow."

7

Stone drove out to the farthest reaches of Brooklyn, to Eduardo Bianchi's elegant Palladian home on the beach. He was greeted at the door by the wiry and slightly sinister butler who had served Eduardo for as long as anyone could remember. Rumor had it that the man had once served as an assassin for Eduardo back in the days when he had been operating as a Mafia chief of such rank that his name was not known even at the capo level. No law enforcement agency had ever recorded him, followed him or, apparently, even known of his existence.

Now Eduardo Bianchi operated at a level where mayors, governors and even presidents sought his counsel, and he served on the boards of a number of New York's most prestigious arts organizations and charities.

Stone joined Eduardo—now probably in his late eighties if not older—at a table shaded by a wide umbrella overlooking the Roman-style pool.

"Stone," Eduardo said, rising and offering his hand, which was cool, dry and strong, "How very good to see you. Please sit down and have some lunch."

Stone took a chair and, once again, marveled at the old man's youthful appearance and elegant tailoring. "You're looking very well, Eduardo."

"Thank you, Stone," Eduardo said, pouring him a glass of Pinot Grigio from a chilled bottle. "What are you working on these days? Your career is always so interesting to me."

"At the moment, I'm trying to locate a gentleman who left a British intelligence agency some years ago with a great deal of knowledge that he put to work in the marketplace."

"Fascinating," Eduardo replied. "And for whom are you trying to locate him?"

"For his former employers."

"You actually know people in British intelligence?"

"Only one person, really, but she is well placed in that community."

"And what will they do with this gentleman when you have found him? Slit his throat in some quiet, English-gentlemanly way?"

"I have been assured that that will not occur, or I would not have accepted the job."

Eduardo smiled. "Ah, you are such an ethical man, Stone. You know, it is often said that violence never solves anything, but I have found over the years that the correct degree of violence, discreetly applied, can solve a great many things."

Stone was surprised; Eduardo rarely made reference to that part of his past.

Lunch was served: langoustine on a bed of saffron rice with much garlic butter. The Pinot Grigio was a perfect accompaniment.

Stone waited until the dishes had been taken away and coffee served before speaking of why he had come. "Eduardo, there appears to be a problem that I need your help in resolving."

"Something requiring violence?" Eduardo asked, a small smile playing across his lips.

"Nothing like that," Stone said. "It's a family matter."

"I was of the impression that all your family had passed on," Eduardo said.

"I was referring to your family, Eduardo."

A shadow seemed to pass over the old man's face. "Most of my family have passed, too, except my sister and my daughters, Anna Maria and . . . Dolce."

"It is of Dolce I speak," Stone said.

"Ah," Eduardo replied.

"She has been spending considerable amounts of time across the street from my house, accompanied by a large man."

"Yes," Eduardo said, "a reliable fellow."

"I have begun to feel uncomfortable about her presence, and my secretary is very worried."

Eduardo looked surprised. "Does Dolce have some problem with your secretary?"

"Oh, no," Stone said quickly. "It's just that her office window is at street level, and she sees Dolce standing there two or three days a week. This has been going on for about a month."

Eduardo looked bleakly into his coffee cup, then took a small sip. "I am afraid I have been foolish, Stone," he said. "Dolce seemed to have improved greatly over the past months, becoming again much the sweet daughter she once was. As a result, I have permitted her to leave the house and make trips into the city, accompanied by Mario, of course. He is quite fond of her."

"I thought that in view of my past . . . difficulties with Dolce that you might wish to know of her visits to my neighborhood."

"Yes," Eduardo said. "You are quite right to inform me of this. You, as well as anyone, have personal knowledge of how dangerous Dolce could be when she was—how shall I put it?—not herself."

Stone nodded. "I am concerned for her safety," he said.

Eduardo shook his head. "I believe you should, perhaps, be more concerned with your own."

"Then you think she may be relapsing?"

"I am very much afraid that she has already relapsed," Eduardo said.

Stone said nothing.

Eduardo took a deep breath and sighed. "She did not come home yesterday," he said.

"She eluded Mario?" Stone asked.

"Mario is recovering in a hospital," Eduardo replied, "from a knife wound. Either he was very lucky to survive or Dolce was extremely skillful. She was taught these things by my man." He nodded in the direction of the butler, who was standing a discreet distance away, watching everything. "She could not have been more than fourteen years," he said sadly.

"I see," Stone said, because he could not think of anything else to say.

"You may be sure that she is being sought by acquaintances of mine," Eduardo said. "I have so far been able to avoid involving the police, and I hope that you will do so as well."

"Of course," Stone said.

"And I would be grateful if your secretary could call mine should Dolce visit your neighborhood again."

"Certainly," Stone replied.

ON THE DRIVE home, Stone felt a dread he had not felt since the day Dolce had shot him. The wound, he realized, had been deeper than he had believed.

He drove around his block, looking for Dolce, before he pulled into his garage and closed the door behind the car.

He went into the house and to Joan's office.

"How was lunch?" she asked, and she wasn't asking about lunch.

"Yesterday Dolce knifed her bodyguard, then disappeared," he said. "I want you to keep the outside office door locked. Don't let anyone in until you have seen who it is."

"Don't you worry," Joan said. She opened her desk drawer, removed the officer's Model 1911 .45, racked the slide, put the safety on and put it back into the drawer with the hammer cocked.

8

When Stone walked into Elaine's, Dino was already half a drink ahead of him.

"You look worried," Dino said, as Stone sat down.

"I didn't know it showed," Stone replied, as a waiter set a Knob Creek on the rocks before him.

"Always," Dino said.

"Dolce's on the loose," Stone said, taking a swig from the drink.

Dino's face fell. "Bring us both another one," he said to the waiter, then turned back toward Stone. "How the hell did she escape?"

"I had lunch with Eduardo a few weeks ago, and to my shock she made an appearance at the table."

"She was running around loose?"

"She appeared to be her old, premurderous self. Eduardo allowed her to go to the city on shopping trips, accompanied by an ape named Mario, and she started hanging around across the street from my house. It gave Joan the willies."

"I'm armed," Dino said, "and it gives *me* the willies."

"Then yesterday Dolce slipped a knife into Mario and vanished."

After looking carefully around the restaurant, Dino summoned a waiter. "Go look in the other dining room and see if there's anybody in there." Elaine used the other room for parties.

"There's nobody," the waiter said. "The lights aren't even on."

"Go look anyway," Dino said, "and look good."

The waiter went, looked and returned. "Nobody in there," he said.

"Thanks," Dino said.

"Don't get all squirrely on me, Dino," Stone said, but he was happy when the second drink arrived.

"I suppose Eduardo's got the troops out looking for her," Dino said. He had once been married to Eduardo's other daughter, Anna Maria, who, in rebellion, called herself Mary Ann. He knew the family well.

"Does he still have troops?" Stone asked.

"Eduardo knows people who know people who have troops. The last thing he wants is for Dolce to do something that gets noticed by the media."

"Like Mario?"

"Mario was smart enough to call somebody. He'd have died on the street before he'd have gone to an ER. You, on the other hand, would be calling 911 before you hit the pavement."

"You bet your ass I would," Stone said, sipping his new drink. "The really weird thing is, Eduardo told me that his butler—what's that guy's name?"

"Pietro," Dino said. "*That* guy really gave me the willies."

"Pietro taught Dolce to use a knife when she was a teenager. Eduardo implied that she was good enough to disable Mario without killing him."

"Now that is very good indeed," Dino said. "Somehow I don't

think she'll have as much consideration for you, unless it's to let you die more slowly. She would want to watch."

"We'd better order dinner before I order another drink," Stone said.

"I think you'd better keep your wits about you," Dino said. "Where's Felicity?"

"She called and said she was hung up in a meeting; she'll join us here." A waiter brought menus.

Felicity came in and sat down before they could order. She gave them both a kiss on the cheek. "Order for me, will you, Stone?"

"Of course."

"But something light. I think I gained five pounds last night."

"How about the Dover sole?"

"Perfect."

He ordered the same for both of them, and Dino ordered pasta. He also ordered Felicity a Rob Roy.

"So," Felicity said, "have you begun our little project?"

"I'm not listening," Dino said.

"You may listen," Felicity replied. "In fact, you may even be of help. Go on, Stone."

"My guy has gotten access to the security tapes at the Seagram Building on or around the dates you gave us," Stone said. "We'll review them tomorrow."

"Good thought," she said. "What else?"

"One of my guys also mentioned an Englishman's love of his tailor, and it seems likely that he's still having his clothes made."

"A very good possibility," Felicity said. "My father practically went into mourning when his tailor died."

"We're looking at New York tailors who make English-style suits."

"Very good."

"Since Dino can listen now, may I show him the photo?"

"Better yet, I'll give him a copy," Felicity said, opening her brief-case and handing the picture to Dino.

"Who's the guy?" Dino asked.

Stone explained. "Do you have access to the FBI's facial compari-son program?"

"I can manage that," Dino said.

"I'm sure Felicity would appreciate it if you'd run that photo-graph. Who knows, maybe we'll get a match."

"It's twelve years old," Felicity reminded him.

"Ask them if they can age him twelve years," Stone said.

"Okay."

"And ask them to give him a nose job, too."

"Yeah, that's quite a honker," Dino said, looking at the man's profile.

Felicity laughed. "Yes, it is quite a honker."

"There's something else I have to tell you," Stone said to Felicity, "which is unrelated to your work."

"And what might that be?" She took a sip of her Rob Roy.

"A woman has been hanging around across the street from my house for . . . a while."

"I'm not surprised," she said.

"The thing is, she's dangerous."

"And what makes her dangerous?"

"Mental illness and a considerable facility with a knife."

"An unattractive combination," Felicity said. "What does she look like?"

"Like a Sicilian princess," Stone said.

"That's a good description," Dino agreed. "It's also what she is, right to the bone."

"Should I go about armed?" Felicity asked.

"It couldn't hurt," Stone said. "I'll loan you something, if you like."

"Oh, I can manage," Felicity said.

9

Stone sat in Bob Cantor's van, parked right outside the Turtle Bay house, and looked at the surveillance tapes from the Seagram Building.

"I've copied them and done some editing and enhancing," Cantor said, "so what you're seeing is the most likely candidates."

Stone watched a videotape of men entering the building and the elevators. An hour later he said, "Stop."

"Which one?" Cantor said.

"The one with the hat, the beefy one."

"Why him?"

"It's his walk, it's not completely natural. Do you see what I mean?"

Cantor rewound and watched the man. "Yeah, I see what you mean about the walk. It's like one leg is stiffer than the other. Maybe he has an artificial leg?"

"I don't think so, but I was told he walks funny."

"Who wears a hat these days?" Cantor asked. "Nobody."

"Maybe an English gentleman," Stone said.

"Are his clothes custom-made?"

"Freeze the shot," Stone said, then looked carefully at the man's back. "I think so."

"How can you tell?"

"For a start, his suit jacket has double pleats; ready-made suits more commonly have a center pleat. Then look at his shoulders: there's no wrinkle near the collar, and there's no puckering on the center seam. The sleeve has four buttons, too, and it looks like they have buttonholes. A man could get that from an expensive shop, but it all adds up to bespoke."

"Bespoke?"

"What the Brits call custom-made. He's showing more shirt collar than usual, too. His shirts are probably custom as well, so make a note to check out shirtmakers, starting with Turnbull and Asser. And the hat is a Trilby, taupe in color. That's very British. See if you can find a shot of him in the elevator."

"Why?"

"Because a gentleman removes his hat in an elevator."

Cantor ran through some more shots at high speed. "Here we go," he said.

"Maybe we can see what floor button he pushes," Stone said, but the man didn't push a button. He removed his hat, though, revealing a head full of dark hair, gray at the temples. The camera was set high, in a corner, and they could see only the back of his head.

"He's not balding," Cantor said.

"Maybe. He didn't push any buttons; he was apparently going to a floor somebody else had already pushed." Sure enough, the man followed another passenger off the elevator.

"That's an express elevator," Cantor said. "It goes only to the higher floors."

"Yeah," Stone said. "The trouble is, none of what we see here actually makes him as our guy. Okay, his clothes look English, and he wears a hat; that's about it. We don't know if our guy has gained a lot of weight over the years or gone bald. I can't tell if he's wearing a toupee. We can't really see his nose, either."

"Well there's one thing about him I like," Cantor said.

"What's that?"

"Of all the people we've looked at on this date, he has the most to recommend him."

"Good point. What's the date?"

"A couple of weeks ago."

"Let's look at the earlier dates, too," Stone said, and Cantor racked up another cassette and began his search. An hour later he was done.

"Nope," Cantor said. "We don't have him on the earlier dates, just the most recent one."

"How many men appear on both dates?" Stone asked.

"I don't know, dozens, maybe many dozens. A lot of them work in the building every day."

"Well, this guy, Mister Smith, doesn't seem to work in the building. I think he's visiting."

"Visiting who?"

"Could be anybody—doctor, lawyer, dentist."

"Are there dentists in the Seagram Building?"

"I don't know. They'd be really, really expensive dentists, though, if they had offices there."

"Nah," Cantor said, "medical professionals need special plumbing and electrical; they mostly stick to buildings that specialize."

"Can we do more to identify the floor he got off on?"

"I've tried," Cantor said, "but people's heads were in the way of the buttons."

"Do we have shots of him returning to the lobby?" Stone asked.

"I haven't seen any," Cantor replied. "I'll go through them again, though."

"Let me know what you find," Stone said, getting up from his seat. "I can't look at that screen anymore." He looked through one of the van's darkened windows across the street. No sign of Dolce. "Bob, there's something else."

"What?"

"I'm being stalked by a tall, slender, dark-haired woman. She stands across the street and stares at my house."

"Maybe she's in real estate."

"No. I know her. She was traveling with a keeper, but she knifed him the day before yesterday, then disappeared."

"You want somebody in the house?"

"Yes, please. Joan is frightened, and I have a houseguest, too. I don't want them hurt."

"Do you want the stalker hurt?"

"No, not if it can be avoided."

"I'll put Peter Leahy on it," Cantor said.

"Tell Peter to cuff her, if he can, but tell him to watch his ass; she's very good with a knife."

"Jesus, Stone, where do you find these women?"

"There's only one like her," Stone replied, "and she found me."

10

Stone sat with Felicity, tucked into a corner table at La Goulue, one of his favorite restaurants. "You seem a little tired," he said, as she took her first sip of her Rob Roy.

"It's the job," she said, "and it doesn't change much when I'm out of the country. Of course, when I'm in New York I have you to, ah, entertain me."

"The pleasure is all mine."

She smiled. "Don't you believe it."

"Tell me about the job," Stone said. "As much as you can anyway."

"There are the usual things," she said. "Agents get themselves killed, sometimes for little or no reason. Last month I had two die in a car crash in Rome. Of course it was on that racetrack the Italians call the Piazza del Popolo. It's insane."

"I'm sorry."

"I have to make the phone calls and write the letters, and even in the case of the car crash, the spouses don't want to believe there wasn't foul play. They've spent years worrying that a husband or wife will be taken out by the opposition, and I think it's something of a letdown when they're lost to a simple accident."

"Is running the firm more fun than working in it?"

Felicity thought about that for a moment. "Marginally," she said finally. It's more fun to know everything instead of just about your own assignment; it's fun to put the pieces together when you have all the information, or at least all of it that's available."

"You don't always have it all?"

"Of course not. Even in my position I can't know everything, and Whitehall and Downing Street are insatiable; they have an almost religious belief that their service is all-seeing, all-knowing. We could be closer to that if they would triple our budget, but that's not going to happen unless there's another war."

"What about terrorism?"

"MI-5 does all the domestic stuff; we're the foreign service, and we did get about a twenty percent bump in the years after 9/11, but inflation has eaten that up. I still have to send one agent out when I'd rather send two or three. Deciding where to allocate the resources is the hardest part of the job."

"Is there anything fun about it?"

"The equipment is fun. We've long since surpassed that Q fellow in the Bond films." She leaned close to his ear. "I have a pen in my purse that can administer a drug without your feeling it. Then I could walk out in the middle of dinner, and you'd be dead of cardiac arrest before you got to dessert. And the autopsy would reveal nothing." She smiled. "We call it the toe tag."

"Is that the sort of information Stanley Whitestone was selling?"

She grimaced. "He was selling everything but, thank God, not the toe tag; that was after his time. If word got out about that, there would be husbands dropping dead every day in their dozens, and not a few wives, too."

"That reminds me," Stone said. He produced his iPhone, pressed a couple of buttons and showed her a minute or so of the Seagram footage. "I don't know if this is the guy," he said, "but we eliminated all the other candidates. This one has the virtue of dressing British and walking funny."

"The quality is very good," she said. "Amazing, in fact. Where did you get the equipment?"

"The cameras are high-definition, off-the-shelf stuff; the iPhone comes from the Apple Store at Fifty-ninth and Fifth."

"Let me see it again," she said, and she watched closely as he reran it.

"What do you think?"

"I think he walks funny," she said, "and I've been trying to picture exactly how and why Stanley walked funny. If this is Stanley, then all that weight he has gained has accentuated his gait." She handed the phone back to Stone. "This is a very good effort," she said. "It would have taken a lot longer if my people had done it. Can you e-mail me the images?"

"Of course." Stone tapped a few buttons. "It's done."

"Now," she said, "can you find this man?"

"If he returns to the Seagram Building," Stone said. "My guy has alerted security there to keep an eye out for him."

"Have we heard from Dino and the FBI yet?" she asked.

"No, the FBI takes longer than my guys and your guys put together, but it's a remarkable system for plucking faces out of the files. Do you think Stanley Whitestone might have committed a crime in this country?"

"I don't doubt it for a moment," she said, "but I'd be very surprised if the FBI or anybody else has caught him doing it."

"Well, if he has been caught at something and his image pops up, the FBI will be all over this."

"And if he should fall into their hands," she said, emptying her drink, "he'll tell them everything he knows about us and all he can make up, just to stay out of prison."

"Perhaps I should have thought of that before asking Dino to do this."

"No, I think it was the right thing; it might turn up something, and we might get to him before the FBI does."

"Whatever you could say. I might still be able to stop Dino."

"No, this isn't going to be easy; we're going to need every resource available. The trail is very cold."

"As you wish."

She looked at him closely. "Subject change," she said. "Why are you still alone?"

Stone blinked. "Why are you?" he asked.

"My work," she replied. "Now back to you."

"I don't know, really. They come and they go. I get dumped a lot."

"Why?"

"I think they think I'm incapable of commitment."

"Is that true?"

"No, I don't think so, but I'm very careful about who I commit to. Don't you think you're blaming too much on your work?"

"I tried to explain this before: it works better if we're both in the service. We are the only people who understand us. Say I married some barrister or stockbroker. There would be a constant schedule of work-related social events, and I would make very few of them. I work all hours, and men get lonely, just as women do. Men are *not* understanding when you tell them *nothing* about what you do. It drives them crazy."

"I suppose I can understand that, but you've told me quite a lot tonight."

Felicity laughed. "If, say, the Chinese or the North Koreans captured you and you told them everything I've told you, they would kill you because you told them nothing."

"See," Stone said, laughing. And then their dinner arrived.

11

Stone was at his desk the following morning when Herbie Fisher appeared at his office door, unannounced. The phone buzzed, and Stone picked it up. "Yes?"

"Mr. Herbert Fisher to see you," Joan said drily.

"Thank you *so* much," Stone said, and hung up. "What can I do for you, Herbie?" he asked.

Herbie came in and took a seat across the desk from Stone. "I know who's trying to kill me," he said.

Stone held up a hand, a stopping motion. "Herbie, think back a couple of years: someone was trying to kill you then, remember? Dattila the Hun?"

"Oh, yeah. I remember that."

"We sued him, remember?"

"Yeah."

"And what happened?"

"Uh, I shot him."

"Right."

"It was easier than suing him."

"Easier for you," Stone said, remembering what he had had to do to keep Herbie from being tried. "If you kill somebody else you think is trying to kill you, the DA is going to remember that little incident with Dattila. You understand?"

"Yeah, I guess so."

"Don't guess, Herbie, *know* it. You can't make a habit of that sort of thing and stay out of prison."

"All right, I know it."

"Now, who's trying to kill you?"

"My bookie," Herbie said.

"And what is his motive?"

"I stopped betting with him."

"You got a new bookie?"

"No, I just stopped betting. I went into the bar he works out of, put a hundred and forty-eight grand on the bar—that squared me with him—and told him I wasn't betting anymore."

"What was his reaction?"

"He didn't take it very well," Herbie said.

"He didn't take it very well how?"

"Well, first he shook my hand and slapped me on the back and offered me a credit line of a quarter million."

"That doesn't sound so bad," Stone said.

"When I told him I wasn't betting anymore he backhanded me across the face and told me if I tried betting with anybody else he would kill me."

"He assumed you would change bookies?"

"I guess."

"I suppose that would upset him."

"I explained it to him: I told him I just wasn't going to bet anymore . . . with anybody. That really pissed him off, like I had violated his constitutional rights or something."

"And you think he took it hard enough to want to kill you."

"Well, if I'm not going to bet anymore, what does he have to lose?"

"Herbie," Stone said, "that may be the first entirely logical thing you've ever said to me. You've just had a lucid interval."

Herbie looked puzzled. "Huh?"

"You paid off your loan shark, too, didn't you?"

"Yeah. I only owed him ninety grand."

"How did he take it?"

"Not very well, either. Of course, he's my bookie's brother, so maybe it runs in the family. He told me I would have to go right on paying the vigorish, and I told him to go fuck himself."

"Who are these people?"

"Joe and Moe Wildstein."

"That sounds like two-thirds of the Three Stooges," Stone said.

"Well, it's not. They're known around town as the Wild Boys."

"Tell me, Herbie—not to digress—why did you decide to stop betting and borrowing with the Wildsteins?"

"The Wild Boys."

"I stand corrected. Why?"

"I thought about it, and I think it's because when you're betting with money you don't have, it doesn't seem real."

"Until they try to collect."

"Well, yeah. But up until that moment, it's like Monopoly money, you know? But if you're laying a bet with money you actually have, it doesn't seem like such a good idea. I mean, you could lose, you know?"

"I can guess," Stone said. "Now let's get back to your lawsuit against the, ah, Wild Boys. Is it both of them you want to sue?"

"They're both trying to kill me," Herbie replied.

"How do you know that?"

"You were in Elaine's when they fired through the window."

"Okay, Herbie, the bullets may have had your name on them—I buy that—but they didn't have Moe and Joe's names on them. The police would have noticed."

"I just have a very strong feeling about it," Herbie said.

"Herbie, being an attorney, as you sort of are, you do understand that your feeling, no matter how strong, is not admissible as evidence in a court of law."

"Well, it ought to be," Herbie said, "when I feel *this* strong about it."

"Let's go back a minute. Did you say that Moe—he's the bookie, right?"

"Right."

"Did he say he was going to kill you?"

"If I bet with anybody else," Herbie said.

"Have you bet with anybody else?"

"I told you, I'm not betting anymore."

"Then Moe has no motive for killing you."

Herbie thought about this. "That's important, isn't it?"

"I think you're getting the picture," Stone said.

"Then I can't sue him?"

"Not until you can prove that he has tried to kill you, and if you're in a position to do that, it would be much faster to let the police take care of it."

"Why?"

"Because, Herbie," Stone said with all the patience he could muster, "lawsuits take months or years, but when the police have good evidence, they make an arrest immediately. That's also cheaper than a lawsuit."

"But he could get bailed out, couldn't he?"

"Not if we can prove that he might try again to kill you."

Herbie nodded gravely. "That makes a lot of sense, Stone."

"Thank you, Herbie. Now, if you'll excuse me, I have other work to do."

Herbie stood. "Yeah, okay, I understand. But . . ."

"But what?" Stone asked and was immediately sorry that he had.

"But what if he hires somebody else to kill me while he's in jail?"

"Herbie," Stone said, "whether it's a civil or a criminal matter, that's a chance you're going to have to take."

"Okay," Herbie said, then left.

Stone took deep breaths, trying to compose himself.

12

Joan came to Stone's office door. "How'd it go with Herbie?" she asked.

"Joan," Stone said, "I'm having a great deal of trouble impressing upon you my desire *not* to see or speak to Herbert Fisher."

"Oh, I completely understand," she said.

"Not completely; otherwise you would not have allowed him into my office only a few minutes ago."

"No, I understand completely," Joan reassured him. "It's just that we have certain ethical obligations to Herbie now."

"Ethical obligations?"

"Yes. We've taken his money, so we owe him our time."

"And just how much of our time do you reckon we owe him?" Stone asked.

"Well, your time, really. About a year: all day, every day, five days a week."

"So you think I should spend all of the next year with Herbie?"

"It's what he's paid you for," she said.

"He didn't pay me, he paid you," Stone pointed out, "and you rashly put the money in the bank and paid all my bills. I'm innocent of this, really."

"You think it's *rash* to put money in the bank, pay taxes and pay bills?"

"Not usually," Stone admitted. "Just when the money comes from Herbie."

"I'm sorry," she said. "I don't see the difference between Herbie's money and that of other clients. I mean, he didn't print it himself, did he?"

"I've been assured it's real," Stone replied. "If it weren't, the bank would have sent the Secret Service over here by now."

The office doorbell rang, and Joan looked over her shoulder. "I hope to God that's not Dolce," she said.

"Can you see who it is?"

"Yes. It's two men in business suits."

"Is there a woman with them?"

"No."

"Then please go and see who they are." Stone rearranged the papers on his desk to appear busy. A moment later, Joan was back with the two men.

"Mr. Barrington, two gentlemen from the Secret Service to see you," she said, and hastily closed the door behind them.

The two men flashed IDs, and Stone shook their hands and offered them seats. "What can I do for the Secret Service this morning, gentlemen?" Stone asked cheerfully, but his stomach didn't feel just right.

"Mr. Barrington," one of them said, "did you make a large cash deposit at your bank recently?"

"No," Stone replied.

"You did not deposit a million dollars in your bank account?"

"Oh, *that* deposit. My secretary did that."

The man removed a plastic envelope containing a banknote and placed it on Stone's desk. "Do you recognize this?" he asked.

Stone leaned forward and examined the note. "I believe I do," he replied. "It appears to be a fifty-dollar bill, United States currency."

"That's what it *appears* to be, certainly, but it is not."

"Then what is it?" Stone asked innocently.

"It's an extremely good counterfeit note," the man replied.

"You could have fooled me," Stone said.

"Have you ever seen it before?"

"I've seen many fifty-dollar bills," Stone replied, "but I don't recall ever having seen this one."

"What was the source of the cash your secretary deposited in your bank account?" the other man asked.

"The funds came from a client."

"And where did he obtain them?"

"From the New York State Lottery, I believe."

"The New York State Lottery does not give people large sums of cash," the man said.

"I thought that was why they were in business," Stone said, "apart from also taking large sums of cash from other people."

"Quite true," the man said, "but their policy is, I believe, to issue a check on the state treasury's funds or to wire transfer winnings to the account of a winner."

"Well, I can't argue that with you," Stone said. "Now that you mention it, when I asked my client where he got the funds and he told me about winning the lottery, I pointed out that very same thing to him."

"And what did he have to say about that?" the agent asked.

Stone shrugged. "I don't suppose it would be a breach of attorney-client confidentiality if I told you he told me he cashed a check."

"On what bank?"

"He didn't mention its name."

"And you think a bank would just give your client a million dollars in cash?"

"After corroborating his balance, certainly."

"Can you tell me how your client managed to include a single counterfeit fifty-dollar bill in a one-million-dollar payment to you?"

"That fifty-dollar bill was not in the cash my client gave me. He gave me only one-hundred-dollar bills."

"Did you look through all the hundreds?"

"No, I did not."

"So, it may have been among the cash he gave you?"

"If it was, it was a mistake of his bank," Stone replied.

"And you don't know which bank it was?"

"No, I don't."

"Would you mind if we asked your client?"

"Not as long as you don't expect me to give you his name," Stone replied. "That would be a breach of attorney-client confidentiality."

"Mr. Barrington," the man said, sighing. "We are agents of the federal government. As an officer of the court you are obliged to help us in our inquiries."

"As long as they don't involve a breach of client confidentiality, I'm happy to help you," Stone replied.

"Could you do this, then: Could you call your client and ask him for the name and address of his bank?"

"I could . . ." Stone began.

"And for his permission to tell us?"

"Now that is something I could do," Stone said. "Will you excuse me for a moment?"

"Of course."

Stone walked to Joan's office. "Will you please call Herbie Fisher and ask him for the name of his bank? Tell him the Secret Service would like to know."

"You mean all that cash was counterfeit?"

"No, apparently only a single fifty-dollar bill was."

"It was all in hundreds."

"I told them that, but they were skeptical."

Joan opened a desk drawer and pulled out a paper band. "There was one of these on each hundred-thousand-dollar bundle," she said.

Stone took the band. "That will do nicely." He returned to his office and handed the band to an agent. "There was one of these around each hundred-thousand-dollar bundle of hundreds," he said. "The name of the bank is printed upon it. Will that do?"

"Yes, I believe it will," the agent said, reading the name of the bank.

"Then I wish you well in your inquiries," Stone said, rising and offering his hand.

"Thank you, Mr. Barrington," the man said, then turned to go.

"I would certainly like to know how all this comes out," Stone said. "If you have a moment to call."

"I'm sorry, but we can't reveal information relating to a case," he said, and then, with his companion, he left.

Stone buzzed Joan.

"Yes?"

"What was the exact amount of the deposit you made?"

"One million dollars."

"Is that on the deposit receipt?"

"Yes, it is."

"Is the receipt stamped and dated?"

"Yes, it is."

"Did you watch the teller count the money?"

"I watched her put it into a counting machine," Joan said.

"And she didn't mention an extra fifty dollars in the stack?"

"She did not."

Stone hung up, baffled.

13

Stone was in his dressing room when Felicity walked in, holding her shoes in her hand. She offered him her lips, and he accepted. "Your feet are tired?" he asked.

"I no longer have feet," she replied, going into the bedroom. "I'm walking on stumps." She began shedding clothes. "What time is dinner?"

"Eight-thirty. We're meeting Dino."

"What a surprise! Wake me in an hour, please."

STONE FINISHED DRESSING, read for a while, then woke her as requested.

"Is it morning?" she asked sleepily.

"Not yet. Another ten hours to go."

She sat up. "A shower," she said.

"Thataway," he replied, pointing.

———

THIRTY MINUTES LATER, she was as fresh as a bouquet of roses.

"How do you do that?" Stone asked.

"Do what?"

"Recover from exhaustion in half an hour?"

"I slept for an hour, remember?"

"Yes, but you still seemed exhausted."

"Not exhausted, just sleepy. I'm quite well now. May we go to dinner? I'm starved."

DINO HAD NOT yet arrived, so Stone ordered a Knob Creek and Felicity's Rob Roy. "How was your day?" he asked.

"Not bad," she replied. "There's someone I'd like you to meet tomorrow."

"Who?"

"I can't tell you."

Stone laughed. "Of course not; it was a silly question."

"I'm thinking of quitting," she said without preamble.

Stone was shocked. "I'm shocked," he replied. "Truly."

"I've got twenty years in, and there's a pension."

"Can one live well on a British civil service pension?"

"One can if one has a comfortable private income, a house in London, another in the Isle of Wight and yet another in the south of France. Daddy died last year, and I was his only child."

"I'm sorry. I didn't know."

"Daddy wasn't sorry," she said. "He had been in pain for a year, and he was glad to go."

"I'm sorry he was in pain. I'm glad he left you well off."

"I would have been *really* well off but for the taxes. Fortunately, Daddy was liquid enough that I didn't have to sell the properties. If I retire, will you come and see me?"

"I will come and see you, retired or not."

She patted his hand. "You're sweet."

DINO ARRIVED, WAVED for his Scotch and sat down. "Good evening, one and all," he said.

"You sound cheerful," Stone said.

"I'm always cheerful," he replied.

"Well . . . no. You are often dour."

"Me, dour?"

"Often."

"Well, I'm not dour tonight," he said.

Felicity spoke up. "Could your good cheer be related to some success with the FBI regarding the photo of Stanley Whitestone?"

"Yes, it could."

"I'm so glad."

Dino pulled an envelope from his pocket. "The FBI photo comparison program pulled this from a bank security camera two blocks up Park Avenue from the Seagram Building." He laid the photo on the table. It was that of a stocky man in a good suit, wearing a hat, entering the bank. "It was a good match."

Stone looked at the photo. "It's no better than the one we got from the Seagram Building," he said.

"Wait, there's another angle," Dino said, producing another photograph and laying it on the table. This one was full face, but from farther away.

Stone and Felicity peered at it.

"Can they enhance it?" Felicity asked.

"This is the enhanced version," Dino said.

"It gives an impression of the same man," Stone said, "but it's too blurry for identification. The Seagram stuff was much sharper."

"The bank equipment isn't as recent," Dino said. "Would you rather have a blurry photograph or no photograph at all?"

"Hobson's choice," Felicity said.

"What?" Dino asked.

"It's Britspeak for no choice at all," Stone replied.

"May I keep these?" Felicity asked.

"Sure," Dino said. "Anybody hungry?" Without waiting for a reply, he waved at a waiter for menus.

"I need red meat," Felicity said. "Sirloin, please, medium rare, *pommes frites.*"

"It shall be so," Stone replied, ordering two.

"Make it three," Dino said.

"DO YOU EVER think of retiring, Dino?" Felicity asked when their steaks were ruins of their former selves.

"Never," Dino said. "I'm going to do the full thirty, and then we'll see."

"You'll have to take a promotion," Stone said.

"Nah, I have an understanding with the commissioner."

"Dino doesn't want to be a captain," Stone explained to Felicity. "He likes to pretend he's still a street cop."

"I don't pretend," Dino said. "I *am* a street cop."

"Yes, but you never see the street, except from the rear seat of your cop-chauffeured car," Stone pointed out.

"I understand, Dino," Felicity said. "Sometimes I wish I were, well, a street agent again."

"They got you cuffed to a desk?" Dino asked.

"A very good description," she replied.

"I wouldn't like that."

"It has its advantages," Felicity said.

"Name one," Dino said.

"I haven't been shot at for quite some time," she replied.

"That's okay if personal safety is important to you."

"It isn't important to you?" Stone asked.

"Nah, I don't mind an occasional bullet in my direction."

"This is news to me," Stone said to Felicity. "I've never heard of Dino's fondness for flying lead."

"I understand what he means," she said. "One remembers the occasions when death was near but passed one by."

"You bet your sweet ass one do," Dino said.

"I remember getting shot in the knee," Stone said. "I didn't find anything to like about it."

"Not even survival?" Felicity said.

"Oh, well, yes," Stone said. "That and not getting shot higher up."

She squeezed his thigh. "I'm grateful for that, too."

14

Stone and Felicity got out of the ambassador's old Rolls-Royce in front of his house. As the car pulled away, the opposite side of the street was exposed, and Stone, standing on his doorstep, fumbling for his key, saw her.

He hustled Felicity inside, locked the door, picked up the nearest phone and pressed the intercom and page buttons. "Willie, pick up any phone."

"I'm here," Willie said.

"Where?"

"In the kitchen."

"She's across the street."

"I'm on it."

"Watch your ass." Stone hung up.

"Your former lady friend?" Felicity asked.

"I wouldn't describe her that way."

"How would you describe her?"

"As the insane daughter of a good friend." They got onto the elevator and started upstairs.

"Isn't it about time you told me about her?" Felicity asked.

Stone sighed. He ushered her off the elevator and into his bedroom, and they began to undress for bed.

"All right," he said. "I met her four years ago. I didn't seek her out; she found me. We saw each other for a while, and it got serious. She suggested we get married, and I didn't refuse her."

"A reluctant bridegroom?"

"No, just one with reservations. She is the daughter of a man named Eduardo Bianchi, an Italian-American of some note."

"The name is familiar, but I can't place him."

"A great many people would say the same thing," Stone replied. "No one really knows Eduardo's true history, but the stories are that, as a young man, he became associated somehow with some Mafia figures. There is disagreement about whether he was ever actually a member, but there is disagreement about almost all the details of Eduardo's life."

"Very interesting," Felicity said.

"There is some evidence to support the idea that he was the man behind, but not a member of, the Commission, which was an organization that tried to impose some order on the criminal elements under it and sometimes succeeded."

"I've heard of that."

"Back in the fifties, when J. Edgar Hoover finally began to believe that the Mafia might just exist, Eduardo is said to have withdrawn even further from the organization, but he is thought to have continued to control it from a distance. Meanwhile, he became a prominent business figure, investing in and serving on the boards of a number of important banks and other financial institutions. Over the years he became a model of respectability in spite of the rumors about his past as well as an important figure in the worlds of the arts and charitable institutions.

"Eduardo lived quietly in a house he built way out in Brooklyn on the water. He maintained offices in Manhattan but did most of his work from home. He entertained judiciously, when it suited him, and sent his two daughters, Anna Maria and Dolce, to fine schools, where they did well. They both worked in various businesses and foundations that Eduardo controlled.

"Anna Maria, who preferred to be called Mary Ann, met Dino at some function in Little Italy, and almost immediately after that she found herself pregnant. It was imparted to Dino that, if he wished his testicles to remain attached to his body, a proposal of marriage would be in order. A boisterous wedding was followed by an even more boisterous marriage, which produced a son, now in a New England prep school.

"A couple of years ago, there was a divorce, and Eduardo insisted on a settlement in Dino's favor, which has enabled him to live well as a newly minted bachelor."

"But you digress," Felicity said. "Tell me about the other daughter."

"We traveled to Venice, where Eduardo was attending a business convocation allegedly attended by the more important members of both the American and Italian Mafias. Dolce and I were married in a small civil ceremony, which was to have been followed a day or two later by a large religious ceremony presided over by a high-ranking Italian cardinal who was influential in the Vatican.

"The day before the second wedding, the husband of a friend of mine was murdered in Los Angeles. You may remember the actor Vance Calder."

"Of course," Felicity said. "You were involved in that?"

"I was involved in the subsequent investigation, and the murderer was identified but never convicted. Dino and I left Venice for L.A., and Dolce began to behave erratically, which was to say, dangerously.

"After a time, the relationship ended, and Eduardo sought psychiatric treatment for Dolce, keeping her in his home. Shortly after that, I received by messenger the torn-out page from the Venetian registry book that Dolce and I had signed. It could only have come from Eduardo.

"The following year, Dolce escaped from her father's house and found me in Palm Beach, where I was working on a case. At a large party she fired several shots at me, but only one struck. Fortunately it was a nonfatal part of my body. She was immediately returned to her father's custody and has remained there since.

"Eduardo and I have remained friends, lunching together several times a year at his home. Recently, Dolce showed improvement, and Eduardo allowed her to be escorted to the city on shopping trips. A few days ago, she knifed her escort and disappeared. She has been seen outside my house several times since then."

"And she still wants to kill you?" Felicity asked.

"I don't know what she wants," Stone said, "but I think it's wise to assume the worst. That's why I had a man in the house, and he's looking for her now. He will have called others to help."

"Do you think we're safe here?" Felicity asked.

"Yes, or I would have sent you away by now."

"That's good enough for me," she said, tossing away the last of her clothes and pressing her naked body against his.

They stood there for some time, savoring each other and becoming more and more aroused. Finally, she climbed him like a tree, wrapped her legs around his body and took him inside her.

Stone supported her weight with his shoulders and his hands under her buttocks for as long as he could, and then he lowered her to the bed and began all over again.

They were both in the throes of orgasm when the phone rang. Stone let the voicemail pick it up, but then it began ringing again.

"Perhaps you'd better answer it," Felicity said.

Stone rolled over and picked up the receiver. "Hello?"

"It's Cantor. Peter and I are on the street, looking for the woman."

"Any luck?"

"We found Willie."

"Is he all right?"

"He's unconscious, but he doesn't seem to have any wounds, knife or gunshot. An ambulance is on the way; we'll be at Lenox Hill."

"See you there." Stone hung up and began rounding up his clothes. "The man who was watching the house went after Dolce, and he has been found unconscious. I'm going to have to go to the hospital."

"Do you want me to come?"

"No, I think you're safer here. Are you armed?"

"There's a gun in my handbag," she said.

He picked up the purse from the floor and handed it to her. "Keep it in your hand until I get home," he said. "I'll ring the phone once, then hang up to let you know, so you won't shoot me."

15

Stone found Bob Cantor and Peter Leahy seated in the waiting area of the Lenox Hill emergency room. Cantor moved his jacket and made room for Stone between them.

"How is he?"

"Awake but with a concussion. They're admitting him for observation."

"What happened to him?"

"A blow to the head with something like one of those flat blackjacks that detectives used to carry."

"That's enough to concuss an ox," Stone said. "Were you able to talk to him?"

"A little. He was confused, and he couldn't remember being hit."

"Just as well," Stone said. "At least she didn't knife him."

"Yeah, I was worried about that until we couldn't find a wound. A nurse found a big bruise under his hair. Where's your houseguest?"

"Locked in with a gun in her hand," Stone said. "Don't worry; she's a very capable lady."

"Isn't she the British spook I heard about a few years back?"

"Yes, but I didn't tell you that."

"Of course not. She's your client, isn't she?"

"I didn't tell you that, either."

"Tell me the truth about this Whitestone guy."

"It's Whitestone like the bridge. You know everything I know. Dino ran the photo through the FBI facial comparison computer program and came up with a surveillance photo from a bank on Park Avenue, near the Seagram Building, but it wasn't as good as what you got."

"If he's going into a bank on Park, maybe he works around there, maybe even in the Seagram Building."

Stone nodded. "Or maybe he lives in the neighborhood."

"That's not a residential part of Park. You don't find apartment buildings until uptown of Fifty-seventh Street."

"Good point," Stone agreed. "Can you round up some more help?"

"Sure. How many you want?"

"I want a man in the plaza in front of the Seagram Building, watching who comes and goes, and I want somebody near that bank, doing the same thing. I want cameras and long lenses, and I want to see the guy's face, preferably without the hat."

"I'm on it as soon as I pay Willie's bill," Cantor said, "which I'll forward to you."

"Right," Stone said.

"There's Willie," Cantor said, rising. Willie was on a gurney, being wheeled toward the elevator. Stone, Cantor and Peter intercepted him.

"How you doing?" Stone asked.

"I've got a headache," Willie replied, "but they gave me

something for it. I'm sorry, Stone. I never saw this coming. Last thing I remember was sitting in your kitchen. Did she come into the house?"

"No. I called you, and you were following her."

"I don't know how she got behind me, then," Willie said.

"You get some rest, and we'll bail you out of here tomorrow."

Stone and Cantor left Peter with his brother and walked outside, where Stone hailed a cab. "You beginning to see what we're up against with Dolce?" he asked Cantor.

"I got the picture," Cantor replied. "I'll put Peter and another guy in the house; next time, we'll double-team her."

Stone nodded, got in the cab and drove away. He took the elevator upstairs and stepped out into the master suite. As he did, he heard a *pffft!* noise, and he was showered with plaster fragments.

"Hey, it's Stone!" he yelled, flattening himself against the wall.

"Let me see you!" Felicity shouted.

"Okay, I'm coming in—don't shoot." He walked into the bedroom and found Felicity sitting up in bed, bare breasted, holding a small semiautomatic pistol equipped with a silencer.

"You were supposed to call," she said, reprovingly.

"I'm sorry. I forgot," Stone said, sitting down on the bed next to her.

"Is your man all right?"

"Concussion, held overnight for observation. He was black-jacked."

"I could use a woman like that," Felicity said. "You think she's job hunting?"

"Go back to sleep," Stone said. "It's three in the morning." He took the gun from her, made sure the safety was on and put it on her bedside table.

Felicity fell back onto the pillow, and Stone tucked her in. "Don't forget our appointment tomorrow morning," she said, closing her eyes.

Stone got undressed and joined her in bed, but he had a hard time getting to sleep. He had a feeling Dolce was going to change her tactics now, and he couldn't fathom what she might do next.

16

Before Stone and Felicity left the house, Peter Leahy did a quick jog down the street and back, then returned. "No sign of her," he said.

Felicity said to Stone, "We can't arrive together in the ambassador's car; people would talk. You get a cab. Did you bring your passport?"

"Yes," Stone said, patting his jacket pocket. "But I don't know why."

"Because you will be treading upon British soil," she said. She gave him the address and then ran down the front steps and into the waiting Rolls.

Stone hailed a cab and gave the driver the address. Ten minutes later he was deposited in front of a large, elegant town house near Sutton Place. He walked up the front steps and tried the knob. Locked. He found a bell and rang it.

A few moments later a middle-aged man in a black uniform

with silver trim opened the door. He was wearing a sidearm in a polished, black holster. "Yes?"

"My name is Barrington. I have an appointment with Ms. Felicity Devonshire."

"Dame Felicity," the man corrected him. "Wait here."

So she was Dame Felicity now. He hadn't known.

The man opened the door a second time and allowed Stone inside. He found himself in a large, marble-floored foyer with a handsome desk to one side. A graceful double staircase climbed into the upper reaches of the house.

"Come this way, please."

Stone followed the man through a door he hadn't noticed into what was apparently the next building, which was plainer in decor. They got into an elevator with a thick, steel door, and the man opened a panel with a key and pressed a button. The car rose quickly to what seemed to be the top floor, and the door opened.

Another man, dressed in the same uniform as the first and also armed, stood waiting. The elevator door closed, and the first man went down with it.

"Your name?" the new man asked.

"Stone Barrington."

"And with whom is your appointment?"

"Ms. . . . ah, Dame Felicity Devonshire."

"Your passport, please?"

Stone dug it out and handed it over. The man carefully compared the photograph inside with Stone's face. He did not return the passport. "Come with me, please."

Stone followed him through two more doors to what he assumed was the rear of the building, and then they entered a room the size of a large closet. "Stand against the rear wall, please," the man said. Stone did so. The man rolled a steel box with a glass top in front of Stone. Etched into the glass were the outlines of two hands. He opened a drawer, opened Stone's passport and placed it inside.

"Place your hands upon the outlines, please, and press down slightly."

Stone did so, and then suddenly three lights flashed, one in front of him and one on either side. He realized that he had just been fingerprinted and photographed from the front and in both profiles. His passport had been photographed, too.

The man pressed a button, and Stone heard a whirring sound from the other side of the door they had entered. "Thank you," the man said, returning Stone's passport. "Come this way, please."

Stone followed him out of the closet and down a hallway into what seemed to be a third building. The man stopped at a steel door and placed his palm on a recognition panel. The door slid open with a hiss, they both stepped through, and it closed behind them. Stone noticed that the inside of the door was sheathed in mahogany panels over the steel. They were in a small sitting room decorated with comfortable leather furniture and hunting prints, along with a few oil landscapes.

"Please take a seat," the man said. "Someone will come for you." He departed through the door they had entered.

Stone sat down and recognized a Vivaldi sonata for flute wafting through invisible speakers, and a stack of magazines was on a table next to him. He picked up the top one and found himself leafing through the current issue of *Country Life*, perusing ads for houses in Kent, Sussex, Devon and other counties. He had about settled on a charming cottage by the sea in Cornwall when a door on the other side of the room opened and a middle-aged woman in a tweed suit stepped into the room.

"Mr. Barrington, I presume?" she said.

Stone rose. "How could I possibly be anyone else?" he asked.

She tried not to laugh. "This way, please." She led him through what was apparently her office and to a set of double mahogany doors, where she knocked twice.

"Come!" a female voice said.

The woman opened the door and stood back for Stone to enter. Felicity, who was seated at an antique desk, stood up. "Ah, Mr. Barrington," she said, extending her hand.

Stone shook it. "Ah, Dame Felicity," he said.

"That will be all, Heather," Felicity said, "until the other gentleman arrives."

Heather closed the door, and Felicity motioned for Stone to sit down. He did so and was about to speak, when she held up a hand. "I trust you've been well since our last meeting," she said, tapping an ear with a fingertip.

So they were being recorded. "Very well, indeed, Dame Felicity, and may I congratulate you on your honor?"

She blushed a little. "Thank you," she said. "It comes with the job."

"And what job is that?" Stone asked mischievously.

"Civil service," she replied, making a face. They were not being photographed. Then there was another knock at the door.

"Come!" Dame Felicity said.

The door opened, and a slight, gray-haired man in a very good but not new suit entered. "Good morning, Dame Felicity," he said.

"Good morning," she said, rising and shaking his hand. "May I present Mr. Barrington?"

The man turned and shook Stone's hand. "Smith," he said.

"How do you do, Mr. Smith?" Stone asked.

"Very well, thank you."

"Please sit, gentlemen," Felicity said.

They sat.

"Mr. Barrington, Mr. Smith is in possession of more knowledge of Stanley Whitestone than I, being his contemporary. I thought it might be useful for the two of you to meet."

"I hope so," Stone replied.

"Mr. Barrington," Smith said, "what questions do you have regarding Mr. Whitestone?"

"Why don't we start at the beginning?" Stone said. "Please tell me in as much detail as possible of the first time you met Stanley Whitestone."

Smith looked at Felicity and got a nod from her, then turned back to Stone and began.

17

Smith gazed at the ceiling for a moment. "We were nine years old," he said, "and we were at Eton. He impressed me immediately."

"How so?" Stone asked.

"He was very bright and quick and had an acerbic wit, especially for a nine-year-old."

"Go on."

"He excelled in his studies and on the playing field, both without seeming to try very hard."

Stone knew that, among the British, not seeming to try very hard was admirable. "What sports did he play?"

"Cricket, track—he was a sprinter—and he was good on horseback. I believe he had grown up with his own horse."

"Anything else from the Eton years that might be of help in identifying him?"

Smith thought for a moment. "He suffered a fall from a horse and acquired a cut on his forehead," he said, pointing to a spot high over his right eyebrow. "Needed stitches. Left a thin line of a scar about two inches long."

Stone took the photograph of Whitestone from his pocket, looked at it and handed it to Smith. "Do you see it here?"

Smith checked. "No," he said.

"He had it removed, then?"

"Possibly. Or it may have moved into his hairline as he grew up. I can't think of anything else that might identify him now. After we left Eton I was at Oxford, and he was at Cambridge. I saw him two or three times at parties in London, then not again until I . . . became employed as a civil servant."

"Did you join the service at the same time?"

"No, I did two years of National Service, which he seemed to have avoided, so he was senior to me when I came aboard."

Felicity spoke up. "Whitestone attended Cambridge as a King's Scholar," she said, "after being recruited his first semester. It was arranged that he did his National Service with us."

Smith seemed a bit miffed. "I rather thought it was something like that," he said. "I was recruited out of the army."

Stone kept himself from laughing at this display of jealousy. "What were your impressions of him at the time of your joining?"

"Much the same as at Eton," Smith said, "only by that time he had acquired considerable charm. Perhaps that happened at Cambridge."

Felicity consulted a file on her desk. "Whitestone joined the theater group there and became adept at comedy. A number of his contemporaries went on to become professional actors, and half a dozen of them did very well. He had that opportunity but was already committed to us."

"Then I would assume that he learned about makeup and disguise in the theater group," Stone said.

"A logical assumption," Felicity replied. "He made good use of that knowledge in the field."

Stone turned back to Smith. "Why did you dislike Whitestone?" he asked.

"Dislike?" Smith asked.

"All right, hate," Stone said.

Smith said nothing.

"Answer him," Felicity said.

"I tend to distrust people who have too much charm," said Smith, who seemed to have very little himself.

"Did he advance in the service faster than you?" Stone asked.

"I told you, he was two years ahead of me; naturally, he would have been promoted sooner."

"Did your record of advancement match his?"

Smith scratched an itch on his forehead. "I don't think anyone advanced as quickly as he."

"Was he considered a candidate for . . . top management?" Stone asked.

"I would have had to be above him to know that," Smith said, looking pointedly at Felicity.

"Probably," Felicity said. "I was junior to him, but—to use an American term—the scuttlebutt was that he was headed for the top."

"Did he leave abruptly?" Stone asked.

Felicity answered. "He didn't turn up at the office one day, and later that morning the interoffice post delivered a one-sentence letter of resignation to the director."

"Have you seen the letter?" Stone asked.

"It's in his file."

"Was it profane or disrespectful?"

"I believe he told the director to get stuffed."

Stone couldn't help laughing. "Mr. Smith, where were you at the time of Whitestone's . . . departure?"

"I was working in his section," Smith replied.

"And what section was that?"

Felicity interrupted. "I don't believe that's relevant."

"Let me rephrase," Stone said. "Was he doing work that could have benefited him financially if he had used the information he had gained in his work in the private sector?"

"Oh, yes," she replied. "I thought you understood that."

"Was his work of a financial nature?"

Felicity stared at the ceiling. "I can't think of a way to answer that question without telling you more than you need to know to accomplish your task."

"I'll try again," Stone said. "Given his experience, might he have gone to work in the financial industry? In the City, perhaps?"

"Nothing as overt as that," she replied. "It's more likely that he would have been employed surreptitiously by someone in a position to profit from his experience."

"Do you have a name of a possible employer?"

"The evidence is inconclusive," she said.

"To whom did the evidence point?"

"I would not wish his name to be bandied about," she said.

"Of course not, but knowing it might be very helpful in learning the whereabouts of Whitestone."

Felicity sighed. "Lord Wight," she said.

Stone's eyebrows went up.

"I believe you may have known him briefly," Felicity said, "during your little sojourn in London a few years back."

Indeed, Stone had met him. Lord Wight was the father of a woman he had been quite attached to for some months in that year, and he had visited the family home in the South of England. "Was this before or after Lord Wight's financial difficulties?" he asked.

"During and after," she responded. "It was rumored that Whitestone was responsible for saving his bacon and recovering much of Wight's fortune and reputation."

Stone was puzzled. "But you were unable to verify this?"

"We verified it to our satisfaction," she replied, "but that did not rise to an actionable level."

"Were crimes committed at the time?" he asked.

"We believe that both Lord Wight and Whitestone benefited greatly from insider information supplied by Whitestone."

"I see," he said.

Felicity looked at her watch.

Smith stood. "Please excuse me," he said. "I have another appointment."

"Of course," Felicity replied. Smith left the room, and Felicity stood. "I hope that what you have heard may be of use to you, Mr. Barrington," she said.

The woman in the outer office suddenly appeared. "May I escort you out, Mr. Barrington?"

Stone got up. "Yes, thank you. And thank you, Dame Felicity."

"Good day, Mr. Barrington," she replied.

Stone followed the woman to the elevator, where she unlocked the panel and pressed a button. When he arrived on the ground floor, his uniformed escort was waiting for him. A moment later he was on the front steps of the house, blinking in the sunshine.

18

Stone took advantage of the good weather and walked home. As he came into his block he saw two things: one that puzzled him and another that frightened him.

He was puzzled by the chauffeur-driven, Mercedes-made Maybach parked in front of his house, and frightened by the woman standing across the street, who did not seem to see him. She was of Dolce's height and build, but she wore a coat or cape with a hood, which was drawn over her head, leaving her face in shadow.

Stone stepped behind a tree and stopped. As he watched, she turned toward Third Avenue and began walking. At the corner, she hailed a cab and was driven away. Stone heaved a sigh of relief and walked on to his house, entering through the office.

Joan sat at her computer, paying bills online. "Morning," she said. "A client is waiting for you."

"Which one?" he asked.

She waved him away with a hand, as if he were breaking her concentration.

Stone walked into his office to find Herbie Fisher stretched out on his leather sofa, his shoes off, sound asleep. Stone sat down at his desk and noisily shuffled some papers, but Herbie slept on. Stone made a couple of phone calls, not bothering to keep his voice low, and still Herbie slept. Finally, his patience ran out.

"Herbie!" he practically shouted.

Herbie raised his head, looked around, and then sat up and began putting on his shoes.

"Will there be anything else?" Stone asked.

"No, I don't think so," Herbie said, and then rose, put on his jacket and did up his necktie. Stone noticed that he had a better haircut than customary and that his nails had been manicured.

"Then I'd better get back to work," Stone said.

Herbie was almost to the door when he stopped. "Oh," he said, "I almost forgot. I'm thinking of buying a house in this neighborhood, and I wanted to ask your opinion."

This was disturbing news. "Where in the neighborhood?" he asked.

"Next door," Herbie said, pointing to the east.

The house was larger than Stone's, and the two back gardens were separated only by a low brick wall. "Not the best choice," he said.

"Well, there's another one available across your back garden, in the next block."

Stone knew that house, and it was very nice. "Herbie," he said, "I'm not sure you're suited to living in a large house alone. The upkeep and, especially, the taxes are just awful. I think you might feel more at home in a good condo building, maybe a penthouse?" Maybe he would fall off the thing.

"That's a thought," Herbie said.

"The ladies love a penthouse. Why don't you ask your agent to show you a few?"

"How about a co-op building?" Herbie asked.

Stone shook his head. "Then you'd have to face a board of directors, and they can be very tough on people with new money. They like a long record of high earnings; some of them even demand a high net worth from applicants, as much as fifty million dollars. None of those problems with condos."

"That's very good legal advice, Stone," Herbie replied, nodding sagely. "I'm glad I retained you."

"I'm glad you're happy with my services, Herbie. That your Maybach waiting outside?"

"Not yet. It's a loaner from the dealer, but I'm considering it."

"How much?"

"A little under four hundred grand," Herbie said. "It's the short-wheelbase model, not the limo. I don't want to be too . . ." He seemed to search for the word.

"Ostentatious?" Stone offered.

"I was going to say flashy, but I guess opsenbacious will do."

"Yes, you want to keep a low profile," Stone said. "Why don't you look at some penthouses today?"

"Good idea," Herbie said, turning toward the door while reaching for his cell phone and pressing a speed-dial button. "Hello, Serena? Herbert Fisher here. I'd like to see some penthouses." He listened for a moment. "High-up ones," he said. "Meet you outside your office in ten minutes? I'm in the Maybach." He snapped the phone shut. "See you, Stone."

"Be sure and look at a lot of apartments," Stone said. "You really want to know what's out there before you decide. And you might ask to see apartments that are already nicely decorated." Stone dreaded to think what sort of decor Herbie might wind up with.

"Yeah, maybe," Herbie said. "You want to come along? It's a nice car."

"Can't, Herbie; too much work to get done. Have a good day."

"You, too," Herbie said, and then walked out.

After he heard the outside door close, Stone walked down the corridor to Joan's office. "You let him use my office?"

"Why? Did he disturb anything?"

"Only me."

"Well, he's our most important client, isn't he? We have to treat him well."

"Did he tell you he's thinking of buying the house next door?"

Joan put the back of a hand to her forehead. "Oh, no."

"If he does, he'll be in here every day."

"Oh, no, no!"

"Wouldn't you be happy to see our most important client every day?"

"No, no. Please, no."

"I'm encouraging him to go high-rise," Stone said. "Assist me in that endeavor, will you? Help me convince him that he belongs in a penthouse in some building on the far Upper West Side or maybe New Jersey."

"New Jersey would be perfect," she said.

"By the way, did you happen to see the woman standing across the street?"

"Oh, God! Was it Dolce?"

"I don't know; she was wearing a hood that obscured her face, and she walked away shortly after I spotted her. Your view must have been blocked by the car Herbie is thinking of buying."

"The Maybach? That's big enough."

"We're supposed to have one of Cantor's people here to deal with Dolce, remember?"

"Oh, there was one here. He said he was going down to Second Avenue to look for a paper."

"Did you offer him the *Times* or *The Wall Street Journal*?"

"I think he's more of a *Post* reader," she replied. "Oh, here he comes."

The door opened, and a large young man walked in carrying a *Post* under one arm. "Hi," he said, offering Stone a hand. "I'm Jake Musket. Everything all right?"

"Yes," Stone said, shaking the hand, "except for the woman who was standing across the street when I arrived ten minutes ago."

Jake Musket reddened. "Oh," he said.

19

Felicity went home to Stone's early, shortly after Joan had left. She came to his office and gave him a kiss. "You did well this morning," she said.

"I did?" Stone asked. "I didn't really learn anything of value."

"Of course you did," she said. "You now know as much about Stanley Whitestone as anyone."

"I now know he once had a scar on his forehead and that, as a boy, he played cricket, ran fast and was good with horses. None of those things is likely to help me find him in New York City."

"But you're getting a feel for him, aren't you?"

"And I know that he was an amateur actor and is good at disguises."

"You see? You know a lot now."

"I also know that your Mr. Smith hated his guts—still does, probably."

"Well, I'm not sure what you can do with that," she said. "Would you like to go to a dinner party tonight? Good," she said without hesitating.

"I guess I'd love to," Stone replied. "Who's giving it?"

"The ambassador."

"He's back?"

"Got back today. He forgot to invite me before he left. It's black tie."

"I own a black tie," Stone replied.

"We're not due there until eight," she said. "Why don't we go upstairs and have a little nap?"

The little nap came only after half an hour of inventive lovemaking, and it was welcome.

THE ELDERLY ROLLS-ROYCE picked them up at eight and drove them to the Upper East Side residence of Britain's ambassador to the UN. They were greeted at the door by a uniformed butler, who led them to the residence's living room and shouted over the conversation of the early arrivers, "Dame Felicity Devonshire and Mr. Stone Barrington."

The first person Stone saw was Mr. Smith, whom he had met earlier in the day.

"Don't speak to Smith," Felicity murmured in his ear.

Stone nodded to the man and received a nod in return.

"He doesn't look important enough to be dining with the ambassador," Stone whispered back.

"I expect he's on call as the odd man," she replied. "I would have been seated next to him if you hadn't come." A succession of introductions ensued, and Stone made an effort to remember at least their surnames. A waiter passed with Champagne flutes, and Stone snagged a pair.

He was surprised when he tasted it. "This is Krug," he said to Felicity.

"That means there is at least one person here who is very important to the ambassador," she said.

"I wonder who it is," Stone replied.

"I'll figure it out before we're done. Come meet the ambassador."

The ambassador, whose name was Sir John Pemberton, was younger than Stone had expected, only fiftyish, and his wife was fifteen years younger and quite beautiful, a redhead in a chic dress with an encouraging expanse of bosom showing.

"I'm very pleased to meet you, Mr. Barrington," the ambassador said.

"Yes," Lady Pemberton echoed. "One meets so few of Dame Felicity's friends; they're such a secretive lot. Are you secretive, Mr. Barrington?"

"Sometimes," Stone replied.

"Oh, good," she said, deftly separating him from Felicity, like a cowgirl with a calf, and steering him toward a corner. "It will be such fun worming secrets out of you."

Stone caught a glimpse of Felicity's face as they moved across the room, and it occurred to him that if her glance were a knife, Lady Pemberton's throat would already have been cut.

"Tell me," Lady Pemberton said, once she had secured him in a corner. "What, as you Americans say, do you do?"

"I'm an attorney at law," Stone replied, "and that is not a secret."

"Solicitor or barrister?" she asked.

"In the United States attorneys frequently do both."

"Oh, of course. I knew that."

"Some attorneys specialize in trial work, while others never see the inside of a courtroom," he said.

"And are you with a big, grand firm of lawyers?"

"I am of counsel to such a firm," Stone said, "but I make my offices in my home."

"How very convenient," she said, flashing brilliant dental work. "Then you're often at home in the afternoons?"

"Often," he replied.

"How nice. I am frequently at loose ends in the afternoons," she said, taking his arm in such a way that his elbow rubbed against one of her stunning breasts.

"May I have my gentleman back now, please?" Felicity said, stepping up and taking the other arm. "There's someone I'd like him to meet."

For a moment, Stone thought a tug-of-war would ensue with him as the rope.

"If you must," Lady Pemberton said. "We'll catch up later, Mr. Barrington."

Felicity towed Stone to the other end of the room.

"Nick of time," Stone said quietly.

"Yes, you'd have been upstairs with her in another moment," Felicity said through a fixed smile that she bestowed upon everyone she passed.

They came to a tall, slender man of about sixty who wore a Royal Navy formal uniform with much gold trim and who stood ramrod straight, sipping whiskey neat from a tumbler. "Stone," Felicity said, "may I present Admiral Sir Ian Weston? Sir Ian, this is my friend Stone Barrington."

"Howjado," the admiral said.

"Very well, thank you," Stone replied.

"Did they fob that fucking awful bubbly off on you?" the admiral asked. Stone nodded. "They've got a proper bar over there with a decent single malt."

"Oh, I'm quite happy with the Champagne," Stone said. "I'm not often served Krug."

"He's pouring the Krug, is he? Must be somebody important here. Wonder who?"

"I was wondering the same thing, Sir Ian," Felicity said. "Sir Ian is the ambassador's naval attaché," she explained to Stone. She looked around the room. "I'll bet it's that American couple over there," she said.

"Could be," the admiral replied.

Stone followed her gaze until it alighted on Bill Eggers and his wife, Suzanne. He laughed. "That gentleman is the managing partner of the law firm to which I am of counsel," he said, "and I'm not certain anyone in diplomatic circles would consider him important enough for Krug."

"Oh," Felicity said. "And whom do we have here?" she asked, looking toward the door, where the butler was about to announce a portly man and his elegant wife.

"Lord and Lady Wight," the butler intoned.

"What a coincidence," Stone said.

"Yesss," Felicity drawled.

20

Stone had not set eyes on Lord and Lady Wight since he had been a guest in their country home a few years before. Wight had been the subject of an investigation by the House of Lords at the time, and the supposition was that he might be stripped of his peerage and perhaps even go to prison. Stone and one of their daughters, Sarah, a painter and sculptor, had been close then.

The Wights spotted Stone and came over. "Barrington, isn't it?" Wight asked.

"It is, your lordship," Stone replied. "Your ladyship, it's good to see you again."

"And you, Mr. Barrington," she replied. "Sarah still speaks of you."

"That's kind of her," Stone replied. "May I present Dame Felicity Devonshire?"

"Howjado," Wight replied.

"So nice," echoed his wife. Both of them looked right through her, having no idea who she was.

"How do you do, Lord Wight, Lady Wight," Felicity said. Then, turning to him, "I believe you knew my father."

Wight looked at her blankly for a moment, then the penny dropped. "Why of course," he said. "You remember General Sir Giles Devonshire, my dear."

"Of course I do," Lady Wight replied. "Such a dear man. How is he?"

"Deceased," Felicity replied. "Last year."

"Saw the obit in the *Telegraph*," Wight replied. "So very sorry."

"Thank you," Felicity said.

Wight narrowed his eyes in thought. "I believe he had a sort of second career after his retirement from the army, didn't he? In Whitehall or someplace?"

"A minor post," Felicity replied, "but it kept him busy."

Lady Wight tugged at her husband's sleeve. "Must check in with the ambassador," she said.

"Oh, Lord Wight," Stone said. "I believe you're acquainted with a Mr. Stanley Whitestone."

Wight looked momentarily alarmed, then he lifted an eyebrow. "Yes, yes, decent fellow," he replied.

"Where is he these days?" Stone asked.

"Oh, dear, I'm not sure I know," Wight replied. "Believe he was in Cairo for a spell; lost track of him after that. Will you excuse us? Must check in with the ambassador." He hustled his wife toward the other side of the room.

"That was very direct," Felicity said. "Very clever, too."

"Thank you, but why?"

"Now we know that Wight knows where Whitestone is," she said.

"We do?"

She shook her head. "Men can be so dense. Didn't you see his reaction when you mentioned him?"

"You mean the lifted eyebrow?"

"You shocked him to the core," she said.

"And you learned that from a lifted eyebrow? I could use you in court when picking a jury or cross-examining a hostile witness."

"I expect you could," Felicity said, and then the butler shouted that dinner was served.

THEY WERE SIXTEEN at dinner; Stone knew because he counted. He found himself at Lady Pemberton's right hand, and he could just make out Felicity at the far end of the table, between the ambassador and Lord Wight. A sliver of foie gras was served.

"Delicious," Stone said.

Lady Pemberton gazed archly at him. "Yes, you are."

Stone felt himself blush. "I hope you didn't send to England for this," he said. "We have quite good geese and ducks in the Hudson River Valley, and they keep us supplied with their livers."

"Oh, we always order domestically," she said, "except for Champagne, of course. Do you expect to be in your office tomorrow afternoon?"

On another occasion, with a less married woman, Stone would have been pleased to invite her over. She was, after all, quite alluring. As it was, Bill Eggers and his wife were halfway down the table, no doubt wondering what the hell they were doing here, and Susan Eggers could spot two people arranging an assignation from across the street. "I'm afraid not," he said. "I have a houseguest at the moment who is taking up much of my time."

"What a pity," Lady Pemberton said. "Perhaps another time?"

"Lady Pemberton," Stone said, "in your position I'm sure you know who Dame Felicity is."

"Of course I do," she replied.

"Then you will know how . . . inconvenient it might become for her to suspect we're having this conversation."

It was Lady Pemberton's turn to blush. "You have a point," she said, "but I expect our paths will cross again here or there."

"As Fats Waller used to say, 'One never knows, do one?'" Stone replied. Lady Pemberton looked baffled for a moment then turned her attention to the gentleman on her left.

AFTER DESSERT, IN the British tradition, the gentlemen departed the dinner table and wandered into Sir John's study for cigars and brandy. In a moment the air was thick with the aroma of burning Cuban tobacco, an odor Stone despised. He would have to have his tuxedo sent to the cleaners tomorrow.

Bill Eggers approached. "What the hell are you doing here, Stone?"

"I might ask the same of you, Bill," Stone replied.

"Oh, Lady Pemberton has taken an interest in early American furniture, and she and Suzanne met at some event or other and got on famously." Eggers was a major collector of eighteenth-century American furniture and owned some pieces that had been loaned to museums for exhibitions. "What's your excuse?"

"An old friend invited me to accompany her here."

"The redhead? She's quite something, isn't she?"

"You have no idea," Stone said. Apparently, the only people here who knew who Felicity was were the ambassador and his wife, Mr. Smith and, possibly, Admiral Sir Ian Weston.

"Is she something with the British UN delegation?"

"Something like that," Stone replied.

"You're not being very forthcoming, Stone. Ordinarily, I can't shut you up."

"Circumstances require me to be discreet," Stone said.

"And who's the heavy gent with the elegant wife?" Eggers asked.

"Lord and Lady Wight. You remember my painter friend, Sarah?"

"I remember you hustling us out of her gallery opening the night the place was bombed," Eggers said.

"The Wights are Sarah's parents."

"Now that I think of it, he's a big developer in the UK, isn't he?"

"He was; then he wasn't. Now he is again, I'm told."

"Someone mentioned him as a possible client," Eggers said.

"I'd be happy to introduce you," Stone said. "Let's wend our way over to the fireplace, where he's warming his backside."

And they did.

21

They found Wight before the fireplace, momentarily alone.

"Lord Wight," Stone said, "I'd like to introduce you to Mr. William Eggers."

Wight nodded. "Howjado?"

"Bill is the managing partner of the law firm of Woodman and Weld. I'm of counsel to the firm."

"Oh, yes," Wight said, suddenly interested. "I believe someone in London mentioned your firm to me in a favorable light."

"That's very gratifying," Eggers said.

"Perhaps we should have a chat in more businesslike surroundings."

"If you're going to be in New York a few days, why don't you come up to our offices and have lunch with Stone and me?"

"I'd like that," Wight said. "Are you available tomorrow?"

"I am," Eggers replied, "and I'm sure Stone is, too."

"Of course," Stone said.

"We're in the Seagram Building on Park Avenue," Eggers said. "May we say twelve-thirty tomorrow?"

"Very good," Wight replied. "I know the building, of course."

The butler stood at the door. "The ambassador invites you to rejoin the ladies," he said more quietly than usual.

As Stone was leaving the study, Smith materialized at his elbow. "A word?" he said.

Stone remained in the study with him while the others made their way out. "Certainly," he replied.

"Are you aware of Lord Wight's former relationship to Stanley Whitestone?"

"I've heard it mentioned," Stone said. "Are you sure it's former?"

"Lord Wight has been at some pains the past few years to make it seem so."

"Perhaps all is not what it seems," Stone pointed out.

"Should you discover that they are still . . . acquainted, you must be careful not to let Wight know that you know."

"Why not?"

"Because Wight is also . . . acquainted with some dangerous people who would not like you or anyone else to know."

"What do you mean by 'dangerous'?" Stone asked.

"Wight is not entirely his own man," Smith said, "and some of his associates have a way of making people who annoy them disappear."

"I'll certainly keep that in mind," Stone said. "Now, shall we join the ladies?" And they did so.

THE EVENING WAS over promptly at ten-thirty, and Stone was careful to say nothing of his impending meeting while they were in the car. They were let into the house by Jake Musket.

"Nothing to report," Musket said, then saw them onto the elevator.

"Who was the man you introduced to Wight?" Felicity asked as they moved upward.

Smith had apparently had a word with her. "The managing partner at Woodman and Weld," Stone replied. "Bill Eggers."

"Why did you make the introduction?"

"Bill asked me to; he's interested in Wight as a possible client."

"Do you think that's a good idea?" she asked.

"Bill does. He and I are having lunch with Wight tomorrow at the firm's offices."

"I don't suppose you can get out of it."

"Why should I want to do that?" Stone asked. "It might give me an opportunity to raise the subject of Stanley Whitestone again."

"I believe Smith had a word with you."

"He did. Told me that Wight has dangerous associates."

They reached the bedroom, and Felicity turned so that Stone could unzip her dress. "Smith is right," she said. "I shouldn't want anything to happen to you."

"Neither would I," Stone said, moving her hair aside and kissing the nape of her neck.

She stepped out of her dress and tossed it onto a chair.

Stone waited until after they had attended to each other's desires before he spoke again. "Felicity, are you telling me all I need to know about Whitestone and Wight?"

"I've told you all I can," she replied.

"That may not be all I need to know," he said.

"Go to sleep," she commanded.

STONE GOT TO the offices of Woodman & Weld a few minutes early and found Eggers alone in his office. He sat down. "What do you know about Lord Wight?" he asked.

"We have a London office, as you know," Eggers said. "It's in a building that Wight's company built and manages."

"So he's your landlord, and that's it?"

"A solicitor I know in London tells me that Wight is a large consumer of legal services," Eggers said.

"Given his past, do you want to be seen to represent him?"

Eggers shrugged. "His reputation in this country is better than in his own, and I happen to know that he has acquired two building sites in midtown. He also owns a building on East Fifty-seventh Street that houses Strategic Services."

Stone knew that Strategic Services was one of the two or three largest private security companies in the United States. "Have you had any dealings with them?" he asked.

"I've played tennis with Jim Hackett a couple of times at the Racquet Club," Eggers replied, referring to the owner of the company. "We had a drink afterward last week, and I think he might be a good source of referrals."

"He sounds worth cultivating," Stone said. "I don't know much about his background."

"He's ex–Paratroop Regiment."

"He's British?"

"Scottish, but you wouldn't know it to talk to him," Eggers said. "He came to this country twenty-five years ago, and he's very much assimilated."

"He has a lot of ex–special ops people on staff, doesn't he?"

"That's the rumor," Eggers said. "And from both sides of the Atlantic. His corporate protection people are mostly former U.S. Secret Service."

"I don't know a lot about his company," Stone said, "but I have the impression that they have been mixed up in some unsavory things, for their clients."

"I've never heard of any evidence to support that," Eggers said, "but any outfit that's as secretive as Strategic Services is bound to generate rumors. They never speak to the press, never comment on their work or so much as acknowledge the name of a client."

"I can see how that might perk up some ears," Stone said.

Eggers's phone buzzed, and he picked it up. "Yes? Please send him to my dining room." He hung up. "Our possible future client has arrived," he said.

22

Lunch was served in Eggers's private dining room, off his office. The room was paneled in walnut, and the bookcases were filled with his collection of old law books, bound in leather. A fire burned cheerily in the hearth, giving off the lovely scent of piñon wood that Eggers had shipped in from Santa Fe.

By the time the soup course plates were being taken away, Stone was bored rigid. The talk was of London clubs that Eggers and Wight belonged to. Stone noticed that the Royal Yacht Squadron, of which Eggers was a foreign member, was not mentioned, and he assumed that Wight had been blackballed by that club. By the time the main course of lamb chops was served, all the talk was of real estate. Stone was having trouble keeping awake and had no opportunity to raise the subject of Stanley Whitestone. Then his cell phone vibrated on his belt.

Stone stepped away from the table and answered it.

"It's Joan," she said. "Herbie Fisher just called, and he's in some sort of trouble. He's in the tank at the Nineteenth Precinct."

"I'll go right over," Stone said, grateful for the interruption. "Excuse me, Bill, Lord Wight," he said to the two men, "one of my clients has an emergency, so I'll have to leave you."

Wight stood up and shook his hand. "I'll speak to Sarah later today, Barrington," he said, "and I'll give her your regards."

"Please do," Stone said.

"I'll call you later," Eggers said.

Stone got out of there. It was a beautiful day, and he decided to walk up to the Nineteenth, which was in the East Sixties. Herbie would appreciate his presence there more if he had to stew awhile.

Stone knew the desk sergeant from the old days, when they had both been patrolmen. "Hey, Mac," he said.

"Hiya, Stone. How's it going?"

"Not too bad," Stone replied. "I believe you're hosting a client of mine, one Herbert Fisher. What's the beef?"

Mac consulted a large ledger. "Disorderly conduct," he said.

"How disorderly?"

Mac hit a few computer keys and read aloud from the arrest report. "Subject was a passenger in a limousine stopped for a traffic violation. While I spoke with the driver, subject got out of the car and began to berate me for stopping his car. I told subject to quiet himself and return to the rear seat, but he refused and assaulted me. I placed subject in handcuffs and transported him to the Nineteenth Precinct."

"You know what kind of assault?" Stone asked.

"I talked to the officer when he brought Fisher in. I believe it was repeated jabs to the chest with a forefinger."

"Trot him out, will you, Mac?"

"Two minutes," the cop replied. "Number two's available."

Stone went to interview room number two, sat down and waited. A moment later, Herbie, in restraints, was escorted into the part of the room on the other side of the thick plate-glass partition. One of his hands was uncuffed so that he could use the telephone. He picked it up.

"Stone," he said, "a cop tried to beat me up."

"Save it, Herbie," Stone replied. "I've heard all about it, and the incident could get you up to a year at Riker's but probably more like thirty days."

"What?"

"I said, 'Save it,' Herbie. Now if you'll behave yourself for half an hour I'll try to get you out of here." Stone pressed a button, and the escorting officer returned. "We're done," he said to the man. Herbie was escorted back to the tank, still protesting.

Stone left the interview room and walked upstairs to the detective squad room. Dino was sitting in his glass-enclosed office at the far end of the room, and he waved Stone in and pointed at a chair. He finished his conversation and hung up. "So," he said, what brings you out of your cozy East Side town house and into this temple of justice?"

"Herbie," Stone replied.

Dino rolled his eyes. "What now?"

"He had an argument with a cop during a traffic stop, and the guy ran him in for disorderly conduct; he's in the tank. I'll buy the next two dinners at Elaine's if you'll get him released and make the report go away."

"Are you attempting to bribe an officer of the law?" Dino asked sternly.

"Yes," Stone replied.

"The next five dinners," Dino said.

"Four, and that's my best offer. Herbie can rot."

"Done." Dino made the call. "You can meet him downstairs. See you tonight?"

"Yeah, and thanks."

"I'm ordering the good wines," Dino said.

"Don't press your luck, pal," Stone replied and went back downstairs.

HERBIE WAS LED from the cells and into the public area, rubbing his wrists. "I want to sue them," he said.

Stone took him by the arm and marched him into the street. "Sue who?" he asked.

"All of them, the whole precinct."

"For what?"

"Disrespect," Herbie said.

"That's not grounds for a lawsuit, Herbie, especially since you've been a guest here before. They tend to remember those things."

The Maybach glided to a halt next to where they were standing, and the chauffeur got out and opened the rear door.

"I think I found the right penthouse," Herbie said. "It's on Park Avenue, up in the nineties."

Stone thought that was probably far enough from his house. "Sounds great, Herbie."

"You want to come and take a look?"

"Can't do it today; I had to leave an important meeting to uncan you."

"I'm going to pick up Sheila and take one more look," Herbie said.

"I'm sure Sheila will give you sage real estate advice," Stone said, "but if I were you, I wouldn't ask her opinion on decor."

"Why not?"

"I think Sheila's tastes might run more to the Bronx than to Park Avenue."

"There you go again, misjudging people," Herbie said. "Sheila is from Queens."

"Of course she is," Stone said.

"By the way, I've got a witness to an assault on me that was instigated by the Wilds," Herbie said.

"Who's the witness?"

"Sheila."

"Herbie, Sheila probably works for someone close to the Wilds."

"Why do you say that?"

"Because she's a hooker, and the Wilds are probably her pimp's loan shark and bookie, respectively."

"I hadn't thought about that," Herbie said.

"Go buy your apartment," Stone said. "If you like, I'll do the closing."

"Closing?"

"That's where you and the seller meet, he gives you documents transferring the apartment to you and you give him money. I should think that an Internet attorney like yourself would know that."

"I knew that," Herbie said. He got into the Maybach and was driven away.

Stone hailed a cab.

23

Joan was on the phone as Stone walked into his offices. "Bill Eggers for you on one," she said.

Stone walked back to his office, sat down and picked up the phone. "Hey, Bill."

"What do you mean walking out on us that way?" Eggers demanded.

"I had a client in the tank at the Nineteenth Precinct, and, anyway, I was of no use to you in a conversation about clubs and real estate. By the way, I noticed you and Wight don't have the Royal Yacht Squadron in common."

"Wight was blackballed," Eggers said.

"I figured. How did the meeting go?"

"He's selling a building he owns in town, and we're doing the legal work."

"Congratulations! I'm glad to have been able to make some rain for you."

"I made my own rain, no thanks to you. You just pointed me at him."

"I introduced you and rather warmly, I believe."

"All right, all right, you introduced us. Thank you."

"You're welcome. I get a referral fee, don't I?"

"Don't press me, Stone; you'll get something when the sale closes and Wight's bill is paid."

"Your word is good enough for me, Bill."

"Which one of your clients was in jail?"

"One Herbert Fisher, who stupidly got into an altercation with a cop during a traffic stop."

"You're handling that kind of crap?"

"He paid me a very nice retainer to do all his legal work. He's buying a penthouse apartment on Park Avenue as we speak."

"Maybe you should introduce him to us," Eggers said.

"Believe me, Bill, you don't want to know him, and I don't want anybody to know that I know him."

"Oh, *that* kind of client."

"You remember when I represented that guy who shot Carmine Dattila, aka Dattila the Hun, in a coffeehouse in Little Italy?"

"Sure. You were famous for a day."

"Herbie Fisher was that guy."

"You're right. We don't want to know him, but since you mentioned it, how did you get him off?"

"I made a case to the DA for self-defense, which was helped by the fact that a NYPD/FBI task force had just disarmed everybody in the coffeehouse and had Dattila under electronic and visual surveillance."

"I should have thought that would have clinched the case *against* your client."

"Sure, but it would have made both the NYPD and the FBI look like asses."

"You're a lucky son of a bitch, you know that?"

"Sometimes."

"You want to play tennis at the Racquet Club tomorrow, with Jim Hackett and me?"

"Sure, what time?"

"Six o'clock."

"See you then."

"I'll leave your name at the door." Eggers hung up, and so did Stone.

Joan buzzed him immediately. "Herbie Fisher called while you were on the phone and said he bought the apartment and he wants to close tomorrow."

"Get him back for me, please." Stone waited until she buzzed, then picked up. "Herbie?"

"Yeah, Stone. I got the apartment."

"How much did you pay?"

"Three and a half million dollars, and I got it furnished. They wanted five and a half, but I'm a good negotiator. I want to close tomorrow."

"It doesn't work like that, Herbie. First we have to do a title search."

"What's that?"

"Have you forgotten all the questions on that bar exam you sort of took?"

"It sounds familiar."

"It means we have to find out if the title to the apartment is good, if there are any encumbrances, like mortgages. If there are, the seller has to pay them off at the closing, so you get a clean deal. It's going to take at least a week."

"Can I move in now?"

"No, Herbie. You don't own it yet."

"But I gave them a check for ten percent."

"You'll have to give them the other ninety percent before you can move in."

"Can I move in on closing day?"

"I'll see that that's in the contract," Stone said. "Is anyone living there now?"

"No. They already moved out and took everything they wanted. The rest is mine."

"Talk to your real estate agent; she'll get the whole thing together and put me in touch with the seller's attorney."

"Are you sure I can't move in today?"

"Herbie, they won't even give you the keys until the closing."

"I can pick a lock."

"Don't you do that, Herbie! You want to go back to jail for breaking and entering?"

"Can I have the living room painted? I don't like the color."

"Talk to your agent; maybe she can get permission."

"Can I break a wall down?"

"Don't even think about it, Herbie. You have to play by the rules!"

"Oh, okay," Herbie replied, sounding dejected.

"Listen, you can go out and buy furniture and pictures and other things and have them delivered the day after closing. You might need sheets and towels, too."

"Yeah, Sheila and I could do that."

"I think I need to have a little chat with Sheila," Stone said.

"What for? You trying to get laid?"

"No, Herbie. I just need to straighten her out on where her loyalties lie."

"Her loyalties don't lie."

"Her loyalties to you, Herbie. Is she going to be loyal to you or to her pimp?"

"I want to marry her," Herbie said.

"In that case, you're going to need an ironclad prenup, and I can do that for you."

"What's a prenup?"

"A prenuptial agreement that sets out what's yours and what's hers, should you get divorced."

"We're not going to get divorced," Herbie said.

"That's what everybody who ever got married believed, until they got divorced. This is absolutely mandatory, Herbie, and I don't want an argument about it. When is the wedding?"

"I don't know; I haven't asked her yet."

"Herbie, if you get married without my having gotten her signature on a prenup, I will stop representing you, and she will take all your money."

"She's not like that."

"That's what everybody who ever got divorced said. Promise me you won't set a date until I say it's okay."

"Okay, I promise."

"Good-bye, Herbie. I'll get your closing set up." He hung up and buzzed Joan.

"Yes?"

"Print out a prenup for me, will you?"

"Sure. Which one?"

"The maximum-strength one."

"Gotcha. You getting married?"

"No, but Herbie probably is."

Stone heard a loud cackle as she hung up.

24

Stone got to Elaine's first, and two couples he didn't know were sitting at the table next to his. One of the men got up, walked around the table, tapped Stone on the shoulder and stuck out his hand. "Stone Barrington, I believe?"

Stone stood up and accepted the hand. "I believe, too," he said.

"I'm Jim Hackett; I understand we're playing tennis tomorrow evening." Hackett was a little shorter than Stone, solidly built and had a broken nose that made him look like an ex-fighter.

"Hi, Jim," Stone said. "I've heard about you from Bill Eggers, and I'm looking forward to our game."

"So am I," Hackett replied.

"I'm a little rusty, so I hope you'll go easy on me."

Hackett smiled. "Don't count on it," he said. "I hope Eggers told you we play for money."

"He didn't, so you can collect your winnings from him. I'm sure he'll find a way to put my losses on his expense account."

Hackett laughed. "See you tomorrow." He went back to his seat.

Dino came in and sat down. "Where's Felicity?"

"Working. Some sort of meeting."

Dino waylaid a passing waiter. "Bring what's-his-name here his usual Kentucky swill and me my usual princely Scotch," Dino said. "And a wine list; Stone's buying."

"Here we go," Stone said, rolling his eyes.

Dino pulled a sheet of paper from his pocket and handed it to Stone. "Here's Herbie's arrest report," he said. "I scrubbed it from the computer, too."

Stone looked it over and then put it in his pocket.

"Aren't you going to burn it?"

"Not until I've shown it to Herbie," Stone replied.

"What's he up to these days, besides annoying honest police officers?"

"He bought an apartment on Park Avenue for three and a half big ones," Stone said.

"Where on Park?"

Stone recited the number.

"Not the penthouse, I hope."

"Well, you can hope," Stone said. "What's wrong with the penthouse?"

"Nothing if Herbie isn't bothered by ghosts."

"Ghosts? What are you talking about?"

"You know, if you read a real street newspaper instead of the *Times*, you'd know these things."

"What things?"

"There was a double murder there about a year and a half ago: man and woman found hacked to death on the living room floor. The ME says the murderers used meat cleavers."

"Why are you telling me this? I don't want to know this stuff."

"Herbie might. The apartment is unsalable; there've been two sightings of ghosts in the place. How much is Herbie paying?"

"I told you, three and a half million."

"I guess that's a bargain, kind of; they were asking five."

"Herbie says five and a half but that he's a great negotiator."

"They should have paid him," Dino said. "That's the kind of thing that hangs over a piece of real estate for decades. I guess he could redecorate."

"He bought it furnished."

"Take my advice: when you draw up the contract, be sure to include a clause that requires the seller—or his estate—to have the living room carpet replaced."

"I'll keep that in mind," Stone said.

"Can you get him out of it?"

"He already gave them a check for three hundred and fifty grand."

"Did he sign the disclosure form?"

"I don't know."

"The murders would be a factor affecting the sale price," Dino said. "If they didn't disclose them, you might be able to get him out of the deal."

"If I were on the other side of the deal, I'd say that a two-million-dollar discount ought to cover the, ah, incident."

"But you're not on the other side of the deal."

Stone took a swig of his drink. "I'm not going to think about this now. Tomorrow is soon enough."

Herbie and Sheila walked into Elaine's.

"Oh, shit," Stone said.

The couple stopped at Stone's table. "Hi, Stone," Herbie said. "You remember Sheila." Herbie was reaching for one of the two empty chairs.

STONE PUT A leg up on one of the chairs. "Sore knee," he said to Herbie. "Good evening, Sheila."

Sheila turned to Herbie. "They don't want us to sit here; let's sit in the back."

"Herbie," Stone said, "when you put down the deposit on the apartment, did you sign anything?"

Herbie looked thoughtful. "Yeah," he said, slapping his pockets and coming up with an envelope.

Stone took the envelope. "I'd better look this over," he said. "See you later." He turned back to his drink, and Herbie took the hint, for a change.

"You going to open the envelope?" Dino asked.

"Not until I've had another drink," Stone said, waving at a waiter, who was way ahead of him. Stone took a sip of his second drink and opened the envelope. "Here it is," he said, reading from the document: " 'Seller acknowledges that he is aware of the previous owners' deaths by violence in the apartment and that his offer is made with due consideration of market consequences of that event.' "

"I guess you could call that disclosure," Dino said, "even though it doesn't mention the meat cleavers or machetes."

"I guess you could," Stone said. "Excuse me for a minute." He got up and walked back to Herbie's table. "May I sit down for a moment?" he asked.

"No," Sheila said.

"Sure," Herbie said.

Stone decided to ignore Sheila and sat down. He handed Herbie the disclosure agreement. "Read paragraph eleven," he said.

Herbie read it. "What does this mean?" he asked.

"It means that the previous owners were murdered in the apartment, hacked to death with meat cleavers."

"Omigod!" Sheila shrieked. "It's *that* building? You read about that in the *Post*, didn't you, Herbie?"

"Ah, no," Herbie said.

"But," Stone interjected, "you did read about it in this disclosure agreement that you signed when you gave the agent your check for three hundred and fifty thousand dollars?"

"Well . . ."

"Herbie," Sheila said, "are you *insane*?"

"Now, wait a minute, Sheila."

"Yes," Stone said, "wait a minute, Sheila. Herbie got a two-million-dollar discount on the apartment because of the murders. That should make you feel better about the deal."

"I don't give a shit about the murders," Sheila said. "What I do give a shit about are the *ghosts*! For God's sake, don't you two guys ever read a newspaper?"

Herbie had turned a lighter shade of his usual pallor. "Ghosts? What are you talking about?"

Stone stood up. "Sheila will explain it to you. I apologize for interrupting your evening," he said, including Sheila. "We'll talk about this tomorrow."

He got the hell out of there and went back to his own table.

"Never mind telling me," Dino said. "I heard it from over here."

25

Stone awoke the following morning to find Felicity lying next to him.

She opened an eye. "You didn't know when I came home last night, did you?"

"I've never seen you before in my life," he said, running a hand up the inside of her thigh. "But this feels familiar."

"It should," she said. "It's wet, too."

"I notice that. It must be some sort of signal."

"It must be," she agreed.

He gathered her into his arms and made the most of things.

LATER, WHEN THEY were lying on their backs, sweating and catching their breath, Stone said. "What do you know about a guy named Jim Hackett?"

"Strategic Services?"

"Yes, that Jim Hackett."

"I met him once at a dinner party in London; there wasn't much opportunity for one-on-one conversation. I looked him up after that: owns a very large private security company, is a contractor for the American and British governments and for many corporations, owns a factory that converts ordinary motorcars into virtual tanks, not averse to being paid in cash by foreign clients and stashing the funds in Switzerland or those little islands south of Jamaica."

"Is he clean?"

"As clean as anyone can be in that business. Nothing outright unsavory about him, as I recall."

"Has your firm used his company's services?"

"No," she replied. "Her Majesty's government frowns on that sort of thing, except when they do it themselves. Why are you interested in Hackett?"

"I'm playing tennis with him at the Racquet Club this evening. It occurred to me that he's the sort of person who might have run across Stanley Whitestone at some point, and I thought I might ask him about Whitestone."

Felicity smiled. "What a good idea," she said. "He is *exactly* the sort of person who might know something about Stanley. You see, Stone, this is why I hired you: you are imaginative as well as lucky. I want a complete report tonight when you come home."

"Does he know who and what you are?" Stone asked.

"I shouldn't be surprised," she replied. "He's the sort who would make it his business to know."

"Mind if I drop your name? It might help."

She thought about that for a minute. "Yes I mind," she said, "and certainly in the same conversation in which the name of Stanley Whitestone is mentioned. I don't want him making a connection between Stanley and me. My position is that Stanley is ancient history and nobody at my firm gives a flying fuck about him. Please remember that."

"How could I forget it?" Stone asked.

"I'm going to have dinner at Elaine's with Dino," Felicity said. "Meet us there when you're done with Mr. Hackett, or vice versa."

IN TENNIS CLOTHES, Jim Hackett was revealed to have a muscularly gnarled body that appeared to have lived through many difficult moments. His broken nose was a perfect representation of the rest of him. His tennis game was murderous; he thought nothing of aiming a shot between the eyes of an opponent who had come to the net. Stone knew this, because he had been struck between the eyes. It tended to make one more cautious on the court, which was exactly what Hackett intended.

Hackett and his partner, Mike Freeman, an employee of his who appeared to have been hired entirely for his tennis game, defeated Eggers and Stone in straight sets, 6–4 and 9–7. Stone felt as if he had played fifty tiebreakers at Wimbledon.

Afterward, at dinner in the member's grill, Hackett bought the drinks and collected a couple of hundred in cash from Eggers. "You two gave us more of a match than I had anticipated," he said.

"Where did you find Freeman?" Eggers asked. "At the U.S. Open?"

Hackett laughed and shook his head. "Mike was a middling pro a very long time ago, but he made a very fine living for many years allowing gentlemen to nearly win their matches at some of the world's finest clubs."

"The man is an assassin," Eggers said.

"That must be what he does for you these days," Stone said. "When he's not assaulting people on the courts."

"No. Jim is a client's man; he has great charm, and he's a fine organizer of teams for special sorts of work," Hackett said. "Stone, what exactly do you do for this upstanding law firm of Bill's?"

Stone looked sideways at Eggers. "Oh, I handle the cases that Bill and his white-shoe colleagues don't want to be seen to handle."

"Is that a good description, Bill?" Hackett asked.

"Not far off the mark," Eggers replied, a little uncomfortably.

"You should be very pleased to have Stone," Hackett said. "Every business needs someone like him, and certainly every law firm." Hackett passed Stone a business card. "Stone, if Bill ever stops appreciating you, give me a call. You'd find a very comfortable home at Strategic Services."

"Jim," Eggers said, "that is an outright attempt at theft, and I resent it. I mean, it's not like you let me win at tennis first."

"On the contrary, Bill," Hackett said, "knowing that you have someone like Stone on the payroll impresses me, makes me more likely to want to hire your firm. He also kept you alive in the second set, even after I knocked him senseless at the net."

"Stone has his uses," Eggers said. "Standing between me and cannon fire is one of them."

"I understand that you two impressed Lord Wight yesterday at lunch," Hackett said.

"We had a pleasant conversation," Eggers said, "even if Stone had to leave to get someone out of jail."

"Hah!" Hackett roared. "I love it! Someone from Woodman and Weld fishing a client out of the pokey!"

"And I have the only record of his arrest in my pocket," Stone said.

"I hope to God he didn't murder anybody," Eggers said.

"No," Stone replied. "He merely pressed a disagreement over a traffic ticket a little too far and got himself a free ride to the precinct."

"That's what I mean," Hackett said. "A firm needs somebody like Stone."

AS EGGERS WAS being shown into his chauffeured car after dinner, he turned back toward Stone. "I hope you didn't take that offer from Jim Hackett seriously."

"I hope you did," Stone said, turning toward home.

26

As Stone arrived at Elaine's, Dino and Felicity were just ordering. He waved away a menu. "No thanks, just a drink; I've already eaten."

Elaine, who was seated with regulars at the next table, reached over and took Stone by a lapel. "What did you say?"

"A business dinner," Stone said, knowing her views on those who dined before they arrived at her restaurant.

"People do business here," Elaine said, freeing the lapel from her grasp.

"I was forced to dine elsewhere, sweetheart," he said.

She looked unconvinced but turned back to her previous conversation.

"So," Felicity said, "what did you find out about Whitestone?"

"It didn't come up," Stone replied. "It would have been awkward to raise the question. Anyway, Hackett probably already knows I'm interested in Whitestone."

"How would he know that?"

"Because I raised the name with Lord Wight, and Hackett was aware of my and Eggers's lunch with him yesterday."

"So you think Hackett and Wight are in league?"

"Wight owns the building that is Hackett's headquarters. I don't know that they're otherwise 'in league,' as you put it."

"Let's suspect the worst," she replied.

"You do that; I'll just try to find Whitestone."

"You're not making a lot of progress on that, are you?" Dino asked.

"We've got the bank and the Seagram Building staked out; that's all we can do at the moment."

"Stone is making progress," Felicity said to Dino.

"Thank you, Felicity," Stone said.

Felicity took a sip of her Rob Roy. "If they are in league, then Hackett knows that you and I know each other, because you introduced me to Wight at the ambassador's dinner party."

"Good point," Stone said. "Also, Hackett seems to be the sort of guy who knows everything about everybody, so we'd best assume he knows everything about us."

"Everything?" Felicity asked.

"Well, not *everything*."

"Hackett also made me a job offer," Stone said. "Sort of."

"What sort of job offer?"

"He gave me his card and said if I ever tired of working for Woodman and Weld, he would make me comfortable at his company."

"Take the job," Dino said. "Then maybe *you'd* know everything."

"I think he did it just to annoy Bill Eggers," Stone said, "and it worked."

"Dino has a point," Felicity said.

"You want me to go to work for Hackett?"

"That would never do," Dino said. "Then Stone would actually have to work for a living."

Felicity couldn't suppress a laugh. "Why don't you drop him a note and manage to indicate some interest?"

"Because Hackett would see that Eggers knew about it, and I'd catch hell from him."

"Then tell Eggers why you're doing it," she said.

"You want him to know about Whitestone?"

"You already mentioned the name in his presence at the dinner party."

"You want me to tell him I'm working for you?"

"Certainly not. You can lie about that."

"Lies have a way of coming back and biting one on the ass."

"Oh, handle it, Stone," she said.

Dinner came, and the waiter began pouring an expensive bottle of wine.

"That's two, Dino," Stone said.

"And two to go," Dino replied.

THE FOLLOWING MORNING Stone was in his office when the phone rang. Joan had gone out for something, so he picked it up. "Stone Barrington."

"You answer your own phone?" Hackett said. "Don't you have a secretary?"

"You place your own calls?" Stone asked. "Don't you have a secretary?"

Hackett laughed heartily. "Let's have lunch today," Hackett said. "There's something I'd like to discuss with you."

"All right," Stone replied.

"The Four Seasons at one?"

"That's Eggers's hangout," Stone replied.

"All right, Michael's?"

"Good," Stone replied. "See you at one." He hung up and called Eggers. The secretary put him through.

"Good morning, Stone," Eggers said. "I thought that went well yesterday."

"I don't know about you, Bill, but it wore me out," Stone replied.

"You should stay in better shape," Eggers said, chuckling.

"You going to get any business from Hackett?"

"I wouldn't be surprised."

"How close are Hackett and Wight?"

"They know each other. I don't know any more than that."

"Hackett just called and invited me to lunch today. I accepted."

"Now you listen to me, Stone . . ."

"Easy, Bill."

"You're not going to . . ."

"Bill, if I were job hunting, I wouldn't be telling you about it, would I?"

"Then why are you having lunch with him?"

"Because I need some information for one of my own clients, and Hackett may have it."

"What client?"

"You know I can't tell you that. I can tell you there's no conflict with Woodman and Weld."

"Well, all right, then, but I want to know if he tries to poach you away from me."

"But then I'd be violating Hackett's confidence."

"Goddamn it, Stone . . ."

"Bill, you're going to have a stroke if you're not careful."

"Don't you accept any work of any kind from Hackett, without my agreement."

"Bill, I'm not trying to screw you. You've been very good to me, from the beginning. I just want to tap Hackett's brain for my other client."

"All right, all right, but you call me after lunch."

"I will, but I don't know how much I can tell you."

Eggers hung up without another word.

27

Michael's was a restaurant on West Fifty-fifth Street that catered to the publishing and media crowd, and Stone wondered why Hackett had chosen it. It was a wide-open room with contemporary furniture and good art on the walls. Michael Mc-Carty, the owner, had opened his first Michael's in Santa Monica, California, in the late 1970s and the New York place not long afterward.

Hackett was already seated at a prime table when Stone arrived on time. They shook hands, and Stone took a seat. "This is a publishing hangout," Stone said. "What are you doing here?"

"It's close to my office, and the food is great," Hackett replied. "That's about all I demand of a restaurant, except for fine wines, good service, attractive decor and beautiful women to look at."

"Who could ask for more?" Stone said.

Hackett had already ordered a bottle of wine and poured Stone a glass. "One of my favorite chardonnays," he said. "Far Niente."

"One of mine, too," Stone said, sipping the delicious wine.

Menus were brought, and Hackett, with Stone's permission, ordered sweetbreads with morel mushrooms for both of them.

"I wasn't kidding yesterday," Hackett said.

"That's what I'd like Bill Eggers to think," Stone said.

Hackett laughed. "You can use me as a ploy, if you like, but I'm serious."

"And I'm seriously appreciative," Stone said, "but I'm very happy with my arrangement with Woodman and Weld. It gives me a lot of freedom."

"What sort of freedom?"

"I can travel pretty much when I like: I enjoy Maine and the Florida Keys. I fly myself around."

"What do you fly?"

"Something called a JetProp. It's a Piper Malibu that's had the piston engine replaced with a turbine. Does two hundred sixty knots at twenty-seven thousand feet."

"I fly myself, too," Hackett said, "except I have a new Cessna Citation Mustang. I just got type-rated last month."

"What did that require?"

"The usual program is two awful weeks in a simulator in Wichita with a lot of classes and an FAA check ride at the end, but I couldn't take that big a chunk of time off, so I hired an instructor and learned everything over about a six-week period, then took the check ride. Who's your tailor?" Hackett asked, suddenly changing the subject.

"Doug Hayward, in London," Stone said. "Doug died last year, but his cutter, Les, is still there, and the shop's open."

"Doug has made my clothes for thirty years," Hackett said.

"I hear you were in the Paratroop Regiment," Stone said.

"Went in at eighteen," Hackett replied, "a fresh little Scot right out of a croft in the Shetlands."

"What happened to your accent?" Stone asked.

"I was led astray by American women."

Stone laughed. "They'll do that."

"God bless 'em," Hackett agreed. "I can still produce a burr on demand, but I've been an American for a long time. How about if I give you an occasional assignment?" Hackett asked.

"If it's something that wouldn't conflict with a Woodman and Weld client, sure," Stone said.

"I'll have to give that some thought," Hackett said. "I'm thinking of becoming a Woodman and Weld client myself."

"That would make it a lot easier for me," Stone said.

"Will you give me your frank personal assessment of the firm? In confidence, of course."

"If I were a business client looking for outstanding legal representation, wide influence and excellent political connections, I'd put my business there," Stone said. "I think that in their various fields they're the best."

"That's very reassuring," Hackett said, "and very much what I've heard from other sources. Do they do patent work?"

"They do, and they do it very well."

"I own a business that builds armored vehicles out of ordinary cars," Hackett said, "and we've developed some parts and processes that I've managed to keep very close to our vest. I'd like to patent them and, eventually, license them to other builders."

"I'm sure the firm would be delighted to handle that for you. Would you include all the company's legal work?"

"That seems a logical way to proceed," Hackett said. "I believe we spent close to two million on legal last year."

"Shall I speak to Bill and have him set up a meeting with a couple of people in patents and intellectual property rights?"

"Do that," Hackett said.

"I have a lightly armored vehicle, myself," Stone said. "A Mercedes E55."

"We've done a couple of dozen of those," Hackett said. "Where'd you buy it?"

"The local Mercedes dealer had taken the order from a fellow reputed to have very serious Italian friends. Unfortunately, his friends caught up with him shortly before it was delivered. I bought it from the widow, through the dealer."

"That's one of ours," Hackett said. "I remember the situation. You ready for a new one yet?"

"Well, it's several years old, now, but with low mileage, so I'm happy for the moment."

"I'll give you a better deal than you got before," Hackett said.

"It actually saved my life, once. Somebody took a shot at me from the back of a motorcycle. It needed a new window, a windshield and a couple of other parts, but it kept me safe."

"I love an endorsement like that," Hackett said. "Usually we get those from Africa or the Middle East; nice to have one at home. Seems we have more and more in common, Stone."

"Yes, it does, doesn't it?"

"Have you ever flown a jet?"

"No, I haven't."

"One day soon, let's go out to Teterboro and take a little trip. I'll let you fly left seat."

"I'd love to do that."

THEY FINISHED LUNCH, Hackett signed the check, and they walked a couple of blocks together.

"I'm sorry you won't think of joining me full-time," Hackett said, "but I will find some projects for you."

"It might be politic to arrange things through Bill Eggers," Stone said.

"Of course. By all means, let's be politic." He stopped, and they shook hands.

"Thank you for a very good and interesting lunch," Stone said. "I'll have Bill arrange a meeting for you."

"I'll look forward to it, Stone," Hackett said. He turned and walked toward Fifty-seventh Street and his offices.

"Oh, Jim," Stone called.

Hackett turned back. "Yes, Stone?"

"Something I meant to ask you: have you ever heard of a man named Stanley Whitestone?"

Hackett scratched his nose. "I have. He got cashiered out of MI6 some years back, dabbled in business with Lord Wight, I believe. Why do you ask?"

"I recently heard the name, and I was curious."

"Would you like to meet him tomorrow?"

Stone sucked in a breath. "Yes, thank you, I would."

"You're in Turtle Bay, aren't you?"

Stone gave him a card.

"I'll pick you up at one tomorrow," Hackett said. "You'll be home by dinnertime."

"Thanks, Jim."

"Don't mention it." Hackett turned and walked away.

STONE WALKED A little farther, then took out his cell phone and called Eggers.

"Stone? How did it go?"

"I believe I made a little rain for you, Bill."

"How so?"

"Hackett would like to meet with your best patents people about a business he owns, making armored private cars."

"Sounds good," Eggers said.

"It's better than that," Stone said. "Please him, and he'll give you all of that company's legal work. He says they paid their attorneys a couple of million last year."

"Very good indeed, Stone. Did you and Hackett come to any sort of private arrangement?"

"No, we didn't," Stone replied. "He offered me some projects, and I asked him to arrange them through you."

"Good man," Eggers said. "Do you want to attend the patents meeting?"

"Not unless I need a good nap," Stone said. "Bye-bye, Bill."

28

When Stone got home from lunch, Joan caught him as he came through the door. "Felicity called, said she won't be home tonight; something's come up."

"I'll call her on her cell," Stone said.

"She said you won't be able to reach her."

"Okay," Stone replied. He got some work done that afternoon, and by the following morning he still had not heard from Felicity, so he called her cell. For his trouble, he got a loud squawk and a recorded message saying the number was not in use.

AT ONE O'CLOCK Stone was standing out on his front stoop when a large, black SUV pulled up in front, and a rear window slid down. Jim Hackett waved him into the car.

"Is this one of your armored specials?" Stone asked.

"Top of the line," Hackett replied. "It will repel the hottest fire, even a roadside bomb."

"I hope you don't run into a lot of those," Stone said. "Where are we going?"

"To see Stanley Whitestone," Hackett replied. Then his cell phone rang and he talked for the next half-hour, while the car rolled through the Lincoln Tunnel and all the way to Teterboro Airport, where Stone kept his airplane.

They stopped at a gate, Hackett spoke some words into an intercom, the gate slid open and they drove through.

"They won't let me drive onto the ramp," Stone said.

"They would if you worked for me," Hackett replied. The car stopped at a Cessna Citation Mustang, which was painted in a red, white and blue livery, with stars and stripes on the tail.

A man in coveralls stood by the door of the airplane. "Your preflight inspection is all done, Mr. Hackett," the man said. "The ground power unit is connected, and the air-conditioning is on." He opened the door and let down a set of steps. "I've entered your clearance into the onboard flight plan."

"Hop in," Hackett said to Stone. "Take the left seat."

"I've never flown a jet," Stone protested.

"Then it's about time you did," Hackett said, pushing him aboard.

Stone got into the left seat and found three large glass displays lit up.

"I'll do the radios and the avionics," Hackett said, putting on a headset and indicating that Stone should do likewise. "You just fly the airplane."

Stone picked up the light headset hanging on the yoke before him and put it on.

Hackett was already on the radio, requesting permission to taxi. "Okay," he said to Stone, "release the parking brake there, do a one-eighty turn and follow the taxi line around to the left."

Stone adjusted his seat and then did as instructed. They stopped at the threshold for runway 1 and were told to wait for final clearance.

"Watch," Hackett said. He pressed a button on one of the throttles, and a set of command bars popped up. He flipped up a switch on the panel. "Pitot heat on," he said. "Now on clearance, taxi onto the runway and stop. Press the heading button and the switch above it, there." He pointed. "We've been given the Teterboro Five departure. That means we fly heading 040 after takeoff and at fifteen hundred feet turn left toward Patterson VOR and climb to two thousand feet." He turned a knob on the autopilot, and "2,000 feet" appeared in a little window on the primary flight display. They were cleared for takeoff, and Stone taxied onto the runway and stopped.

"Hold the brakes and push the throttles all the way forward," Hackett said.

Stone did so, and the engines came to a roar.

"Release the brakes, and I'll call the speeds for you," Hackett said.

Stone released the brakes, and the airplane leapt down the runway.

"Airspeed's alive," Hackett said. "Seventy knots, V1. Put both hands on the yoke and . . . rotate. Keep the flight director at the command bars."

Stone rotated and watched the screen, then did as he was told.

"Seven hundred feet, autopilot on," Hackett said, "heading 040. Fifteen hundred feet, turning left." He turned the heading knob, and the airplane followed its instructions. "Two thousand feet, leveling off, reducing power," Hackett said. "Pull the throttles back to sixty percent." He tapped a gauge.

Air traffic control came on and gave them 6,000 feet and direct Brezy, which Stone knew from his own experience was an intersection near the Carmel VOR.

"Where are we going?" he asked.

"Fly the airplane and don't ask questions," Hackett said, dialing in the new direction and altitude. Soon they were over Connecticut and handed off to Boston Center. They were given 35,000 feet for a new altitude, and Hackett made the control changes. "The autopilot has the airplane," he said to Stone. "Now you can talk."

"Where are we going?" Stone asked.

"To Bar Harbor, Maine," Hackett replied. "We'll find Whitestone near there."

The airplane climbed to 35,000 feet and leveled off. "This is awfully easy to fly," Stone said.

"It is, once you've been trained. You already know how to fly; learning to operate the new avionics and handle emergencies is the hard part." Hackett began giving Stone a lesson in using the switches and displays. The logic was much the same as that on Stone's airplane, since the avionics manufacturer of both was Garmin. Shortly, they were given direct Bar Harbor, and Hackett showed him how to accomplish that.

"There's nothing else to do but monitor the gauges until we descend." An hour later they were descending into Bar Harbor Airport in gloriously clear weather. Hackett talked Stone through the landing, and shortly they were at the ramp.

Stone followed Hackett to the parking lot, where another of his black SUVs was waiting, but this time Hackett drove. They crossed a short bridge onto Mount Desert Island and, ignoring the turn for Bar Harbor, drove toward the village of Somersville.

Once in the tiny eighteenth-century clapboard village, Hackett drove past a church and then pulled over. "Follow me," he said, getting out of the car.

They walked along a well-tended path through a cemetery, and Hackett stopped and looked around. "Would you say we are alone?" he asked.

Stone looked around. They were out of sight of the road now. "I'd say we are," he replied.

"Let's keep going, then." Hackett strode off with Stone behind him trying to keep up. Then Hackett abruptly stopped.

"STONE," HE SAID, "may I present Mr. Stanley Whitestone, late of London, England, but resident in this country for some years."

Stone looked down and saw the granite headstone with Whitestone's name and dates on it.

"I buried him nearly two years ago," Hackett said.

29

They returned to the car, and Hackett drove on for another mile. Then he turned left onto a paved road that became gravel, continued to the end and through a gate and stopped in front of a shingle-style house. They got out of the car and entered through the front door, which was not locked.

"This way to my study," Hackett said.

Stone followed him down a hallway and into a large, paneled room filled with books, with a computer desk built into one corner.

Hackett began rummaging through filing cabinets, muttering to himself. "I know they're here somewhere," he said. Finally, he extracted an envelope. "Have a seat and inspect these," he said, pointing to a chair before the fireplace. He switched on a lamp so that Stone could see better.

Stone opened the envelope and extracted some eight-by-ten color photographs. A naked man lay on a gurney with a cloth laid over his crotch. His chest was badly bruised, and there was a cut on his chin. He looked very much like an older version of the Stanley Whitestone photograph Felicity had given him.

Hackett sat down on the sofa next to Stone's chair. "Whitestone was my guest up here two years ago. I loaned him a car so that he could see some of the island. We had a dinner reservation, and when he had been gone for several hours I called the police to report him missing. I was passed on to an officer who asked me to describe Stan and the car he was driving. I did so, and he told me that Stan had been badly injured in a head-on collision with a fully loaded dump truck, a few miles from here.

"I went to the Bar Harbor Hospital and found that he had died only a moment before my arrival. I took those photos with a pocket camera I occasionally carry."

Hackett sighed. "I knew that he wasn't married and that his parents were dead. There were no siblings, either, so there was no one I knew of to inform. Finally, after the body had been in the hospital morgue for a couple of days, I called Lord Wight, who had recommended that I interview him for an open position in my firm, and he couldn't help, either. He did tell me that the man, who I had been told was named Robert Foster, was Stanley Whitestone. I had heard something of him on the grapevine. I made arrangements with the local funeral directors and bought a plot in the churchyard. Apart from the funeral director, I was the only person at the burial. There's another envelope inside the envelope in your hand."

Stone extracted a smaller envelope, opened it and found a death certificate. "Had you ever met him before he came to see you?"

"No, he called from New York and flew commercial up here, and I put him in the guesthouse. We talked for a while over lunch the following day, and I was impressed and had about decided to offer him the job. Then he went sightseeing, and I didn't see him again until he was dead."

"What did he tell you of his background?" Stone asked.

"He was the son of a career Royal Army officer, a colonel, educated at Harrow and Sandhurst, served for some years in the army as an intelligence officer, rose to the rank of major, then left and traveled for several years. He had an inheritance, I believe."

"What impressed you?"

"Intelligence, wit, knowledge of the political situation in a number of countries, especially in the Middle East. I needed someone to work out there, to be based in Saudi Arabia."

"Did he tell you where he had traveled?"

"Middle East, North Africa. I believed he lived in Morocco for a while." Hackett looked at his watch. "I said I'd have you back by dinnertime. You can keep the photographs if you like. I expect Dame Felicity would like to see them."

Stone didn't reply to that. He stuffed the items back into the envelope and took it with him.

Back in the airplane, he followed Hackett's instructions again and flew them back to Teterboro, where he flew an instrument approach into the airport. "I'm very impressed with the airplane," he said, as they shut down the engines. "Thank you for letting me fly it."

"Come to work for me, and you'll have one of your own next year," Hackett said.

"I don't think I could afford to run it," Stone replied.

"I'll see that you can," Hackett said as they deplaned. The man who had seen them off was there to tend to the airplane.

Back in the car, Hackett pressed a switch, and a thick glass window between the front and rear seats slid up. He turned toward Stone. "You think I'm Stanley Whitestone, don't you?"

"It crossed my mind," Stone said.

"I invite you to check out my background as thoroughly as you like," Hackett said. "I'm sure Dame Felicity would want you to."

Stone still didn't acknowledge the reference.

"Have you known her for long?"

Stone said nothing.

"Oh, come, Stone," Hackett said. "The two of you were together at the ambassador's dinner, and you introduced her to Wight. You can't deny that you know her."

"I don't deny it," Stone said.

"How did you meet?"

"In London some years ago. I was doing some work for a client there."

"Did you know what she was at the time?"

"She didn't talk about her work. Ours was a social relationship."

"Interesting that Whitehall is still interested in Whitestone," Hackett said. "I'm sure that's where the inquiry originated, not with Dame Felicity. Whitestone was before her time. I mean, they may have overlapped, but she would have been in the field when he was in Cambridge Circus."

"Cambridge Circus?"

"That's where their offices are, or were at the time of White-stone's departure."

"What did you hear about the reasons for his departure?" Stone asked.

"Some sort of row occurred in the higher reaches of the firm, I think, and Whitestone lost. His position became untenable as a result, and he left."

"Why would Whitehall want to find him now?" Stone asked.

"Interesting question," Hackett said. "I'm curious enough to want to know the answer. Would you like to find out for me?"

"I don't think so," Stone said.

"Oh, right: conflict of interest."

Stone didn't address that.

"Shall I drop you at home?" Hackett asked.

"Eighty-eighth and Second Avenue, if it's not inconvenient," he replied.

The car deposited him at his corner, and he walked the few feet to Elaine's. Dino was there, and so was Felicity.

30

Stone sat down, and a Knob Creek on the rocks was placed before him. "Evening, all," he said, placing the envelope on the table. He turned to Felicity. "Where have you been?"

"Away," she replied.

"I tried your cell phone and got a message that it was not in service."

"It's back in service," she said. "Where have you been?" She took a sip of her Rob Roy.

"Meeting Stanley Whitestone," he replied.

Felicity choked on her drink, and Stone had to pat her firmly on the back. "Start at the beginning," she said, dabbing at her watering eyes with a napkin.

Stone started at the beginning and gave her a blow-by-blow account of his afternoon.

Dino spoke up. "Hackett let *you* fly his jet?"

Stone ignored him. He handed Felicity the envelope and watched as she opened it and peered at the photos.

"It *could* be Whitestone," she said. "And he *could* have died as a result of a motorcar accident." She looked at the death certificate and the fingerprint card.

"Run the prints," Stone said. "That should settle it."

"Was he cremated?" Felicity asked.

"Hackett didn't mention cremation. I shouldn't think he'd have bothered with buying a cemetery plot if the body had ended up in an urn. And it's unlikely that there's a crematorium anywhere near the island."

Felicity put the photos and documents back into the envelope and stuffed it into her briefcase.

"That will be a hundred thousand pounds," Stone said.

"You haven't earned your fee yet," she replied.

"Well, I'm not performing an autopsy. Hackett didn't say if the body was embalmed, but if it wasn't, it's either mush or dust by now."

"I want everyone involved in Maine to be talked to: the hospital doctors and nurses, the police, the undertaker, the lot."

"My assignment was to locate Stanley Whitestone and report his whereabouts to you. I have done so. You said that after you knew where he was, others would deal with him."

"I think Hackett is Whitestone," Felicity said.

"I considered that. In fact, he brought it up himself. He invited me—or you—to investigate his background thoroughly."

"I will certainly have that done," she said. "I'd like you to handle the task on this side of the water."

"I will be happy to accept a new assignment," Stone said, "just as soon as I've been paid for the previous one."

"Your fee was predicated on success," she pointed out, "and we have not confirmed who, if anyone, is buried in that churchyard on Mount Desert Island."

"I've given you photographs of the body, a death certificate and his fingerprints. What more could anyone ask? If the prints aren't

Whitestone's, then we can talk," Stone said. "You can open the grave and examine the corpse if you like, after having obtained the proper permissions, of course. But . . ." He leaned forward for effect. ". . . if the fingerprints fit, you must remit. Agreed?"

"Spare me the Johnny Cochranisms, please," she said.

"Spare me a hundred thousand quid," he replied.

"Give me your bill," she said, "made out to the Foreign Office. If the prints are Whitestone's, I'll countersign it and submit it. You should have your check in a few weeks."

"Weeks?" Stone asked. "I have incurred considerable out-of-pocket expenses, mainly surveillance, both electronic and manned."

"I'll need the tapes for our files," she said.

"You may have them tomorrow," he replied, "and I would be grateful if you would see that payment is expedited." He took his checkbook from his pocket, tore out a check, voided it and handed it to Felicity. "You may wire-transfer the funds, in dollars, to this account, using the current exchange rate."

She added his check to her briefcase. "I'm starved," she said, and they ordered dinner.

"Hackett knew I was working for you," Stone said, when the waiter had left.

She looked at him askance. "You told him?"

"No, Lord Wight told him of meeting us together, and he figured it out. When he asked me, I did not confirm it."

"I don't like someone like James Hackett knowing about this."

"Then perhaps you shouldn't have taken me to that dinner party," Stone replied. "By the way, did you ever figure out who the VIP was who deserved to be served the Krug?"

"I expect it must have been Wight," she said. "No one else there was of much importance."

"Bill Eggers tells me that Wight's reputation is better here than at home."

"At home, his past is no more than a smudge on his copybook," she said. "He's been back in business for a while, now."

"Well, now we know that he was in touch with Whitestone right up until his death."

"Yes. He lied about that, didn't he? Said he thought Whitestone was in Cairo, when he had actually recommended him for a job with Hackett, and under an assumed name, too."

"Is there a crime in there somewhere?" Stone asked.

"No, it's not criminal to conceal the identity of a former member of the service, and we can't prove that he did anything criminal in conjunction with Whitestone."

"Hackett was curious about why the Foreign Office is still interested in Whitestone. I'm curious, too. Did the inquiry originate with them or with you?"

"Why do you want to know?"

Stone smiled a little. "Well, Hackett offered to hire me to find out."

She looked at him, shocked.

"I declined, of course," he said quickly.

"I should certainly hope so," she said. Then, looking thoughtful, she added, "I wonder why Hackett wonders why the F.O. is still interested in Whitestone."

"Maybe Whitestone isn't dead," Stone said. "Maybe the photos were faked. Hackett said he wanted to hire Whitestone—though he said he didn't know who he was at the time—to represent his company in the Middle East. Maybe Whitestone is, at this moment, representing his company in the Middle East."

"I want to know more," Felicity said.

"Look, Hackett is a very smart man. If he's protecting Whitestone by faking his death, you may be sure that all the people you want talked to in Maine have been bought."

"Or," Felicity said, "perhaps, Hackett and/or Whitestone found a look-alike, murdered him, battered the body and buried him, first taking photographs and Whitestone's fingerprints. In that case, he wouldn't need to buy anybody, would he?"

"There are all sorts of possibilities."

Felicity nodded. "And I don't like it when there are all sorts of possibilities."

31

When Stone awoke the following morning, Felicity's side of the bed was empty. Before he could order breakfast, she returned.

"I've used your scanner," she said. "The fingerprints are Whitestone's."

"You'll have my bill before noon," Stone said. "What would you like for breakfast?"

"Two fried eggs, wheat toast and blood sausage, please. And English breakfast tea."

"I don't believe we stock blood sausage," Stone replied. "God, but that's a disgustingly British thing to eat at breakfast."

"All right, any sort of sausage."

Stone got Helene on the intercom and ordered for both of them.

"I'll expedite your check," Felicity said, "but there's one more thing I want you to do for me."

"What's that?"

"I want you to obtain James Hackett's fingerprints."

"He's a naturalized citizen; they'll be in the FBI database."

"No. I want you to obtain them directly from the source."

"Oh, I see. You want me to go over to his office, hold him down and print him?"

"I would be grateful if you could be more subtle than that."

Stone thought about it. "All right, let's invite him to dinner."

"Here?"

"Why not? I have a dining room, a kitchen and a cook. At a restaurant I might have trouble confiscating his wineglass."

"All right," she said.

"And you must be here."

"Why on earth should I be here?"

"Because it will guarantee his acceptance. If he's Whitestone, it will be an opportunity to demonstrate his invulnerability to your identifying him."

"Oh, all right. Who else will you ask?"

"I think Bill Eggers. It would be an opportunity for them to get to know each other better."

"You need one more couple."

"How about Dino?"

"Why Dino?"

"Why not? Hackett, being in the business he's in, would love to get to know an NYPD lieutenant."

"We need someone who's not a drinking buddy of yours."

"Do you have a request?"

"You know the former police commissioner, don't you?"

"Yes, we have a cordial acquaintanceship. It might be a little uncomfortable, though."

"Why?"

"He's married to a woman I, ah, knew . . . rather well."

"Ask him, and get over it."

"I *am* over it."

"Not if you're uncomfortable inviting her to dinner with her husband."

"Oh, all right. I'll get Joan on it; we have to find an evening when everyone's available." He picked up the phone, buzzed Joan and asked her to arrange the dinner.

Their breakfast arrived on the dumbwaiter, and they sat up in bed with trays on their laps. Felicity stole his orange juice.

"You didn't order orange juice," Stone pointed out.

"I just did," she said. "Oh, all right, we can share."

Stone refilled the glass from the pitcher, and they shared.

"I was just thinking," Felicity said, stabbing a sausage link and making it disappear.

"Uh, oh," Stone said. "What now?"

"You said that Hackett had offered you employment."

"On three occasions," Stone said.

"Why don't you accept?"

"Well, first of all, I'm very happy with my current employment status."

"Take a leave of absence. Hackett would probably pay better, anyway."

"I can't argue with that," Stone said. "The problem is, you want me to work for him so that I can prove he's Whitestone and you can destroy him. That would leave me out of work, and I'd have to go crawling back to Bill Eggers, not to mention my own clients."

"Why do you think I want to destroy Hackett?" she asked.

"You clearly would like for something bad to happen to Whitestone, and if he's Whitestone . . ."

Stone's phone buzzed. "Yes?"

"Your dinner is arranged for tomorrow evening," Joan said. "You may expect your guests at seven."

"Wow," Stone said, "that was fast work."

"Yes," she said, "it was, wasn't it?" She hung up.

Stone turned to Felicity. "We're on for tomorrow evening. Drinks at seven." Stone cleared away their trays and sent them down to the kitchen on the dumbwaiter.

"You have a very efficient secretary," Felicity said. "What is her name again?"

"Oh, no you don't. You'll hire her for some secret mission."

"I might just do that," she replied, sipping her orange juice.

"I'm not telling you her name."

"It's Joan."

"I'm not telling you her last name."

"Oh, come on, Stone."

"I'll tell you if you'll tell me why you and/or the Foreign Office want to find Stanley Whitestone."

"That's just eating you up inside, isn't it?"

"It is. And I think I deserve to know."

"Hah!"

"Tell me," he said, kissing her on the ear.

"Let's not bring sex into this," she said.

"Why not? Sex goes with everything." He kissed her on the neck and ran a hand under the covers.

She turned toward him. "Maybe," she said, "when we're finished."

THREE-QUARTERS OF AN hour later, Stone lay panting and sweating. "All right," he said. "Tell me why you and/or the Foreign Office want to find Stanley Whitestone."

"I didn't say I'd tell you that."

"Oh, yes, you did."

"I said maybe."

"The implication was that, if I performed well, you'd tell me."

"You may have inferred that; I certainly didn't imply it."

"All right, my participation in this project ends now."

"What are you going to do about your dinner party?"

"I'm going to use it to cement the relationship between Hackett and Eggers, so I'll get a nice bonus. I'm not going to bother to get Hackett's fingerprints."

Felicity leaned over and kissed his penis, then slipped it between her lips.

"That's not fair," Stone breathed.

"I can stop at any time," Felicity said, pausing.

"Don't stop."

"You'll get Hackett's prints?"

"Yes."

Felicity continued.

32

Stone had his bill typed up and handed it to Felicity on her way out. "You'll expedite it?" he asked.

"I said I would."

"Paid in days, not weeks?"

"Probably."

"What?"

"I can do only so much. As it is, I'll have to phone the foreign minister personally. I may not be available for dinner tonight."

"You know where to find me."

"Thank God I like the food at Elaine's," she said, and headed for the ambassador's Rolls.

Stone walked back to his office to find Joan waiting for him.

"Here," she said, placing a pile of papers on his desk, "these are the closing documents for Herbie's new penthouse."

"When is the closing?"

She looked at her watch. "In eight minutes."

"Does Herbie know?"

"He's waiting outside, clutching a cashier's check for three million one hundred fifty thousand dollars. He wanted to bring cash, but I wouldn't let him."

"Why did he want to bring cash?"

"He had some idea that the IRS would find out about the apartment."

"Why would they care?"

"I tried to explain that they wouldn't be interested, but he wouldn't believe me."

"Send him in."

Herbie appeared at the door in another new suit, and his hair had grown out enough to make him look like a normal person. "Hey, Stone," he said.

"Come in, Herbie, and sit down." Herbie sat down. "What's all this about the IRS?"

"I just don't want them to know that I own an expensive apartment."

"Why not?"

"What if they try to take it away from me?"

"Why would they do that?"

"To make me pay my taxes."

"Herbie, when the lottery people gave you the check, they paid both the state and federal taxes on that income in full."

"They did?"

"That's the way they work."

"So I don't owe the IRS anything?"

"I didn't say that. How much did you make last year?"

Herbie shrugged. "A hundred and a half, maybe."

Stone was surprised. "From what source?"

"Some from the ponies, some from poker."

"But you had to pay your bookie and your loan shark a bunch of money, didn't you?"

"That was how much I lost," Herbie said. "A hundred and a half was how much I won."

"Well, if you combine those numbers, you ended up with a loss."

"I did?"

"Your accountant will explain it to you. He will also explain how, if you're going to earn your living as a gambler, you'd better keep some records."

"But if I do that, the IRS will tax me."

"If you had kept records for the last year, you'd have a very large deduction to take, and you wouldn't owe any taxes."

"Oh."

"Please, talk to your accountant."

"I don't have one."

"You need one desperately," Stone said, digging a card out of his desk. "Call this guy; he's first-rate."

"Can't you be my accountant?"

"Certainly not. I'm your lawyer; I have little financial expertise. That guy can tell you how to hang on to your money and to live on the income from it."

"Okay, I'll call him. By the way, I want the apartment in Sheila's and my names."

"Too late," Stone said. "All the documents are in your name; it would take a long time to change them, and you couldn't move into the apartment today."

"Oh, we moved in last week," Herbie said.

"How did you do that?"

"I swiped a key from the real estate lady."

"Herbie, we close today, with the apartment in your name."

"But I told Sheila . . ."

"You tell Sheila to call me for an appointment. I'll sort it out."

Joan buzzed. "The seller and his attorney and the real estate agent are here."

"Send them in," Stone said, moving to the conference table. "Herbie, say nothing during these proceedings. All you do is sign your name where I point, and keep your mouth shut."

Somewhat to Stone's astonishment, Herbie did just that, and in a little over half an hour everything was signed and the transaction completed. The seller's team left.

Stone handed Herbie two sets of keys. "Here are the keys you're supposed to have. You can move in now."

Herbie pocketed the keys and shook Stone's hand. "Thanks, Stone, you've been great."

"See that accountant, Herbie, or soon you won't have any money left."

"I'll call him tomorrow," Herbie promised and then ran out of the office.

Joan came in. "How'd it go?"

"Very smoothly," Stone replied. "Good job on the document package."

"It's what I do," she said.

"Among many other things. Felicity was very impressed with how quickly you put together the dinner party for tomorrow night."

"It was easy, once each guest knew who the other guests would be."

"Oh, you'd better hire a waiter and somebody to help Helene in the kitchen."

"I have already done so."

"I suppose you've planned the menu, too."

"Hot hors d'oeuvres, then crab soup to start, followed by beef Wellington, *pommes soufflées* and haricots verts. Crème brûlée for dessert. You can pick the wines."

"Thank you very much, and give yourself a ten percent raise."

"Oh, good!" she squealed and gave him a big hug.

Stone reflected that if she quit, he'd have to shoot himself.

33

Stone went into the dining room to check the table setting and to distribute the place cards. The hired waiter came into the room, and Stone took him to the chair where Hackett would be sitting. "Is Bob Cantor here yet?" Cantor was coming to handle the fingerprinting.

"Ten minutes ago," the waiter replied.

Stone picked up the three wineglasses at Hackett's place and polished them with his linen handkerchief. "Now these three glasses are free of fingerprints," he said. "When you clear away each course, take the empty wineglass into the kitchen, holding it by the stem, not touching the bowl, and give it to Bob, understand?"

"Got it," the waiter said.

BILL EGGERS AND his wife arrived exactly on time for dinner, which meant ten minutes before anyone else. The waiter served them drinks.

"I wanted to tell you, before the others arrive, that Jim Hackett met with our intellectual property people this afternoon, and they pleased him. He's on board with Strategic Services, and he's said that if we do a good job, he'll give us more business."

"I'm delighted to hear it," Stone said.

"You'll find your rainmaking reflected in your bonus."

"I'm delighted to hear that, too."

"Jim has also said that he'd like you to take on some projects for him."

"I'm glad to do that as long as you're on board with it."

"I am."

"Did he say what sorts of things he'd like me to do?"

"No. In fact he specified that, while nothing he assigns you will be a conflict of interest with Woodman and Weld, the details of your assignments would remain strictly between you and him. I'll rely on you to avoid conflicts."

"I will do so."

Felicity came downstairs and was reintroduced to the Eggerses, then the doorbell rang, and the former commissioner and his wife, Mitzi, walked in. It was the first time Stone had seen them since the wedding. Stone shook the commissioner's hand, and Mitzi offered him a cheek while Felicity observed, then was introduced.

Jim Hackett was the last to arrive, with a beautiful woman called Vanessa, to whom, Stone surmised, Hackett was not married. They settled in for cocktails, while the waiter brought hot hors d'oeuvres.

"Stone," Hackett said, "I expect Bill has told you I met with his people this afternoon."

"Yes, he has."

"I was pleased with what I heard, and I thank you for arranging it," Hackett said. "Dame Felicity, it's good to see you again after so much time has passed."

"I'm pleased to see you, Mr. Hackett," Felicity replied.

"It's just plain Jim, please."

"And it's just plain Felicity." Her gaze seemed to be boring into Hackett. "We met at a dinner party in London some years ago, as I recall."

"That's correct."

"I thought at the time you seemed familiar. Had we ever met before that?"

"No, I don't believe so, though I did meet your father once, at lunch at the Garrick Club. He was a very impressive gentleman."

"The Garrick was his favorite," Felicity said. "I understand you are a native of the Shetland Islands."

"I am."

"You grew up there?"

"Yes. My father was a crofter—he tended the sheep—and my mother was the weaver."

"You've made quite a leap from those days, haven't you?"

"From those days to these required a number of leaps," Hackett said. "The army got me out, and then I got out of the army."

"How did you come to be in the security business?"

"I was in the Paratroop Regiment, and on occasion we served as armed guards for various high-ranking officers and other dignitaries. A mate of mine left the regiment and joined a security firm, and then invited me to join when my enlistment was up. The two of us were adept at devising new security procedures, and eventually we went out on our own. My partner was killed in a car-bomb explosion, and I was left with the business."

"What was his name?" she asked.

"Tim Timmons," Hackett replied. "He had no family, so his half of the business came to me."

Stone could practically see her memorizing this information.

STONE HAD PICKED particularly good wines from his cellar, and they went down well at dinner. Even Felicity and Mitzi seemed to take to each other, and Hackett went out of his way to be charming to Felicity. Stone tried to just watch and listen. The waiter appeared to be doing his job with Hackett's wineglasses.

WHEN THE GUESTS had gone, Stone went into the kitchen and found Bob Cantor. "How did it go?" he asked.

"I've got clear prints of the thumb and four fingers of his right hand," Bob said, handing Stone a sheet of paper. "I've scanned and printed them for you."

"Great job," Stone said. "Talk to you later." Stone went back into the living room and handed Felicity the prints. "All five fingers, right hand," he said.

"Perfect," she replied. "I'll get them checked in the morning."

They went upstairs and undressed for bed. "Well," he asked, "what did you think about Hackett?"

"I was mesmerized," she said.

"Was there anything about him that reminded you of Stanley Whitestone?"

"Everything and nothing. First I would think that I had detected some word or movement that was Whitestone, then it would be gone, submerged in Hackett's personality. He gave a bravura performance."

"So you think it was a performance?"

"At least to the extent that everyone performs at a good dinner party, and, by the way, it was a good dinner party. You're an excellent host."

"I suppose your people will be checking out this Tim Timmons?"

"Oh, certainly," she said, "and I expect we'll find that the facts will jibe with Hackett's account of them."

"Then why bother?"

"Because everyone makes mistakes, even James Hackett, and when he does, I want to be on top of things."

"I have to tell you that I'm convinced Hackett is who he says he is."

"Why?"

"Because nobody could so completely morph his identity into that of another. I mean, you knew Whitestone, and Hackett had no hesitation in talking to you all evening."

"You know the films of Laurence Olivier, don't you?"

"Yes, of course."

"That's what Olivier did—submerge himself into character—and I think that's what Hackett has done. I think Hackett is the Olivier of liars."

"What is Whitestone's background?"

"You've heard some of it: Eton and Cambridge, recruited there."

"Who was his father?"

"The bastard son of a marquess who was sent into the church and served out his years as a small-parish vicar."

"Has all that been substantiated?"

"Of course. When one is at both Eton and Cambridge, one leaves indelible footprints that anyone can follow."

"Hackett says that when Whitestone met him, seeking employment, he said he was Harrow and Sandhurst, son of an army colonel."

"A person with such a background would leave equally indelible footprints and if he lied would easily be found out. It is impossible to believe that Whitestone would have invented such an easily penetrated legend."

"What about Hackett's 'legend,' as you put it?"

"More difficult, at least his early years. The Paratroop Regiment is another thing, though. After all, they keep records."

"And you've already read them?"

"It's being looked into," Felicity said.

Stone reflected that he would not enjoy Felicity looking into some lie of his own.

34

Stone was at his desk the following morning when Joan buzzed him. "Mr. Jim Hackett on one," she said.

Stone picked up the phone. "Good morning, Jim," he said.

"A perfectly wonderful dinner last night, Stone, and with very fine company."

"I'm glad you enjoyed it, Jim. We were happy to have you."

"Dame Felicity turned out to be much more . . . approachable than I had surmised from our first meeting."

"A couple of glasses of Champagne will do that."

"Well, thanks again. Now to business: you're mine for the next two, two and a half weeks. I've cleared this with Bill Eggers, so clear your decks."

"All right. What do I do?"

"Someone is sitting in your outer office at this moment who will explain everything. I probably won't speak to you again until you've completed your assignment, so have a good time."

"I'll try," Stone said, but Hackett had already hung up.

Joan buzzed. "A Ms. Ida Ann Dunn to see you, representing Mr. James Hackett."

"Send her in," Stone said.

A handsome woman of about fifty entered his office carrying a satchel and followed by Joan, who was carrying two other cases. "Good morning, Mr. Barrington," she said, dropping her heavy satchel on his desk and opening it.

"Please call me Stone."

"And you may call me Ida Ann," she replied, hefting a large three-ring notebook from her satchel and dropping it with a thump before him. "Over the next five days or so, you will memorize this," she said. The cover read *Operators Manual, Cessna 510*. "And this," she said, placing a smaller book on top of it, the title of which was *Garmin G-1000 Cockpit Reference Guide*.

"After the five-day study period with me, you will meet Mr. Dan Phelan, who will instruct you in the actual flying of the Cessna 510. After thirty or forty hours in the airplane, you'll take a check ride with an FAA examiner, who will issue you a type rating for the 510. Any questions? No, never mind. I'll ask the questions; you start reading."

Stone opened the operator's manual. "Why am I doing this?" he asked.

"If you'll forgive me, Mr. Barrington—Stone—that's a rather stupid question. You are doing this because Mr. Hackett is paying you to do so."

"Of course," Stone replied. He picked up the phone and buzzed Joan.

"Yes?"

"Clear my schedule for the next two weeks," he said. "Make that two and a half weeks."

"That will be easy," Joan replied. "The only thing we have scheduled for the next two and a half weeks is a visit from the Xerox man and, probably, several visits from Herbie Fisher."

"You deal with the first fellow, then tell Mr. Fisher I'll be unavailable. And hold all my calls, except those of Felicity Devonshire."

"You betcha," she replied and hung up.

Ida Ann Dunn now had a laptop projector set up on the conference table and a screen hung on a wall. "Come over here, please, Stone, and bring the operator's manual with you."

Stone took a seat at the conference table, and Ida Ann began. By the time Stone was allowed to have a sandwich at the conference table, she had covered structural systems, electrical systems and lighting with slides and animation, while he kept up the pace in the manual. She ate wordlessly, flipping through her notes.

After lunch, Ida Ann covered the master warning system, the fuel system, auxiliary power system and power plant. Promptly at five p.m., Ida Ann switched off the projector and handed Stone several sheets of paper.

"Quiz time," she said. "As you will note, the examination is multiple choice. You have forty minutes."

"May I be excused to go to the restroom?" Stone asked.

"Be quick about it," she replied.

Stone was quick, and then he tackled the exam.

Ida Ann ran quickly through it. "You missed a question," she said. "Let's review the fuel system again."

Twenty minutes later, satisfied that he understood his error, she dismissed him, said she would see him at nine the following morning, then was gone.

Stone stood up and stretched, rubbing his neck.

"And what was that all about?" Joan asked from the doorway.

"I'm being taught to fly a jet airplane," he said.

"At the conference table?"

"First, ground school, then flying."

"And Hackett is paying you to do this?"

"He is. Call Eggers's office later this week and find out how much to bill him."

"Will do. Oh, Felicity called and said she'd meet you at Elaine's at eight-thirty."

"Then I have time for a nap," Stone said, heading upstairs, exhausted.

STONE ARRIVED AT Elaine's to find Dino already there, as usual, and the two ordered drinks while they waited for Felicity.

"How was your day?" Dino asked amiably.

"You won't believe it," Stone replied. "I spent it in ground school, learning to fly a Cessna Mustang."

"Isn't that a jet?"

"It is."

"But you don't own a jet."

"I do not."

"Are you planning to buy one?"

"I have a new client, Jim Hackett, who says that if I come to work for him, I'll be able to buy one next year."

"You're leaving Woodman and Weld?"

"No. Hackett is hiring me through the firm for special projects."

"And the first special project is learning to fly a jet?"

"You guessed it."

"And he's paying you for this?"

"You guessed it again."

"How long will it take?"

"Two, two and a half weeks."

"You can learn to fly a jet that fast?"

"You forget, I already know how to fly; I'm just learning a new airplane."

Felicity made her entrance forty minutes late. "Apologies," she said. "Drink."

Stone waved at a waiter and secured a Rob Roy.

"How was your day?" she asked.

Stone gave her a brief account of it.

"And it takes only two weeks to learn?"

"If I'm lucky."

"I'm not flying with you," she said. "Let me know when you have a hundred hours."

"I already have three thousand hours," he said.

"A hundred hours in type."

"Right. What have your day's investigations produced?"

And she began to complain.

35

Felicity took a sip of her Rob Roy. "Turns out that the records of the Parachute Regiment at the time Hackett alleges he was a member are stored in an army warehouse in Aldershot, south of London."

"So?" Stone asked. "Are they available?"

"They are available," she replied, "but they are a sodden, mold-infested mess, having been placed in a corner of the warehouse that has been flooded twice by huge rainstorms in the past two years."

"What can you do about that?"

"I've been able to spare two document specialists who are trying to dry and extract the relevant pages," she replied, "but quite frankly, if I had a dozen people to spare for a year, that might not be enough manpower or time to find Hackett's and Timmons's records."

"In this country," Stone said, "if you are fingerprinted for anything—military service, for instance—your prints end up in the FBI database. Is the same true in Britain?"

"Yes, and we've already been to the police, but that far back, none of the records have been computerized, so a search of paper records has to be done by hand. The problem that arises is that hardly anyone with the police is old enough to know how to accomplish such a search, as opposed to a computer search. We are being defeated by the lack of old skills among younger employees. What's more, the records from that time have also been stored in a warehouse in boxes that were poorly labeled."

"So you have no hope of finding a record of Hackett's fingerprints?"

"Very little hope. It's just barely possible that we might get lucky."

"I have a suggestion," Stone said.

"Please make it a good one."

"Hackett is a naturalized American citizen," Stone pointed out. "He would have been fingerprinted at the time of submitting his application for citizenship, and the State Department would have his application on file."

Felicity brightened. "That is a very good suggestion, Stone. I'll have the ambassador make inquiries tomorrow." She wrinkled her brow. "I wonder what the State Department would make of a foreign ambassador inquiring about the fingerprints of an American citizen."

"Good point," Stone said. "It might be better to have your police make the request through the FBI."

"Perhaps so," she said. "I'll phone the commander of the Metropolitan Police tomorrow and make the request." She took another sip of her drink. "Why do you suppose Hackett wants you to learn to fly a jet aeroplane?"

"I can only guess," Stone said. "When he was trying to persuade me to come to work for him he told me that, in a year, I'd be able to afford my own jet."

"That must be very alluring for you," Felicity said.

"It's interesting, but not alluring."

"I'll bet you've had little-boy fantasies for years about flying your own jet."

"I'm afraid you're right," Stone admitted.

"Then why don't you go to work for him?"

"That's what I'm doing right now; Woodman and Weld has assigned me to Hackett."

"So what's the difference?"

"The difference is, if you can prove that Hackett is Whitestone, you're going to do something terrible to him, and Strategic Services would probably come crashing down without him to run it. Then where would I be?"

"Not at Woodman and Weld."

"Exactly."

"If that happened," Dino pointed out, "you could sell your hypothetical jet and live on the proceeds."

"Sell my hypothetical jet?" Stone asked. "Never!"

Felicity managed a laugh.

"You should do that more often," Stone said. "You've been working too hard."

"No harder than usual."

"Who's minding the store in London while you're here?"

"I have a very competent deputy who handles the administrative side. The rest I am doing from the office here."

"Don't you ever have to make an appearance?" Dino asked.

"Eventually," Felicity replied. "It's not as though I'm the prime minister or some other public figure. I don't have to appear in the newspapers or on television every day or be interviewed by anyone."

"How much longer can I count on having you as my houseguest?" Stone asked.

"At least until we get to the bottom of the Hackett/Whitestone riddle," she replied.

"Then I'll have to work more slowly," Stone said.

36

Stone submitted to the tender ministrations of Ms. Ida Ann Dunn for the remainder of the week. Felicity was little seen and reported no further progress on substantiating the identity of James Hackett.

On Friday afternoon Ida Ann closed the operator's manual, switched off her projector and handed Stone a thick sheaf of papers. "Your final examination," she said. "You have three hours." She tucked the manual in one of her cases. "So you can't cheat," she said. "I'll be back."

Ida Ann disappeared and came back in two and a half hours. "Are you done?" she asked as she walked into Stone's office.

"You said I have three hours," Stone replied.

"I didn't say you had to *take* three hours."

"Give me a minute, all right?"

"Take your time," she sighed.

Ten minutes later, Stone handed her the completed answer sheet.

She placed a template over it and ran down the columns with a finger. "My, my," she said.

"That bad?"

"That good. One hundred percent."

Stone sagged with relief, because he knew that if he had missed any answers he would have had to undergo a further lecture on the misses.

Ida Ann tucked the answer sheet into her briefcase and offered her hand.

Stone shook it.

"Tomorrow morning at eight o'clock, please meet Mr. Dan Phelan, your flight instructor, at Jet Aviation at Teterboro Airport. And take along your logbook, license and medical certificate."

"But tomorrow's Saturday," Stone complained. "Don't I get the weekend off?"

"You do not," she replied, and with a little wave over her shoulder she departed.

THE FOLLOWING MORNING at eight, Stone walked into the pilot's room at Jet Aviation and looked around. Various uniformed corporate crews sat around gazing blankly at CNN on a large television set. A man in a battered leather flight jacket, dark trousers and a white shirt stood up and walked over.

"Stone Barrington? I'm Dan Phelan." They shook hands.

"I guessed."

"Let's go sit down in a quiet corner for a few minutes." They took a vacant table and two chairs. "Let me see your license, your medical certificate and your logbook."

Stone handed them over, and Phelan started with the license. "I understood you've been flying a JetProp," he said. "How come you have a multiengine rating?"

"I got it in anticipation of buying a Beech Baron twin, but then I changed my mind and bought a Malibu, and later had it converted."

"So the only twin time you have is your training for the rating? Six hours?"

"That's correct."

"Well, by the time you take your check ride for your Mustang-type rating, you'll have a lot more." He examined Stone's medical certificate and handed it and the license back to him, then he began flipping through the logbook. "I see you've flown in and out of Teterboro a lot over the past few years."

"I'm based here," Stone replied.

"That will stand you in good stead," Phelan said. "Teterboro is the busiest general aviation airport in the country; if you can handle an airplane here, you can handle it anywhere." He handed Stone a sheaf of copies of New Jersey instrument approaches. "Today, we're going to fly out west of here to a practice area and do some air work: steep turns, slow flight and stalls. Then we'll grab some lunch and fly some approaches at other airports. When we're done, we'll come back here and fly whatever approach is in use. Got it?"

"Got it," Stone said.

Phelan opened his briefcase and unfolded a very large photograph of the Garmin G-1000 instrument panel in the Mustang. "I understand you've already got a couple of cross-country flights in with Mr. Hackett, so you must be a little familiar with this."

"Jim did all the avionics operation," Stone said. "I just flew the airplane. I have read the cockpit reference guide, though."

Phelan produced a checklist for the airplane and had Stone go through it step-by-step and show him where the controls were for each item. Then they did it again. An hour and a half later, Phelan said, "Okay, let's go flying."

They took over an hour to do a detailed preflight inspection of the aircraft, then go through the checklist of the startup procedures, entering the weights of people, baggage and fuel to be carried; getting a clearance; and entering a flight plan into the G-1000. Finally, they were ready to taxi, and fifteen minutes later they were in the air, climbing to 10,000 feet and headed west.

Phelan explained each air-work procedure they would do and then gave Stone the throttle settings and speeds for each. Stone performed them twice—a little shaky on the first try but much more confidently on the second—then they flew an instrument approach into an airport, had a hamburger and got back into the airplane. They flew another half-dozen approaches into various airports, a couple of them by hand without the help of the autopilot, then headed back to Teterboro and flew an instrument landing system to a full-stop landing.

They put the airplane to bed and walked back into the terminal.

"You did well," Phelan said. "You're clearly up-to-date on your instrument procedures, and you did a pretty good job of hand-flying the airplane."

"Thank you."

"Tomorrow we start on engine-out procedures: approaches, missed approaches and landings, all on one engine. It'll be fun."

Stone shook the man's hand, walked back to his car, got in and rested his head on the steering wheel. He felt as though he had been machine-washed and fluff-dried; every muscle ached. He got out his cell phone and called Mei, a Chinese lady, and scheduled a massage before dinner.

BY THE TIME Mei had finished with him, he felt human again and hungry.

Dino was waiting for him at Elaine's. "You look like shit," he said pleasantly.

"Let me tell you how I got that way," Stone said, taking his first, grateful sip of his Knob Creek.

37

When Stone walked into his bedroom, he found Felicity sitting up in bed, reading from a folder with a red stripe stamped across it. She closed the folder and put it into her briefcase, which was next to her on the bed. "How goes the flying?"

"Pretty good, but I'm exhausted," he said, peeling off his clothes and getting in bed beside her.

"No playtime tonight?"

"I'll do better in the morning," he said. "How's the search for Hackett's Paratroop Regiment records going?"

"Extremely slowly," she replied. "If my documents people don't find something soon, I'm going to have to pull them off the job."

"How about the search for his fingerprints with the State Department?"

"Oh, we found those," she said. "They're the same as Hackett's current prints."

"I hate to let the air out of your balloon, Felicity," Stone said, "but when Hackett came to this country twenty-five years ago,

Whitestone was still working in your service, was he not? And he couldn't be in two countries at once."

"Don't you think we've thought of that?" she asked. "It's funny, but the more convinced I become that Whitestone is Hackett, the more convinced you are that he's not. Could that be because he's letting you fly his jet airplane? Could that be because you like him?"

"I do like him," Stone confessed, "and I suppose that could mean I have a bias in his favor, but it doesn't affect the facts of the situation, and you have a lot of facts that you just can't reconcile."

"Yes, we do," she admitted, "but you don't have any facts to support Hackett's innocence."

"Of course I do. Whitestone could simply not have worked for your service on a full-time basis while simultaneously establishing a fabulously successful business in this country. That is a fact."

"No, it's not; it's a factoid."

"What's a factoid?"

"Something that seems to be true, but isn't what it seems, like a humanoid in a sci-fi movie?"

"Well, I don't know what else to do to help you. As it is, I'm spending all my time getting type-rated in an airplane I'm never going to be able to own or even fly, except with or for Jim Hackett. How is that helping you?"

"You're gaining his confidence," Felicity said, "and he's paying you to do it. That sounds like a win-win situation to me."

"Maybe for me, but not for you."

"When you've earned his confidence it will be easier to poke holes in his legend."

"When are you going to tell me why your people still care about Whitestone?"

"When I'm allowed to but not before," she replied. "And I may never be allowed to."

Stone pulled the covers up. "I can't think about this anymore," he said.

"See you in the morning," she replied and switched off her bedside lamp.

THE NEXT DAY Stone and Dan Phelan were taking off from Teterboro with Stone at the controls, when Phelan pulled the left throttle back to idle and said, "You've just lost an engine; handle it."

Stone applied right rudder and used the rudder trim to take the pressure of holding it off his leg.

"Very good," Phelan said.

"The airplane doesn't really handle any differently on one engine as long as the rudder is neutralized," Stone said.

"That's right; the airplane is very benign. Now let's go fly some single-engine instrument approaches and missed approaches."

AFTER THEY LANDED at Teterboro and secured the airplane, Phelan said, "You're doing well, but you're going to have to pay a lot more attention to your heading, airspeed and altitude when you're handflying the airplane. Your FAA check ride will be to Air Transport Pilot standards, and that means plus or minus five degrees of heading, ten knots of airspeed and a hundred feet of altitude."

Stone nodded wearily. "I know," he said.

FOR THE FOLLOWING three days Phelan ordered Stone around the sky while he honed his skills in every phase of piloting the airplane. On the fourth day Stone arrived at Teterboro to find Dan Phelan talking with a tall, slim, red-haired man.

"Stone," Phelan said, "let me introduce you to Craig Bird."

Stone shook the man's hand.

"Craig is an FAA examiner, and he will be conducting your check ride today."

"Today?" Stone asked, astonished. He had not prepared himself mentally for this.

"Today," Phelan said. "I'll leave you two to get on with it." He walked to the other side of the pilot's lounge, picked up a newspaper and began to read it.

"Let's sit over here," Bird said, and they settled at a table. "I gather you weren't expecting this, but Dan feels you're ready, and we've already completed the paperwork for your check ride. You'll probably do better for not having worried about it."

"I hope so," Stone said.

Craig Bird began asking him questions about the Mustang's systems, and Stone supplied the correct answers that had been ground into his brain by Ida Ann Dunn. An hour later, Bird said, "All right, you seem to know the airplane well; let's go fly it."

Bird watched as Stone performed the thirty-minute preflight inspection that he had performed for every day of his training. Then they got into the airplane and closed the door.

Stone picked up his voluminous checklist and turned to the first page. Bird took it away from him. "We're not going to use the checklist," he said. "Don't worry if you forget something, I'll remind you. I'm not going to break your balls. I just want to know if you can fly this airplane well and safely."

Stone worked his way across the instrument panel from left to right, putting them in their proper positions from memory, then started the engines.

THREE HOURS LATER Stone performed the best landing he had made during all his training. "Congratulations," Craig Bird said, "you're now single-pilot type-rated in the Cessna 510 Mustang."

Back at Jet Aviation, Phelan greeted them in the pilot's lounge. "How did it go?"

"He did just fine," Bird replied. He got on his computer and produced a document that was Stone's temporary license and type rating, pending receipt of his new license from the FAA. Bird shook his hand and left.

"I told you you'd do all right," Phelan said. He handed Stone a key to the airplane. "Mr. Hackett asked me to congratulate you and give you this," he said. "He said to use the airplane whenever you like. Just check the schedule with his secretary first."

Stone drove home with his type rating and the key burning a hole in his pocket. He wanted to fly somewhere.

38

Stone arrived home, garaged his car and walked into his office to find Felicity and Joan sitting on the leather sofa, sipping tea. Felicity looked shaken.

"Is something wrong?" he asked.

Joan spoke up. "Felicity had an encounter with Dolce," she said.

"I was getting out of the Rolls," Felicity said. "My driver was holding the door open for me, and suddenly this woman appeared out of nowhere with a knife in her hand. She swung it at my throat, but my driver got an arm in the way and took a bad cut on his forearm. Fortunately, the woman ran away."

"Was he badly hurt?"

"We had the police and an ambulance, and he was taken to an emergency room. He'll be back at work tomorrow morning."

"And you . . . How are you?"

She held up her teacup. "Joan has kindly administered the cure-all for any British subject," she said. "A nice cup of tea. I'm just fine."

"Does Eduardo know about this?" Stone asked Joan.

"I called him as soon as it was over. He was shocked, of course, but he took it well. He said he would do everything possible to see that such an incident not happen again, but he advised you to leave the house for a few days while he takes care of it."

"I can go back to the embassy," Felicity said.

"I've got a better idea," Stone replied. "What do you need to work besides a phone, a fax machine and a computer?"

"Those are my basic tools while I'm here," she said.

Stone went to the phone and called Jim Hackett's direct office line.

"This is Heather Finch," a voice said.

"Ms. Finch, this is Stone Barrington."

"Oh, yes, Mr. Barrington. Congratulations on your success with the jet. Dan Phelan has faxed us a glowing report on your performance."

"I'm calling because Jim kindly offered me the use of the airplane if he didn't need it."

"He's out of the country at the moment and won't be back for another week or ten days, so I'm sure that will be all right. Just leave me a number where I can reach you."

Stone gave her the number and his cell number, thanked her and hung up. He walked back to where Felicity sat. "Pack a bag," he said. "I'm taking you away from all this tomorrow morning."

THE FOLLOWING MORNING Stone backed out of his garage and drove Felicity to Teterboro Airport, with a black SUV in tow, containing two armed guards. An hour later they were in the air, headed to the Northeast.

"I don't understand why you won't tell me where we're going," she said, when they were at 33,000 feet and Stone was no longer so busy with navigating his way out of New York airspace.

"If I didn't tell you, then you couldn't tell anybody else," he said, "and I didn't want anybody else to know. Once we're there, you can tell whoever needs to know."

"Once we're *where*?" she demanded.

"I expect that, in the course of your work, you must have met Richard Stone."

"Of course. Dick was the CIA station chief in London some years ago," she replied. "He directed the agency's European operations from there. I was very sad to hear of his death."

Stone nodded. Dick Stone and his wife and daughter had been murdered on an island in Maine. "Dick was my first cousin," Stone said, "and in his will he left me the use of his Maine house for my lifetime. After I'm dead it will be sold, and the proceeds will go to an agency foundation set up for the widows and orphans of person-nel killed in the line of duty."

"I had heard that you two were related and that you were respon-sible for the solving of the murders."

"I was able to help," Stone said.

"Where is the house?"

"It's on the island of Islesboro, in the village of Dark Harbor, in Penobscot Bay, the largest bay in Maine. Dick had a very well-equipped office there, with everything you'll need."

"I can establish secure computer and other communications links with my office, then."

"I rather thought you could," Stone said. A little later, as they were descending through 11,000 feet, he pointed to the airport at Rockland before turning for Islesboro and beginning his final descent through the last 3,000 feet to the airfield, which lay dead ahead several miles.

"Can you land a jet on that little strip?" Felicity asked.

"We're about to find out," Stone replied. "I'm going to make an approach, and if I don't feel good about it, we'll go back to Rockland and get someone to fly us to Islesboro in something smaller."

"Nothing like experimentation," Felicity said.

Stone canceled his flight plan with Augusta Approach and descended toward the Islesboro airfield. He retarded the throttles, lowered the landing gear and put in a notch of flaps to lose speed. "The key is to cross the threshold at Vref," he said, "which is the final approach speed, given the landing weight of the airplane. We've burned off a thousand pounds of fuel, and there are just the two of us, so we're light."

"That's terribly reassuring," she said, looking unconvinced. "Exactly how long is that runway?"

"Two thousand four hundred and fifty feet," Stone said.

"Have you ever landed on a runway that short?"

"No, but I've landed on several that were only three thousand feet and with plenty of room to spare. Our speed is right on the money, and it takes only twelve hundred feet to stop the airplane once it's on the runway, so it shouldn't be a problem. Trust the airplane."

"I hardly *know* the airplane," she said.

"*Shhh*, I have to concentrate now."

"*Please do*," she muttered.

As Stone cleared the treetops near the end of the runway, he pulled the throttles back to idle and aimed just under the numbers. The little jet settled onto the paved strip, and Stone deployed the speedbrakes and stood hard on the brakes, which were excellent. They turned off the runway and taxied to a parking spot.

"May I open my eyes now?" Felicity asked.

"Of course," Stone said. "We had about seven hundred feet to spare when we turned off the runway."

"I suppose you're very pleased with yourself," she said.

"I am," he replied, setting the parking brake and working through the shutdown checklist. He turned off the last switch, got out of his seat, opened the door and deployed the little set of stairs. A man stood outside the door, and Stone handed him his briefcase. "Hello, Seth," he said, shaking the man's hand. Seth Hotchkiss was the caretaker of the Stone property, and he drove a 1938 Ford station wagon, beautifully restored.

"Hello, Mr. Stone," Seth replied. "You have a new airplane, I see."

"I'm afraid it's only borrowed," Stone replied, unlocking and opening the forward luggage compartment.

Felicity appeared at the airplane's door. "Is there actual earth I can set foot on?" she asked.

"No, there's just tarmac," Stone replied, taking her hand. "Seth, this is Felicity Devonshire." The two shook hands.

He put the engine plugs in place, the pitot covers on, and switched off the airplane's battery to preserve its charge.

TEN MINUTES LATER they were at the house, a handsome and roomy shingle-style home, and Seth's wife was giving Felicity the tour. Stone dug a card from his pocket and called an extension at state police headquarters in Augusta.

"Captain Scott Smith," a deep voice said.

"Captain, it's Stone Barrington." The two had met when Stone was investigating his cousins' murders.

"Mr. Barrington, how are you? Are you in Maine?"

"I'm well, and I'm on Islesboro."

"How can I help you?"

"I've just flown a friend here from New York. Yesterday she and her driver were attacked outside my house by a woman of my acquaintance wielding a knife. The driver was hurt, and the woman got away, but in the past she has been unusually persistent in finding me."

The captain asked for her description, and Stone gave it to him. "Tell you what," the captain said. "I have a regular patrol in the Camden-Lincolnville area. I'll have the car swing by there whenever the outbound ferry is boarding and keep an eye out for her. They'll see that nobody matching that description gets on until they've contacted you. I assume you're at the Stone house."

"That's correct, and I appreciate it, Captain."

"Glad to be of help."

Stone hung up as Felicity entered the room. He unlocked Dick's little office and showed her the room, with its computers and other equipment.

"This will do nicely," Felicity said, taking a seat at the desk. "Now, if you'll give me an hour or so, I'll start letting my people know I'm still alive." She looked at him over her reading glasses. "I hope the takeoff will be less exciting than the landing," she said.

39

Felicity was taking a nap when the phone rang, and Stone picked it up. Must be a wrong number, he thought. Nobody knew he was at this number in Maine. "Hello?"

"Stone, it's Jim Hackett."

Stone was stunned. How on earth had he been found? "Hello, Jim. This is quite a surprise. I'm at what Dick Cheney used to call 'an undisclosed location.'"

"You're at Dick Stone's house on Islesboro," Hackett said. "Did you think I wouldn't have a locator on my airplane?"

"I should have known," Stone said.

"I have a satellite photograph of it on the ramp at Islesboro, too. Oh, by the way, congratulations on your type rating," Hackett said. "Dan Phelan was impressed with your ability to learn quickly, and so am I. Frankly, I thought it would take you at least another week to pass your check ride. And congratulations on your landing in Islesboro; I wouldn't have attempted that."

"It's an easy airplane to fly, once you know the avionics," Stone said.

"You're too modest. Are you and Dame Felicity all right?"

"I'm very well," Stone replied. He wasn't going to play that game.

"I understand your former wife took exception to Dame Felicity's presence in your life."

"How do you come up with this stuff?" Stone asked, baffled.

"Stone, give me a little credit," Hackett replied. "I own one of the largest private security firms in the world; I have access to all sorts of information."

"I'm impressed," Stone said.

"Does Dame Felicity still think I'm Stanley Whitestone?"

"I can't tell you what she thinks."

"I understand she's having some difficulty verifying my identity," Hackett said. "I would have thought my fingerprints would have helped, but you'll get a package tomorrow that may help."

"A package of what?" Stone asked.

"Hang on." Hackett began a muffled conversation with someone else in the room and then came back on the phone. "I have to run," he said. "Stay in Maine with the airplane for as long as you like. If you need to contact me, call Heather Finch at my office, and she can patch you through to wherever I am."

"Where are you?" Stone asked, but Hackett had already hung up.

THEY DINED AT the Dark Harbor Inn, a handsome house on the outskirts of the village. There were only two other couples in the dining room, and neither of them, Stone thought, looked like anyone who would be surveilling them.

"You're thinking what I'm thinking," Felicity said.

"What?"

"About our fellow diners. I shouldn't worry; no one has any idea where we are, except my office in London, not even the ambassador."

"I'm afraid that's not so," Stone said.

"What? You told someone where we were going?"

"Only Joan, and she's completely trustworthy."

"Who else could know, then?"

"While you were napping I had a phone call on the house phone from Jim Hackett."

Felicity nearly choked on her Rob Roy. "Then we're blown?"

"Not exactly; the airplane is blown. Jim has a locator on it, and he knew about the house. I told him about it when we visited his place on Mount Desert Island."

"My God," she said, "if Hackett knows where we are, then what's the point in coming up here?"

"To keep Dolce from killing you," Stone said. "Remember?"

"Well, there is that, but if Hackett can find us, maybe she can, too."

"She is not acquainted with Hackett, and she doesn't have the resources to find us. She doesn't even know of the existence of the house here."

"Well, if Hackett knows, then Stanley Whitestone knows."

"We don't know that Hackett is Whitestone, but I have to tell you I have underestimated Jim Hackett. He knows of your people's difficulties in confirming his identity. He knew that you were running his fingerprints."

"That's impossible."

"He told me he's sending a package that will be here tomorrow that will be helpful."

"How could he possibly get a package here tomorrow?"

"That part is easy; Federal Express delivers five days a week."

"He told you he was going to help confirm his identity?"

"I've told you exactly what he said. After all, as he pointed out, he owns one of the largest private security companies in the world; he has access to all sorts of information."

"He knows too much," Felicity said. "If he knows about my running his prints, then there's a leak in my service."

"From what little I know about him," Stone said, "I wouldn't be surprised if he has one or more of your people on his payroll and maybe some CIA employees, too, as well as the FBI and the NYPD. He knew about Dolce's attack on you, and the department is the most likely source of that information."

"Good God! Next, he'll have sat shots of us in bed together."

"I doubt that; Dick's house was built to be very, very secure. He does, however, have a sat shot of his airplane sitting on the tarmac at the airport here."

She made a small moaning noise.

"That's my fault; I could have as easily flown my own airplane, but I wanted to fly the jet." He managed a rueful grin. "I wanted to impress you with my newly acquired skills."

She laughed. "Well, you certainly did that with your landing. Frankly, I thought you were mad."

"No, as part of my training I practiced short-field landings, so I was pretty confident we wouldn't end up in the trees."

"I think you're the most confident man I know," she said, taking his hand across the table.

"I don't always feel that way," he admitted. "Only when I know what I'm doing, which is only some of the time."

"If you were British, I'd be trying to recruit you, just as Hackett is."

"You mean, I'd have to be British to be recruited as a spy? You have a very narrow view of the work of espionage, don't you?"

"Oh, we have an American or two on the payroll, but they're not on the inside, just as you couldn't be."

"It has occurred to me that, if the American government knew what I'm doing for you now, I might be arrested for spying for a foreign government."

"Should I conceal your payment for this job?" she asked. "I can, easily."

"Please don't. I don't think it's treason for me to do an investigative task for you, but if you concealed the source of the payment and someone stumbled on that, well . . ."

"It wouldn't look good, I suppose."

"I'll be sure to declare the income on my tax return, too, and list the source as the Foreign Office."

"That should put a stop to any inquiry," she laughed.

THEY DINED ON filet of venison and drank a bottle of a very good Australian Shiraz, then went home and fell asleep in each other's arms. Stone dreamed that Jim Hackett was downstairs, waiting for them to wake up.

40

They both must have been exhausted, because they slept until nearly noon, showered together, then had a late breakfast that Seth's wife, Mary, prepared. They had no sooner finished than Felicity headed for Dick Stone's little office and sat down at the computers while Stone tagged along.

Felicity typed in a few keystrokes and was connected with a security program that demanded her staff number and palm print. She turned toward Stone, who was standing in the doorway. "I'm sorry. I have work to do." She reached over and closed the door in his face.

Chastened, Stone went into the living room, sat on the sofa and picked up *The New York Times*, which had come over on the ferry earlier. The doorbell rang, and Stone got up to answer it. There was a FedEx truck parked in the driveway and a young woman in a FedEx uniform at the door holding a box emblazoned with the company's logo. "Ms. Felicity Devonshire?" she asked. "I need a signature."

"I'll sign for it," Stone said.

She allowed him to do so and then left.

Stone took the box into the living room and examined it. The sender's address was a Mount Street, London, number. Stone knew Mount Street, because it was where his tailor's shop was located, and the Connaught Hotel was just down the street. Should he open it? He thought not; it was addressed to someone else.

He read the *Times* for an hour and was about to start on the crossword when Felicity emerged from Dick's office.

"Everything all right?" Stone asked.

"Pretty much," she replied. "Is that the package from Hackett?"

"I assume so; it's from a London address in Mount Street, and it's addressed to you, so I didn't open it."

"That's very discreet of you," she said, patting his cheek. "Open it."

Stone pulled the tab, opened the box and shook out a heavy, dun-colored envelope of the sort that British businesses used.

"Open the envelope," Felicity said, resting her cheek against his shoulder, as if she didn't want to touch the package.

"You were expecting a bomb, maybe?"

"If I were expecting a bomb, I would be in another room," she said. "Open it."

Stone ran a finger under the flap and opened the envelope. A thick, brown file folder fell into her lap.

"Don't touch it," she said. "We need latex gloves. I saw some in a drawer in Dick's office. I'll get them." She got up, ran to the office and returned with two pairs. She handed Stone one, and they each pulled theirs on. "Now," she said, "open the folder."

Stone opened the folder and was presented with what appeared to be the Royal Army Reserve service record of one James Hewitt Hackett, aged twenty upon enlistment. A photograph of a young man with a very short haircut was stapled to the upper right-hand corner. The photograph, yellowed with age, appeared to be the twenty-year-old Jim Hackett, whose nose had not yet been broken. "Looks like Jim," Stone said.

"The folder and the paperwork look well aged," Felicity said. "I'll have that checked into. Keep turning pages."

Stone went very slowly through the dossier, finding reports on the initial training of the young Hackett; his marksmanship scores, all of which were at the expert level; his physical training results, which pronounced him fit and fleet; his medical records, including the setting of the broken nose suffered during training, which pronounced him hale; and his annual evaluations by his superiors, which pronounced him of good character and high intelligence. He had been steadily promoted to his final rank of company sergeant, and the dossier included a recommendation that he be sent to Sandhurst and, upon graduation, be commissioned into the Royal Army. The file ended with a copy of a letter from the regimental commander regretting Hackett's decision to leave the army at the end of his enlistment, imploring him to reconsider and, finally, wishing him well in civilian life.

"That's quite a record," Stone said.

"You notice," Felicity replied, "that this dossier and everything in it appear untouched by water, whereas all the other regimental records lie, sodden, in a warehouse in Kent?"

"That seems to be the case," Stone admitted.

"So, if the dossier is genuine, it was removed from the regimental records before they were shipped to Kent."

"Apparently. How long ago were they shipped?"

"That information is as damp as the files themselves," she replied, "but we estimate the transfer as having taken place about twenty years ago, leaving Sergeant Hackett about a five-year window for the appropriation of his dossier, which is, of course, the property of the Royal Army. He could be done for that."

"Surely there's a statute of limitations for such a crime," Stone said, "which doesn't seem of any great magnitude."

"Perhaps there is such a statute, but I assure you, the Royal Army would not look kindly upon such a theft."

Stone picked up the FedEx box to be sure it was empty and then extracted another, folded FedEx box and a sealed envelope addressed to Dame Felicity. Stone handed her the envelope, but she motioned for him to open it. Stone did so and extracted a letter, which he read aloud:

My Dear Dame Felicity,

I hope the enclosed dossier will be of help to you and your people in your endeavors to ascertain my identity. Perhaps you are wondering if it is genuine? It is. Perhaps you are wondering how I came to possess it? Some years after leaving the regiment I visited its headquarters on Salisbury Plain for luncheon, at the invitation of my former colonel. After a good lunch, during which much wine and port were consumed, the colonel took me into the regimental offices, where many boxes of old records were being packed to be sent for storage. He instructed a corporal who was working there to unearth my dossier, which the young man did with dispatch. We then returned to the colonel's office, where he read the dossier to me and then presented it to me as a gift, saying that, since I was now an alumnus of the regiment, they would have no further use of it.

Having read it yourself, and no doubt having copied it into your service files, I would be grateful if you would return the dossier to my New York office in the box and with the FedEx waybill provided, since I hold a sentimental attachment for the history.

Cordially,

The letter was signed "Jim."

"Well, he's right about one thing," Felicity said, standing and picking up the dossier. "It's going to be copied into our files." She went back into the office and closed the door behind her.

41

They packed a lunch, then walked down Dick Stone's dock to where two boats awaited them: a Concordia and a Hinckley picnic boat. "Do you sail?" Stone asked.

"A little as a child, but that's all," she replied.

"Then we'll take the picnic boat," he said, stepping aboard and helping her to follow. He put their lunch in the galley, got the engine started, and Felicity cast them off. They motored slowly past the little Tarrantine Yacht Club and its dock and moorings, then Stone pressed the throttle forward and, with the warm sun on their backs, they ran across the open water of Penobscot Bay to a little cove called Pulpit Harbor, where Stone slowed the thirty-six-foot runabout and, finally, dropped anchor in the sheltered waters. Two other small sailing yachts also were anchored there, but there was room for everyone with privacy to spare.

Felicity went below for a few minutes, then brought up a tray with their sandwiches and soup while Stone opened a bottle of California chardonnay from the little fridge.

"Well," Stone said, when they were munching away, "did the receipt of Hackett's army service record do anything to convince you he is who he says he is?"

"Certainly not," she replied, forking a piece of lobster into her mouth.

"Why don't you get in touch with his old colonel and check out the story about how he got the file?"

"It's being done as we speak," she replied.

"So, if a retired colonel, living in a cottage somewhere in Sussex or Cornwall, declines to admit that he had too much wine at lunch one day and gave one of his old soldiers his own dossier that was about to be stored forever, Hackett is Whitestone?"

"Not necessarily. But if the story doesn't check out, he may not be Hackett, and that's a start."

"God, I'm glad you're not checking into *my* background," he said, laughing.

"What makes you think I haven't?" she asked coyly.

"You didn't; you wouldn't."

"Let's see: son of a West Massachusetts family who did well in the textile business in the nineteenth and early twentieth centuries; father disowned because he had Communist tendencies and chose to follow a career in carpentry and cabinetmaking instead of an education at Yale; mother disowned because she married your father. They moved to Greenwich Village, where your father found work as a handyman, then gradually built a business making cabinets and designing furniture; your mother became a painter of some renown, whose work is sought today in the art market. How'm I doing?"

"Couldn't find anything juicier than that?"

"Not until you left the police, passed the bar exam and went to work for Woodman and Weld. It got a lot more interesting after that. My God, the women!"

Stone reddened. "You're a prying woman."

"I'd be a fool not to be, with a staff of researchers and a curious nature," she said blithely.

"Do you pry so deeply into the backgrounds of all the men you meet?"

"All the ones I sleep with," she said, "before I sleep with them."

"And have you turned up any cads?"

"One cashiered army officer who embezzled his regiment's funds," she said. "One self-styled entrepreneur who turned out to be a bookmaker, haunting the tracks every day, and one murderer."

"Tell me about the murderer," Stone said.

"I had been seeing him for about a year," she said. "I had just turned thirty and had been promoted to a position in my service that gave me access to a great deal of information. There was talk of marriage. He inherited quite a lot of money and a fine country property from his elder brother, who had died in a farming accident, and he proposed. I vetted him and found that he had been a suspect in the death of an elderly aunt in Scotland, and I brought that to the attention of the police. A few days later two detectives arrived at a restaurant where we were dining and took him away, charging him with his brother's murder. It was revealed at the trial that he had driven a tractor over the poor fellow and then harrowed him. Tried to make it look like he'd fallen off the machine and under the harrow."

"And you turned him in?"

"Most certainly," she replied. "I am an upstanding subject of Her Majesty and an upholder of the law. If he'd been acquitted," she added, "I'd have married him. As it was, he got life."

Stone's cell phone buzzed at his belt. He looked at it and saw Dino was calling. "Excuse me," he said, and answered it.

"Hello, Dino."

"Where the hell are you?" Dino asked.

"It's a secret."

"I can find out, you know; I'm a detective."

"Far, far away," Stone said.

"Well, you'd better get your ass back here," Dino replied.

"Why?"

"Because your esteemed client, Mr. Herbert Fisher, has been arrested for the murder of his girlfriend, one Sheila Seidman. My guys say he tossed her off his penthouse; she made a mess on Park Avenue."

"I don't believe it," Stone said.

"I don't know why not," Dino replied. "If she'd been my girlfriend I'd have offed her a long time ago. Anyway, Herbie's back in the tank, and he won't talk to anybody but you. What time will you be here?"

"I'm in Maine, Dino; it'll have to be tomorrow."

"Stay another week, for all I care. I just wanted to give you the message."

"Tell Herbie tomorrow afternoon," Stone said.

"Okey dokey," Dino replied. "Felicity with you?"

"That information is classified," Stone said.

"That means she's with you. It wouldn't be classified, if she weren't."

"You're too smart for me, Dino."

"I always was," Dino replied and then hung up.

Stone put the phone back in its holster.

"So what difficulty has Mr. Fisher got himself into now?" Felicity asked.

"Apparently, Herbie's girlfriend, an unbearable woman named Sheila, a prostitute by trade, has taken a dive from the terrace of his new penthouse, and the squad at the Nineteenth like Herbie for it. I have to go back tomorrow morning and deal with the situation, Herbie having paid me a large retainer to look after him."

"You think he did it?" Felicity asked.

"Let me put it this way," Stone said. "Today is going to be either the worst day or the best day of his life."

42

The following morning Stone was loading their luggage into the 1938 Ford when Mary called to him from the house. "Phone for you, Mr. Stone."

Stone went back into the living room and picked up the phone. "Hello?"

"It's Jim Hackett," a voice said. "When are you planning to return to New York?"

"In a matter of minutes," Stone said. "One of my clients is in a jam, and we're just leaving for the airport. Do you need the airplane?"

"No, no, it's not that. I have a G-550 for long-distance travel; the Mustang is for personal pleasure. I'm calling from the Gulfstream now, on my way home. There are some things I want to discuss with you."

"I'll be in the city by noon," Stone said.

"Then come and see me in my office tomorrow morning at eight," Hackett said. "Where are you staying?"

"In my own home," Stone replied.

"Not a good idea; the crazy lady is still on the loose. The company keeps a suite at the Plaza for important guests. Tell them I sent you, and stay there until it's safe."

"How will I know when it's safe?"

"I'll tell you."

"All right, Jim. See you tomorrow morning." Stone hung up and went back to the car.

At the airport, after a long preflight inspection and a careful reading of the checklist, Stone positioned the airplane at the very end of the runway, did his pre-takeoff check, then shoved the throttles to the firewall while standing on the brakes. When the instruments showed the engines were producing every drop of available power, he released the brakes and the airplane pressed him back into his seat. He kept one eye on the rapidly disappearing runway and the other on the airspeed tape until the little R landed on the pointer, then he put both hands on the yoke and pulled it back until the flight director told him he was at the correct angle for takeoff.

The airplane rose, just as it seemed there was no runway left, and climbed as it had been designed to.

"Well," Felicity said, "it's reassuring to know this little airplane can do that. For future reference."

"I always knew the airplane could do that," Stone replied, "because it's in the flight manual." He climbed to altitude and moved the throttles back to the cruise detent. "By the way, Jim has suggested that, since Dolce is still at large, we stay in his company's suite at the Plaza. That okay with you, or do you want to move into the embassy?"

"I'll stick with you," she replied. "The ambassador's wife drives me mad."

"Good."

"I'm going to need more clothes, though."

"Give me a list, and I'll have Joan pack a case for both of us and messenger them over to the Plaza." Stone used the sat phone to call Joan.

"Did Dino get hold of you?" Joan asked.

"Yeah, I'll go see Herbie this afternoon." Stone gave her a list of what to pack for both of them.

THE PLAZA SUITE had one bedroom and a large living room, both overlooking Central Park. Felicity approved. "No good sniper position out there," she said, peeking through the sheer curtains.

"Are you often the victim of sniper attacks?" Stone asked.

"It's just a standard security concern," she said. "After a while, the handlers get you trained; makes their work easier."

The cases Joan sent over were already in the bedroom, and Stone and Felicity unpacked. Then they lunched on room service, and Stone left Felicity, who was watching a movie on the large TV screen in the bedroom.

HERBIE LOOKED AWFUL, and the orange jumpsuit didn't help. "Where have you been?" he demanded of Stone. "I've been in here for nearly a whole day!"

"I was several hundred miles away when I heard, Herbie. I got here as soon as I returned to town. Now tell me, what happened?"

"It was yesterday morning," Herbie said. "Sheila and I had breakfast in bed, and we were watching some morning TV when we got into an argument about you."

"About *me*?"

"Yeah. This is all your fault."

"Herbie, calm down and tell me what you're talking about."

"You know what I'm talking about, Stone. It was you who insisted."

"Insisted on what?"

"On the prenup."

"Ah, yes. I did insist, didn't I?"

"Yes, you did. So I told Sheila to go and see you about it, and she went absolutely nuts: ranted and raved and started crying. It upsets me when she cries."

"Does she . . . did she cry a lot?"

"Only when I tried to get her to do something she didn't want to do, like not go shopping."

"Or talk to me about a prenup."

"Yeah."

"Did you explain to her that she would need to see her own lawyer?"

"I thought all she needed was you," Herbie said.

"Let me explain this to you, Herbie," Stone said. "It would be unethical for me to represent both of you at the same time, so Sheila would have needed her own attorney. I would have insisted on that had she called me."

"Even if we were going to get married?"

"Especially if you were going to get married. If she had signed a prenup without her own counsel and you later got divorced, she could get the prenup invalidated on the grounds that she was not properly represented."

"Oh."

"Now go on. What happened next?"

"Well, I couldn't stand the yelling anymore, and I said I would talk to her some more about it after I went to the john, and I went to the john."

"For how long?"

"Long enough to read most of a magazine."

"How many minutes, Herbie?"

"I don't know . . . twenty minutes, half an hour. Who's counting? So I got dressed, and when I came out of the bedroom, Sheila wasn't there. I looked all over for her, but she was gone. I figured she was out doing some revenge shopping and she'd be back when she cooled off, so I sat down in the living room to watch some more TV. Then I heard all these sirens, and they would get louder and louder and then stop, like they were in front of the building. So I went out on the terrace—the sliding glass door was open—and looked over the, whatchacallit, the edge."

"The parapet."

"Yeah, like that. And there were a couple of cop cars and a fire truck down on the street, and people were running around. So I went back inside and watched some of *Ellen*. Maybe five minutes later, the doorbell rang, and there were these two uniforms standing there."

"What did you tell them?"

"They asked me if I knew a woman that sounded like Sheila from their description, and I said yes, that sounded like my fiancée. They asked where she was, and I said I didn't know for sure, but I thought she might have gone shopping. Then these two detectives arrived, and they asked me a lot more questions, and I started to get the idea something was wrong. Then they told me Sheila was down on the sidewalk. I ran to the . . ."

"Parapet."

"Yeah, and I looked down, and the ambulance was driving away and the doorman was scrubbing the sidewalk. The four cops all followed me out, and I said I had to go to the hospital. A detective said there was no need to do that, since she was dead."

"Did you tell them about your argument with Sheila?"

"Well, yeah. I told them everything I knew, then they arrested me and took me down here to the precinct."

"Did they tell you why they were arresting you?"

"Yeah, they said for murdering Sheila. Honest to God, Stone, all I did was ask her to go see you."

"Herbie, you said the sliding glass door to the terrace was already open when you went outside."

"Right. Sheila closed it when we came in last night. We were going out to dinner."

"You didn't touch the door?"

"No."

"Do you know when it was last cleaned?"

"Yesterday. The maid came."

"Did you touch the sliding door after the maid came?"

Herbie thought about that. "No. Sheila opened it when we went out there for a drink, and she closed it when we came in."

"Where did you go to dinner?"

"At that place you told me about, Sette Mezzo."

"Did you have a good time there?"

"Oh, yeah. Sheila was in a great mood, which she wasn't always in, but she was last night. We laughed a lot."

"Herbie, during the argument, did you happen to hit Sheila?"

"No, no. I never hit her in my life."

"What was she wearing when you went into the john?"

"Silk pajamas," Herbie said.

"Okay, you sit tight. I'm going to see if I can cut this short, before they arraign you."

"Okay, hurry back."

"I'll do my best," Stone said, and left the interview room.

43

Stone walked up to Dino's office and was waved in and introduced to an attractive young woman who was sitting in one of Dino's chairs.

"This is Carla Rentz," Dino said. "She's prosecuting your client, Mr. Fisher."

Stone sat down and tried to look puzzled. "Prosecuting him? For what?"

"For murder," the young woman replied.

"On what evidence?" Stone asked.

"Mr. Fisher was the only one present when she was thrown off the roof," she said.

"Excuse me," Stone said. "What evidence do you have that she was *thrown* off the roof?"

"Well, she's dead."

"Have you considered suicide?"

"Why should I consider suicide?"

"Because it's one of two possibilities," Stone said. "Either she was thrown off the roof, or she jumped."

"What is her motive for suicide?"

"What is Mr. Fisher's motive for murder?"

"I'm sure that will emerge."

"Well, if a motive emerges, you *may* have cause to arrest Mr. Fisher but not now. Tell you what. Send a couple of Lieutenant Bacchetti's detectives over to a restaurant called Sette Mezzo, on Lexington near Seventy-sixth. Mr. Fisher and Ms. Seidman had dinner there last night. Ask the headwaiter and their waiter what their demeanor was during dinner there. You'll be told that they were very happy, enjoying each other's company. You see, he was in love with her, and they planned to marry."

"If they were so happy, why would Ms. Seidman commit suicide?"

"Anger is a motive for suicide; people kill themselves all the time, because they think it will hurt the people they're mad at."

"You say he was in love with her. Was she in love with him?"

"In my opinion, no," Stone replied. "Ms. Seidman was a working prostitute who had serviced Mr. Fisher on a number of occasions, and when Mr. Fisher won a large sum in the New York State Lottery, her interest in him became more . . . acute, shall we say. And so did the interest of her employer."

"You still haven't given me a motive for suicide," Ms. Rentz said. "Why was she angry?"

"She was angry because Mr. Fisher had asked her to sign a prenuptial agreement. She didn't want to go back to her pimp and tell him that, so she was between a rock and a hard place. I had already spoken to her earlier about a prenup, and she became angry at the mention of it. She was uncontrollably angry before she jumped."

"We didn't find a prenup in the apartment," she said.

"That's because I hadn't given it to Mr. Fisher yet. He asked her to go and see me about it."

"Without her own attorney?"

"I would have insisted on that," Stone said.

"Why didn't you give Mr. Fisher the prenup earlier?"

"Because I've been out of town for a few days, in Maine. I just got back today. My secretary will be happy to give you a copy of the prenup I had prepared." He gave her the address and Joan's name.

"When the detectives arrived, Mr. Fisher feigned not to know that Ms. Seidman had . . . met her death. How could he have missed that?"

"Because he was sitting on the toilet, reading a magazine, when she jumped. When he was finished there, he got dressed and went to look for her, but she was gone. He thought she had gone shopping, because that's what she usually did."

"How can he prove that?" she asked.

"Mr. Fisher will agree to a colonoscopy," Stone replied.

Dino burst out laughing.

"From speaking to Mr. Fisher a few minutes ago, I have reason to believe that your detectives, if they bother to check, will find that Ms. Seidman's fingerprints will be on the sliding glass door to the terrace but not Mr. Fisher's, because he didn't touch it after the maid came and cleaned it yesterday."

"We'll look into that," Ms. Rentz said.

"You may look into anything you like, and my client and I will cooperate with your investigation, but the fact remains that you don't have enough evidence to arraign him, let alone convict him, and the other available evidence will support my client. For that reason, I'd like him released immediately."

"Mr. Barrington has a point," Dino said. "We can always arrest him later if new evidence comes up."

Ms. Rentz looked at the floor, then at the ceiling. "All right," she said to Dino, "spring Mr. Fisher." She stood up and grabbed her briefcase. "But this isn't over."

Stone stood and offered his hand. "Let us know whatever else you need from us."

She shook his hand and left.

"Nice work," Dino said.

"You don't think Herbie tossed her, do you?"

"Nah, but it's good to see you break a sweat."

THE FOLLOWING MORNING Stone was at Strategic Services promptly at eight and was shown into Hackett's large corner office, where the man was polishing off a full Scottish breakfast. He sent the tray away and pressed a button on his phone. "Mike, join us, will you?" He hung up. "You remember Mike Freeman, Stone; we played tennis?"

"Of course."

Freeman entered through a door between his office and Hackett's and shook Stone's hand, and the three men moved to a seating area by the window.

"Stone, we want to give you something of an overview of Strategic Services," Hackett said. "Mike is my right-hand guy, and he's here to tell you anything I forget."

"Shoot," Stone said.

"We're best known for providing corporate security," Hackett said. "We have a dozen offices around the world, and if we get a call from a client telling us he's paying a visit to, say, Hong Kong, our people and vehicles are at the bottom of his jet stair when he arrives to greet him and take care of him while he's there. That service is a big revenue producer for us, and we've never lost an executive yet, not to a kidnapping or a roadside bomb. Sometimes, though, an executive is kidnapped while not in our custody, and in that case we handle negotiations for his release."

Freeman spoke up. "Or, if necessary, send in an extraction team. We employ large numbers of former Special Forces and Navy SEAL personnel, who are very good at that."

Stone couldn't place Freeman's accent, and he must have been looking at him oddly.

"I'm Canadian," Freeman said, smiling. "Montreal, so my English sometimes has a French inflection. You're not the first to wonder."

"Also," Hackett continued, "we provide armed guards to government agencies both at home and abroad. The State Department is an especially good client."

"Do you provide meals and domestic services for the armed forces as well?" Stone asked.

"No, I have no interest in the catering business, even on that scale. We're strictly security. We also have a division that installs security systems in corporate and government offices, the most sophisticated systems in the world. The new HD cameras are just wonderful. We can now use facial recognition software on the images we get from a camera no bigger than a golf ball."

"That's impressive," Stone said.

"Do you have a good security system at home?" Hackett asked.

"Yes, I have an ex-cop who does that work for me."

"Good. Just remember, we're here if you need us."

Hackett continued through the morning, outlining to Stone the depth and breadth of his company, from the armored vehicle business to investigative services. "You may have noticed," Hackett said, "we can find out just about anything about anybody. That is a particularly important service for corporate boards these days, as any hint of scandal in a potential executive's life can turn up on the Internet at any moment."

Finally, they broke for lunch, which was brought in on a rolling table.

"Everything all right for you at the Plaza?" Hackett asked.

"Just perfect," Stone replied. "Thank you for the shelter."

"Eduardo Bianchi is an old friend of mine," Hackett said, "and it distresses me almost as much as Eduardo that his daughter is in such a state."

Stone had been wondering how Hackett had known that he and Dolce had been briefly married, and now he knew.

"Did sight of my service record make any impression on Dame Felicity?" Hackett asked.

"I can't comment," Stone replied, "but it made an impression on me."

AFTER LUNCH, STONE'S briefing session continued until mid-afternoon. Hackett showed him to the elevators. "I'll have an assignment for you before long. In the meantime, the Mustang is there if you need it."

Stone walked back to the Plaza, enjoying the afternoon. At the hotel there was a message from the Assistant District Attorney, Carla Rentz, and he returned the call.

"We've completed our investigation of Sheila Seidman's death," she said, "and I agree that there is insufficient evidence to prosecute Mr. Fisher."

"Insufficient evidence?" Stone asked. "You mean no evidence at all, don't you?"

"All right, all right, no evidence. Her prints, not his, were on the sliding door, and that did it for my investigators. Mr. Fisher is off the hook."

"I'll let him know," Stone said. "Thanks for calling."

"Would you like to have dinner sometime?" she asked.

Stone was stopped in his tracks for a moment. "I have a guest in town at the moment, but maybe in a week or two."

They exchanged cell numbers.

44

The Plaza was boring. Felicity sent to her office for a computer system, and after it arrived at the hotel she was mostly fully occupied while Stone watched old movies on TV and talked to Joan on the phone.

"Herbie came by," Joan said. "He was pitifully grateful to you for getting the murder charge dropped."

Stone sighed. "Well, that's what he pays me for. I thought he was a fool for giving me such a large retainer, but I'm beginning to suspect I'm going to earn every buck."

"Nothing unfair about that," Joan said.

"Seen anything of Dolce?" Stone asked.

"If I had, she'd be dead," Joan replied. "I've been to the range a few times to practice my shooting."

"Please do *not* shoot anybody," Stone said, "not even Dolce."

"Why not?"

"Because it's a lot more trouble than not shooting anybody. Talk to you later." Stone hung up.

Across the room Felicity was just finishing a call. "Well," she said, hanging up, "we found Hackett's old colonel just as you said, at his cottage in Sussex."

"And . . . ?"

"He remembers hosting Hackett at lunch one day and drinking a lot of port, but he doesn't remember giving him the dossier; maintains he was too drunk."

"He admitted being drunk at lunch, but wouldn't admit giving Hackett his dossier?"

"My man believed him about being too drunk," she said. "Looks like we're at a dead end."

"Are you convinced now that Hackett is not Whitestone?"

"Not entirely," she said.

"I think it would be best if we both proceeded on the premise that Hackett is Hackett and Whitestone is dead," Stone said.

"That would be convenient for you, wouldn't it?" she said archly.

"It would be realistic for both of us," Stone replied. "May I now be released from the bondage of your investigation?"

"Not quite," she said. "I still expect you to report any new information that arises from your working relationship with Hackett."

"That would be a conflict of interest," Stone pointed out.

"Not when you took the work at my suggestion, so I could find out more."

"You are a spider," Stone said, "who toys with her victims mercilessly."

"That's an inappropriate metaphor," she said. "I am simply tenacious where my work is concerned. The safety of my country depends on it."

The phone rang, and Stone picked it up.

"It's Jim Hackett."

"Hello, Jim."

"You're in the clear; Dolce appears to have left town."

"How could you know that?" Stone asked.

"We've been watching her bank accounts but, regrettably, not her bank. She went into the head office yesterday and cashed a check for half a million dollars. The manager knew her personally and said she arrived and was taken away in a chauffeured black car. Said she was taking a vacation. When our computer caught the transaction I spoke to the manager."

"Why do you think she left town?"

"Because she bought one-way airline tickets to Hong Kong, Rome, Johannesburg and Dubai, using her credit card, and all those flights arrived before we learned about it. I had each of them investigated, and a woman answering her description was on each flight."

"So she still could be in New York?"

"I think we've made things too hot for her here," Hackett replied. "It seems more likely that she was actually on one of those flights; we just don't know which one."

"So you think it's safe to return to my house?"

"I do. I'll send a car for you."

"Don't bother; I'll take a cab," Stone replied. He thanked Hackett, hung up and reported the conversation to Felicity.

"All right," she said. "If you think it's safe, we'll go. I'll pack and send someone over for the computer."

AN HOUR LATER Stone walked into his house. Everything seemed perfectly normal, and Joan was in her office. Felicity had taken another cab to her office.

"Did you have a nice vacation?" she asked.

"I suppose so," Stone replied.

"Herbie came by again to thank you."

"Don't let him know I'm home, please. I don't want to be thanked again."

"Will you be home for a while now?"

"I believe so; it seems Dolce has left the country." He told her about his conversation with Hackett.

"I don't buy it," Joan replied, "and I'm not letting down my guard." She took the .45 from her drawer and placed it on her desk. The phone rang, and she picked it up. "It's Felicity," she said to Stone.

Stone went into his office and picked up the phone. "Well, hello, there. Long time no speak."

"I've just had a call from London," Felicity said. "My document-recovery people at Camberly have found James Hackett's service record."

"You mean he has two service records?"

"Since no soldier does, I very much doubt it."

"What does it contain?"

"A solid mass of sodden pages, now one."

"So it can't be read?"

"No, it cannot, but there's something else."

"What's that?"

"The photograph attached to the dossier is just barely legible, and it is not the one of the young James Hackett on the dossier he furnished."

"So Hackett is Whitestone?"

"We don't know that."

"You're confusing me."

"That's not surprising, since I am confused myself," Felicity admitted.

"Do you want me to confront Hackett with this information?" Stone asked.

"I don't know yet," she replied. "I've got to think about that. I'll be working late tonight on this, so don't count on me for dinner. If I finish in time, I'll drop by Elaine's."

"Okay, see you there," Stone said. He hung up and tried to sort through everything he knew about Hackett, tried to make sense of it.

It didn't work.

45

Stone joined Dino at Elaine's.

"What's the matter?" Dino asked, sipping his Scotch.

"Why do you think something's the matter?" Stone asked.

"It's obvious," Dino said. "You think I can't read you by now?"

Stone told him about the latest development in the Hackett/Whitestone saga.

"Now I know why you look the way you do," Dino said. "I'm baffled, too."

"So are Felicity and her people," Stone replied. He looked up to see Herbie Fisher walk into the restaurant with a young woman, very pretty, very nicely dressed.

"You see what I see?" Stone asked.

"I do," Dino replied. "I guess the tradition in the Fisher family is abbreviated mourning."

"I guess," Stone agreed.

Herbie stopped by their table. "Hey, Stone. Hey, Dino. I'd like you to meet Stephanie Gunn, with two *n*'s. Stephanie, this is Stone Barrington and Dino Bacchetti."

"How do you do, Stephanie," Stone said.

"I'm very well, thank you. And you?"

"Very well. So is he." He nodded toward Dino.

"Can't he speak for himself?" she asked.

"I'm very well, thank you," Dino said.

"See?" Stone said. "Fully functioning person."

"I'm relieved to hear it," Stephanie said. "I believe I've heard Herbert mention your name, but not Mr. Bacchetti's."

"Dino is hardly ever mentioned by people who know him," Stone said.

Stephanie laughed.

"Well," Herbie said, "if you'll excuse us." He led the girl toward their waiting table.

"What's wrong with this picture?" Stone asked.

"Well, both Herbie and his girlfriend sounded uncharacteristically normal," Dino replied.

"That's it: I'm unaccustomed to that. Maybe Herbie has entered another lucid interval. If so, that's twice it's happened."

"That's a record for Herbie," Dino said. "Do you suppose that having his girlfriend jump off his penthouse terrace to her death has somehow matured him?"

"There were signs of maturation before," Stone replied. "Like when he asked Sheila to sign a prenup."

"I agree, that's unusually sensible of him," Dino said. "Have you talked with Bob Cantor about this?"

"No, Herbie's uncle Bob wouldn't believe me if I told him."

They ordered dinner and were halfway through when Felicity showed up, sat down and ordered a single-malt Scotch on the rocks.

"No Rob Roy?" Dino asked.

"Not tonight," she replied, taking a swig of the pungent liquid. "I need to go directly to the source, without the sugar and fruit."

"I know the feeling," Dino said.

"You look perplexed," Stone said.

"I think that sums up my mood very nicely," Felicity replied, "at least, until I finish this drink and start another one."

"What is driving you to drink?" Stone asked.

"I've been back and forth with my documents people for the past four hours. They've found the photograph of Hackett that was on the file I sent them but not on his own folder; it was affixed to the dossier of one Timothy Timmons, another soldier in the regiment."

"That's a familiar name," Stone said.

"Oh? How?"

"Hackett told me that he had a friend called Tim Timmons, who left the regiment before he did and went to work for a security company. He later persuaded Hackett to leave and join him there. Eventually they both left and formed their own company. Timmons was later killed in some sort of bomb blast, and Hackett got his share of their company."

"That's very interesting," Felicity said, "since it's all we're going to learn about Mr. Timmons."

"Why is that?"

"His dossier was in the same state as Hackett's: sodden. Only the photograph survived." She emptied the glass of Scotch and signaled a waiter for another. "I'm increasingly baffled by all this."

"Let me suggest the simplest explanation," Stone said.

"Please do."

"Some addled clerk in the regimental offices inadvertently stapled the same photograph to two dossiers."

"That's too simple," she said. "He affixes the same photograph to the dossiers of two men who were friends, later business partners? I don't like coincidences."

"Like them or not," Stone said, "they happen."

"There's more," Felicity said. "In addition to faxing my people Hackett's dossier, I snipped slivers from the folder and several pages and had them analyzed."

"And?"

"And they were identical in makeup and age to the folders found in storage at Camberly."

"So the dossier is authentic?"

"Either that or Hackett has gone to a great deal of trouble to make it seem so."

"I gather you're inclined to the latter explanation."

"Well, yes, I am," she said, sipping the new Scotch.

"Felicity," Stone said, "I think there is only one way for you to proceed in this matter."

"And what is that?" she asked.

"Since you are unwilling to accept any evidence that Hackett is Hackett and not Whitestone, you will just have to operate on the basis that they are one and the same. Otherwise, you'll go crazy."

"I may have already gone crazy," she said. "I reported to my superiors this evening that Hackett is very likely Whitestone."

"And you're having second thoughts?"

"And third and fourth thoughts."

"Have you had their reaction to this report?"

"No. They'll read it first thing in the morning, when they arrive at their desks in London."

"And what is their reaction likely to be?"

She pulled at the Scotch again. "I'm not sure," she said. "And I'm very worried about that."

"Are you afraid of what they will ask you to do about Hackett/Whitestone?"

"Yes, very much."

46

Stone and Felicity lay, sweating and panting, in each other's arms. They had awakened at daylight and had made love in various ways until they had both crashed and burned in an overwhelming mutual orgasm.

A noise pervaded the otherwise silent room. Stone frowned; he knew that noise. It was the clanging of an old British telephone, old enough that it didn't have a volume control and, thus, loud enough to play havoc with an eardrum.

"That can't be your cell phone, can it?" he asked.

She sat up in bed. "Oh, yes," she replied. "They control that ring from the other end." She scrambled out of bed and ran naked across the room to where she had left her purse. "It's the sound of a red telephone ringing," she said, digging through her bag. "Yes, Minister?" she said, finally.

Stone could hear the tinny blare of a man shouting from across the Atlantic.

"Yes, Minister," Felicity said. "Yes, Minister." There was a long pause and more blaring. Then Felicity said emphatically, "No, Minister. Most certainly not on the available evidence." She held the phone away from her ear as the shouting resumed.

Stone could nearly understand the shouted words. He was almost certain he heard the word *termination*, but he could not be sure in what context.

"Then I suggest you do exactly that, Minister," Felicity said. "I have one or two other suggestions for you that I may offer at a later date, but you may have my resignation within the hour if that is your wish." She held the phone away again, in anticipation of more loud noises.

This time Stone thought he heard a more placating sound.

"Perhaps we should talk later in the day, Minister," she said, "when we have both had time to consider our positions. Good-bye, Minister." She snapped the phone shut and threw it at her pillow, which was next to Stone.

Stone picked up the phone and placed it on the bedside table next to him. "Come here," he said, raising an arm. She got back into bed and snuggled close to him.

"I knew he would go off the deep end," she said.

"Which minister was that?" Stone asked. "Foreign or home?"

"It's better you don't know," she replied.

"From what little I just heard, I would suspect that your position is stronger than you may have thought."

"Yes," she replied, "he did climb down off his high horse just a bit toward the end, didn't he?"

"I also suspect he has realized that, if he can't get you to do what he wants you to, he has little chance of getting your replacement to do it, either."

"I hope that is true," she said, "but if he digs down deep enough in the dung heap, he'll find somebody who will cheerfully accomplish that particular mission."

"Dare I ask what that mission is?" Stone asked.

"You dare not," she said.

"Because then you'd have to kill me?"

"Ha!" she said. "Finally you've found a situation that fits that cliché."

"You did the right thing," Stone said. "If he sacks you, then you can spend more time with me."

"Yes, and more time with my horses and dogs, too."

"The dogs, maybe, depending on how many you have. I don't think I can house the horses."

"Then you would just have to come and see me, wouldn't you? I'll introduce you to the English country life."

"Would I enjoy it, do you think?"

"You'd be bored rigid, I do think." She explored his crotch with a hand. "Not that there's anything wrong with that."

STONE WALKED OVER to Jim Hackett's offices in something of a quandary. He had two clients whose interests were antithetical to each other's, and he was being forced to choose sides. He did not want to choose sides.

Hackett received him with his usual good cheer. "Coffee?" he asked, waving at a silver Thermos on the table before the sofa.

"Thank you, yes," Stone replied.

"You look tired," Hackett said. "First time I've seen you look tired."

"A little," Stone said, sipping the strong coffee. A large shot of caffeine was what he needed.

"Yesterday you seemed to absorb quickly what Mike and I had to tell you."

"Thank you. I found it extremely interesting."

"This company's activities are a lot to absorb in a single

day," Hackett said, "but you'll have other opportunities to learn more."

"Jim," Stone said, "yesterday you spent a lot of time telling me about the company's personal protection services."

"I suppose I did. Do you require personal protection?"

"No," Stone said, "but I'm afraid you do."

"I don't have even one bodyguard," Hackett said. "I travel alone or with an assistant. The only times I'm guarded are in combat zones, like Iraq and Afghanistan. What do you know that I don't know, Stone?"

"The odd thing is, I don't *know* anything. I only suspect, but I suspect that you should be in a place, at least for a while, where you can see a threat coming from more of a distance than you can on a New York City street."

Hackett crossed his legs and stared out the window at the city skyline. "Felicity has been talking, has she?"

"No," Stone replied, "she hasn't. She's said absolutely nothing. This morning I was privy to one side of a transatlantic telephone conversation, and while I couldn't hear what was being said on the other end, I was alarmed by her reactions."

"Can you tell me any more than that?"

"I don't know anything more than that."

"All right, then," Hackett said. "I accept that. I don't suppose your relationship with Felicity precludes you from offering advice, does it?"

"No, I don't think so."

"Then what would you advise me to do?"

"I believe I would advise you to disappear for a while, to go to someplace—Maine, perhaps—no, some place not known to me, so I can't inadvertently give you away. I think you should abbreviate your communications with this office to the bare minimum or communicate through third parties, and I don't think you should use a cell phone or any landline known to anyone else. I think you should stay indoors, not in view of the sky, and that you should post armed guards around you."

Hackett did not respond for a long moment, then, finally, he said, "It's as bad as that, is it?"

"I hope I'm wrong," Stone replied, "but I believe it is as bad as that."

47

Stone got back to his office and found Herbie Fisher waiting for him. Stone tried not to groan.

"Can I talk to you, Stone?"

"Yes, Herbie. Come on in," Stone said.

Herbie followed him into the office and closed the door behind him.

"What's wrong, Herbie?"

"Nothing's wrong," Herbie replied.

"What did you want to talk to me about?"

"I want you to go to Sheila's funeral with me," Herbie said.

"Why, Herbie?"

"Because I don't want to go by myself. There might be people there who would try to hurt me."

"I'm not a bodyguard, Herbie, but your uncle Bob can have one or two of the retired cops he knows take care of you."

Herbie looked away. "I can't ask Uncle Bob for anything else," he said. "I've asked him for too much over the years, and I've promised him that I'll stand on my own two feet from now on."

"I see," Stone said, searching for a way to turn him down.

"I want Dino to come, too."

Stone brightened. "Tell you what, Herbie, if you can get Dino to come along, I'll go, too."

"That's great, Stone."

"When is the funeral?"

"In forty-five minutes; we've just got time to make it."

"I don't think you can corral Dino that quickly, Herbie."

"He's outside in my car," Herbie said.

Stone was now trapped.

"You can charge me for your time," Herbie said.

Stone sagged. "All right, Herbie." He stood up and followed Herbie out.

"I'll be back in a couple of hours," Stone said to Joan.

Dino was, indeed, waiting in Herbie's Maybach, sipping a Scotch.

Stone got into the back and took a rear-facing seat. "A little early, isn't it?"

Dino shrugged. "What the hell," he said.

"Is there any bourbon?" Stone asked Herbie.

Herbie leaned forward and pressed a button. A lid rose, revealing a small bar. "I'll join you," he said. "Ice?"

"Please," Stone replied.

Herbie poured the drinks and sat back.

"Where's the funeral?" Stone asked.

"At a cemetery in Queens," Herbie said. "My driver knows the way."

"So it's just a burial, not a funeral?"

"What's the difference?" Herbie asked.

"A funeral usually takes place in a church, a synagogue or a funeral home chapel," Stone said. "A burial takes place in a cemetery."

"Oh," Herbie said. "The only funeral I ever went to was my mother's, and that was in a cemetery."

Dino poured himself another drink. "Whatever," he said.

THE BIG CAR drove through the gates of the cemetery, which turned out to be the one that can be seen from the Long Island Expressway, an incredibly crowded forest of stone.

"How did you get Sheila a plot here?" Stone asked. "I didn't think there could possibly be any room here."

"My mother bought it forty years ago," Herbie said. "Sheila doesn't have any family, and I didn't think the plot ought to go to waste."

The car stopped, and the three of them got out. Herbie led the way, and Stone and Dino followed.

Stone tugged at Dino's sleeve. "How the hell did Herbie get you to do this?" he asked.

"He paid me," Dino replied.

"Paid you? How much?"

"That is an indecorous question, under the circumstances," Dino replied. "A woman is dead."

"I feel as though I'm in some bizarre dream," Stone said. "Is this really happening?"

"Seems to be," Dino replied.

The coffin was perched over the open grave, and a man wearing a black robe stood by it, along with another, shorter man in a black suit. Herbie spoke quietly with the robed man and handed him an envelope.

"Shall we begin?" the robed man asked.

"Just a minute," Herbie said, looking back toward the road.

Three men in suits were coming their way, looking uncomfortable.

Stone whispered to Dino. "At least one of them is packing," he said.

"All three of them are," Dino replied, "but so am I."

The three men walked around to the other side of the coffin, all three glaring at Herbie.

The robed man began to speak in Hebrew.

Stone and Dino watched the three men, who continued to glare at Herbie. Dino took his badge out and hung it in the breast pocket of his suit. The three men looked even more uncomfortable but stopped glaring.

Stone had a sudden urge to burst out laughing but controlled himself.

The robed man stopped speaking, stepped back and nodded at the other man, who was apparently the funeral director. The shorter man reached down to the frame supporting the coffin and did something, and the coffin began to lower into the grave. Herbie picked up a little dirt from the pile beside the grave and tossed it onto the descending coffin, then the three men did the same.

"God bless you all," the robed man said, then turned and began walking back toward the road followed by the three men.

Stone, Dino and Herbie gave them a head start, then followed. They got into the Maybach, the robed man tossed his robe into a Toyota and got in, and the three men got into a Cadillac. They all left.

"Who were the three men?" Stone asked.

"The tall guy was her pimp," Herbie replied. "The other two used to be my bookie and my loan shark."

"And who was the guy in the robe?"

"He used to be a rabbi," Herbie said, "but something happened, I'm not sure what. The funeral guy found him. I think Sheila was Jewish."

"That was thoughtful of you, Herbie," Stone said. "I thought the three guys were going to start shooting at one point, but Dino stopped them with his badge. Nice move, Dino."

"It was better than getting shot," Dino replied.

———

WHEN STONE GOT home, a small package had been delivered for him. Inside was a small black box and a note from Jim Hackett:

> *Directions: Go to your master extension—the one that your office phone system is programmed from—unplug your telephone, plug the wire into the box, then plug the wire from the box into the telephone. This will cause all your telephone extensions to be encrypted when you are called from another encrypted phone. Talk to you soon.*

Stone did as instructed.

48

Felicity called late in the afternoon. "Can we meet for dinner somewhere different? I'm gaining weight."

"How about Café des Artistes?" Stone suggested.

"Fine. Eight o'clock? I'll be working until then."

"Good." Stone hung up and asked Joan to book the table.

FELICITY ARRIVED WITH her omnipresent attaché case, and Stone held a chair for her. He ordered them *Champagne fraise des bois*, glasses of Champagne with a strawberry liqueur at the bottom.

"I've heard this place is about to close," Stone said.

"What? Why?"

"The owner is getting very old, and the lease may be a problem, too. It's been here for more than ninety years and has had only two owners."

"How sad."

They both looked at the Howard Chandler Christy murals of

nubile, nude young women greeting conquistadors in a jungle setting.

"Have you noticed," Stone said, "that while the girls have different faces, they all have the same body?"

"I hadn't, but you're right," Felicity said. "I hope someone will take care of them."

"So do I," Stone replied. "What happened today?"

"Today has been devoted to keeping things from happening," she said.

"Any luck?"

"All I've got to fight with is my resignation, and they know that if they accept it I may talk to other people about why." Stone began to speak, but she held up a hand. "And I still can't talk about it," she said.

"If they accept your resignation, then can you talk about it?"

"Maybe."

"So I'll just have to sit on my curiosity."

"All right, I'll tell you some news, but in the strictest confidence."

"Of course."

"The grave Hackett showed you in the churchyard in Maine is empty. That is, there is no corpse or even a coffin or an urn in it. It's not a grave at all, in fact, just a headstone."

Stone sucked in a breath through his teeth. "So Hackett lied to me about that."

"He not only lied to you; he also went to considerable lengths to deceive you by creating a phony grave."

"And phony photographs of a corpse and phony fingerprints."

"Did you notice that there were no fingerprints in the army service record he sent me?" she asked.

"Now that you mention it," Stone replied. "Do your superiors know about all this?"

"Not yet," she replied, sipping her Champagne.

"Are you going to tell them?"

"I haven't decided."

"If you do tell them, are you going to have to resign?"

"Very likely so."

"I wish I knew some way to get you out of this," Stone said.

"Oh, that's easy," Felicity replied. "Just deliver a living, breathing Stanley Whitestone to any British immigration officer."

"Or his corpse."

"If it can be authenticated, and since we don't have any photographs or fingerprints, that will be extremely difficult."

"Whom do we have to convince?"

"Only the foreign secretary, the home secretary and their appointed authenticators."

"Only them?"

"Only them."

"Order dinner," Stone said, handing her a menu, "while I think about it."

They ordered dinner and another glass of Champagne.

"Have you thought about it?" Felicity asked.

"Yes."

"And have you thought of a way to accomplish this?"

Stone sighed. "What I need to do is to speak to Jim Hackett and tell *him* to accomplish this."

"Hackett has already tried and failed, which destroys his credibility in the eyes of my masters."

"There is that," Stone agreed.

"Soon they will begin to erode his company's position in the UK, and eventually they will destroy his business there."

"Does Hackett have important contracts in the UK?"

"Oh, yes."

"Government contracts?"

"A few. Those will go first, then the government will begin to let Hackett's clients know that it would be unwise to continue to engage

Strategic Services, and the fruits of Hackett's labors will wither and die on the vine."

"Perhaps he should be told that," Stone said.

"Perhaps so, though I should be very surprised if he hasn't already thought of it. Will you call him?"

"I can't."

"Why not?"

"Because Hackett has disappeared," Stone replied.

"What do you mean, disappeared?"

"Just that. He's gone, and I don't know where. I doubt if anyone else does, either."

"Then he may have signed his own death warrant," Felicity said.

49

Stone was in his bathroom, brushing his teeth, when the phone rang. He closed the door and sat down on the toilet lid. "Hello?"

There was a sort of scraping noise, and then a voice seemed to come through a long tunnel. "Stone?"

"Jim?"

"Yes. I'm sorry about the quality of this thing, but we're still working out the kinks. When we do, it will be a hot new product for us."

"I can understand you," Stone said. "That's hot enough for me. Can you tell me where you are?"

"I don't think that's a good idea, but you may consider that I am at a sufficient remove to prevent unexpected events."

"How did you travel there?"

"In someone else's transport," Hackett replied.

"That's what I was thinking; they could have tracked your tail number."

"I have reason to believe that I arrived here unnoticed by anyone."

"I'm relieved to hear it, because, I have to tell you, I have even more reason to believe that your life is in danger."

"Is Felicity hunting me?"

"She is the least of your problems."

"Then what has changed?"

"I'm not sure that anything has changed, but I know more now than I did before. I should tell you that your ruse in the churchyard has been uncovered, so to speak, and that if that news makes its way to London the danger will become acute."

"That news has not made its way to London yet?"

"No, but that could change."

"I'm sorry I had to lie to you, Stone, but I did not consider you as much a friend as I now do."

"Let's put that behind us. I believe that your business interests in the UK may be in as much danger as you are."

"I had anticipated that, and I've done what I can to minimize the risk."

"Tell me, Jim, why was there no fingerprint record in the dossier you sent?"

"I don't know; I received it exactly as you saw it."

"And why does your dossier and that of Timothy Timmons bear the same photograph?"

Silence.

"Hello, Jim?"

"I'm still here. I didn't know the two dossiers had the same photo. I assure you that the photo you saw on my dossier was of me. I can't answer for Tim's dossier, because I never saw it. Where on earth did they find it?"

"At a storage facility for old records."

"Was there anything of interest found in it?" Hackett asked.

"What would you expect to be found in it?"

"I've no idea what's in it," Hackett replied, "and I'm very surprised that there would be any interest in Tim's dossier."

"Why not? He was your partner," Stone pointed out.

"I suppose I should have expected that."

"Jim," Stone said, "are you Stanley Whitestone?"

Something like a sigh could be heard down the long tunnel. "Stone, I won't lie to you, but I can't answer that question now. Perhaps later, I don't know."

"Why not?"

"I'm sorry, but you're just going to have to accept that I can't answer you. I'm going to have to go now."

"Jim, is it possible for me to contact you if I need to?"

"No, I'm afraid not. If you have something important to tell me, you'll have to wait for me to call you again. Good-bye." Hackett hung up.

Stone hung up and walked back into the bedroom, where Felicity was waiting for him, sitting up in bed, reading something from her briefcase.

"Who were you talking to?" she asked.

"A client."

"Do clients often call you at this hour?"

"Sometimes. I can't refuse to speak to a client, whatever the hour may be."

"Was it Hackett?" she asked.

"Go to sleep," Stone said, kissing her on the cheek.

She closed the file, put it back into her briefcase, reset the combination lock, then switched off her bedside lamp.

"You're fired," she said. "I hope that will make it easier for you to deal with this."

"Maybe it will," Stone said, switching off his lamp.

STONE WOKE UP later than usual, and Felicity was gone. She had left a note on the bed, saying that she would meet him for dinner at Elaine's.

Stone showered, shaved, dressed and went down to his office, where Helene brought him a light breakfast at his desk.

Joan buzzed him. "Mr. Fisher to see you."

Stone sighed. "Send him in."

Herbie came in and sat down. "It's going very well with Stephanie," he said. "I may have to get you to do a prenup yet."

"Herbie, slow down," Stone said. "You're going to have to learn to restrain yourself sometimes if you're ever going to grow up."

"You think I'm not grown up?"

"Not quite yet, Herbie."

"I want to buy a jet airplane," Herbie said. "I can afford it."

"How much money do you have left, Herbie?"

"A little over ten million."

"You could buy a used jet airplane for around two million," Stone said, "but flying it and maintaining it would cost a lot every month. You'd have to hire a pilot, maybe a copilot, too, depending on which airplane you bought, and when something breaks on a jet, Herbie, it is very, very expensive to repair."

"Oh," Herbie said. "I didn't know that."

"I suggest you explore the idea of first class on the airlines."

"I don't like the airport experience," Herbie replied. "I especially don't like going through security. They always suspect me of something."

"Then join one of the share programs," Stone suggested.

"I've seen those in magazine ads. Which one should I join?"

"I don't have any experience with that, Herbie. I suggest you call, say, three of them, then compare the deals."

"How much does it cost?"

"Again, I don't know, but it will depend on the size of the jet you buy into."

"Okay, I'll look into it," Herbie said, getting up. "I'll tell Stephanie to come see you about the prenup."

"Herbie," Stone said, "tell her *attorney* to call me. Please."

———

IN THE EARLY afternoon, Joan came into Stone's office and handed him a sheet of paper with a number on it. "The bank called," she said. "We received a wire transfer from London in that amount, which is, I assume, your fee from Felicity in dollars."

Stone looked at the number. "I see the dollar is down against the pound," he said, smiling. "First time I ever got a good deal on a currency exchange. Go spend it."

Joan did so.

50

Stone met Dino at Elaine's for dinner, and they were on their second drink before Felicity arrived, looking oddly happy.

"I was going to ask what's wrong," Stone said, "but I suppose, given your mien, I should ask what's right."

"You are very perceptive," she said. "What's right is that I appear to have won."

"I don't suppose you'd care to say what you've won in the presence of Lieutenant Bacchetti," Stone said, nodding at Dino.

"My lips are sealed," Dino said.

"I don't distrust your lips, Dino," Felicity replied, "but forgive me if I talk in riddles."

"Riddle away." Dino went back to his drink and ogled a young woman at the bar.

Felicity leaned in close to Stone. "I've won the argument with my betters."

"Whitestone?" Stone mouthed.

"Have you ever heard of lip reading?" Felicity asked. "And you're facing the window."

"Whitestone?" Stone whispered without moving his lips.

"Yes, that argument," she replied. "I believe the contretemps involving my former colleague has abated, to the point of nonexistence."

"How did you manage that?"

"My hint that I might discuss the situation with those outside my service seemed to do the trick."

"You mean your betters are afraid of being exposed?"

"Exactly. I don't think anyone in my position has ever even hinted at a public discussion of any matter."

"You got their attention, then," Stone said. "I congratulate you. I tried that with the NYPD once, and it got me early retirement."

"I'm too young to retire," Felicity said, "but my betters are not. I think visions of questions in Parliament followed by lurid headlines finally did the trick."

"Should I let my client know?"

"I think you may do so," she said. "Do you know how to reach him?"

"Now that you mention it, no."

"Well, next time he reaches you, then."

"Will do."

"Tell me, did you tell him that his little trick with the cemetery plot didn't work?"

"I can't divulge a conversation with a client," Stone said, "or even that such a conversation has taken place, but I have reason to believe that he is aware that that little jig is up."

"Good. I shouldn't like him to think that he can fool me so easily."

"If I should ever speak to him again," Stone said, "I will convey that thought to him."

"Yes, please."

———

WHEN STONE GOT home, the message light on his bedside phone was blinking. He pushed the necessary buttons to get the recording and heard the now-familiar voice from a barrel.

"A flight plan will be filed for you tomorrow morning for a departure at ten a.m. local," Hackett said. "You may get your routing from Teterboro Clearance Delivery. Pack for two nights." Hackett hung up.

"Was that your client?" Felicity asked from the other side of the bed.

"If it were, I couldn't tell you," Stone replied.

"Well, if you're finished with your telephony, would you kindly devote your attention to me?"

Stone got out of his clothes and did so, taking her in his arms and kissing her.

"I received payment from the Foreign Office today," he said between kisses.

"I'm so glad our business has been concluded," Felicity said, moving his hand to a receptive part of her anatomy, while taking a part of his in her hand. "Is there lubricant available?" she asked.

Stone reached for a bedside drawer and produced a small bottle, squirting it at the appropriate places.

"Much better," she said, moving her hand.

They continued until both of them had achieved a satisfactory conclusion.

"By the way," Stone said before they fell asleep, "I'm going to be away for the next couple of nights."

"I have only a few days left in New York," Felicity said, "so don't be away too long."

THE FOLLOWING MORNING, Stone drove to Teterboro, did a thorough preflight inspection on Hackett's Mustang, then got into the cockpit and started the engines. When he had run through the lengthy checklist, he called Clearance Delivery. The controller gave him a routing that took him north for a few miles, then northeast across Connecticut and Massachusetts and into Maine. To his surprise, his destination was Islesboro, where his own Maine house was.

He got taxi instructions to runway 1, then took off and followed his routing. An hour later he was lined up for landing on the little paved airstrip on Islesboro. As he touched down and began to roll out, applying the brakes, he saw a car parked beside the runway.

He got the airplane stopped, then taxied back toward the car. As he shut down the engines, a window rolled down, and Hackett beckoned.

Stone secured the airplane, then locked it and tossed his bag into the rear seat of the car and got into the passenger seat.

"How are you?" he asked Hackett.

"I'm very well, considering that I'm cut off from all my usual contacts," Hackett replied. "Let's not talk now; I'll devote my attention to driving."

He drove into the village of Dark Harbor and turned toward the Tarrantine Yacht Club.

For a moment, Stone thought he was driving to his own home, but Hackett turned into a driveway a mailbox short.

"Well, this is a surprise," Stone said, getting out of the car before a shingled cottage. "We're next-door neighbors, but from my house I can't see this place for the trees."

"I couldn't go to my own home on Mount Desert," Hackett said, "so I chose your location instead, almost."

"Who would have thought it?" Stone asked, getting his bag from the rear seat and closing the door.

Inside, Hackett directed him to an upstairs room. "I'll see how lunch is doing," he said.

Stone went upstairs, hung his jacket in the closet and unpacked his bag. His room was small but comfortable, and he had his own bath.

Hackett called from downstairs, "Lunch is ready!"

"Be right down," Stone called back.

51

They sat at the kitchen table, where a housekeeper served them a lobster salad, Stone's favorite, and Hackett cracked a bottle of good California chardonnay.

"I have news for you," Stone said.

"Good news, I hope."

"Yes, indeed. You're off the hook."

Hackett stopped eating and looked at him. "The Whitestone thing?"

"That very thing."

"Tell me all."

"It is my understanding that the people in London . . ."

"The home secretary and the foreign secretary?"

"Yes, those people—have called it off."

"Do they accept that I'm not Whitestone?"

"I don't know about that, but I am reliably informed that they have no further interest in you."

Hackett put down his fork and rested his forehead in a hand, his elbow on the table. "Thank God," he said.

"Congratulations."

"I was beginning to think I'd be on the run for the rest of my life."

"Not anymore. Tell me, do you really think that British intelligence has the wherewithal to track you anywhere and cause your demise?"

"Well, they're not the CIA, but they do have a long arm. As you have seen, finding one man is not all that hard, especially if he has as many business interests as I do."

"Somehow I think of them as a smaller, cozier operation."

"Again, compared to the CIA, perhaps they are. But over the years they have built up very good resources. Remember, they were in business before the United States had any kind of intelligence service."

"I suppose so," Stone said, "seeing that ours only goes back to World War II and the OSS."

"Which became the CIA after the war," Hackett pointed out.

"Do they have assassins on the payroll?" Stone asked.

"I should imagine so, though that service would be used rarely enough that they could rely on contract agents."

"Are there really contract assassins in the world of intelligence?"

"Oh, yes," Hackett replied. "I could put you in touch with two or three, should you ever require their services. Not that I have ever used them, of course."

"Jim, from what you and Mike Freeman have told me about Strategic Services, you seem to be running your own private intelligence agency."

"Yes, we are, but not on a governmental scale. And no national intelligence service would have our divisions for manufacturing, like our armored vehicle operation and our electronics section. Just between you and me, those divisions sell to several intelligence ser-vices on a regular basis."

"Things like the telephone scrambler that we've been using?"

"Yes, but we still have a little more work to do on that," Hackett replied. "In a few weeks we should have a prototype with much-improved sound quality on the level of, say, a cell phone."

"I would imagine there would be a big demand for that from the business community," Stone said.

"Indeed, yes. We're already drawing up marketing plans. And it will work just as well on a single hotel room line as on an office system like yours. Also, the final prototype will be smaller than the unit you have."

"I'm impressed."

"Thank you."

Stone took a deep breath and asked, "Jim, are you Stanley White-stone?"

Hackett raised an eyebrow. "Probably not."

"You're not going to give me a straight answer on that?"

"Stone, it might be dangerous to do so, given your connections."

"Dangerous for whom?"

"For Stanley Whitestone."

Stone laughed. "All right, then, if you won't answer that ques-tion, perhaps you'll answer another."

"You can ask," Hackett replied.

"What was this all about? Why would the foreign secretary and the home secretary be so anxious to find and, perhaps, kill a man who left their service a dozen years ago?"

"Didn't Felicity tell you?"

"I'm not entirely certain she knows," Stone said. "If she does, she wouldn't tell me."

"Well, I don't suppose it would do any harm to tell you. After all, you've shown me that you know how to keep a confidence."

"I'm all ears," Stone said.

"Felicity probably didn't tell you that both the foreign secretary and the home secretary, earlier in their careers, had connections with MI6."

"No, she didn't."

"The home secretary, whose name is Prior, had a more informal connection, but the foreign secretary, whose name is Palmer, was actually, for a time, an agent."

"I've never heard that," Stone said.

"And you didn't hear it here," Hackett replied.

"Did they know you—rather, Whitestone—on a professional basis?"

"They did, Palmer more closely, since he worked with Whitestone. They were such good friends that Palmer invited Whitestone down to his place in the country for a weekend on one occasion."

"Sounds chummy."

"Oh, it was. Prior was there, too. He was a parliamentary private secretary to a previous home secretary at that time."

"Does their enmity for Whitestone date to that weekend in the country?"

"I suppose you could say that in that weekend lay the germ of their enmity."

"What happened there?"

Hackett sighed. "All right, here goes. Pay attention. Palmer had a daughter, a beautiful and brilliant girl, who was a doctoral candidate at Cambridge. She was twenty-four."

"How does she come into this?"

"In spite of the age difference, she and Whitestone were drawn to each other, and an affair ensued."

"Are you telling me that this whole business hinges on a May-September affair?"

"It went further than that," Hackett said. "The girl found herself pregnant, as the British like to say."

"And Whitestone was the father?"

"He was the only candidate," Hackett said. He was gazing out the window at Penobscot Bay now.

"Wouldn't he marry her?"

"Alas, he was already married, and a divorce would have taken two years to achieve, assuming his wife was agreeable to the split."

"So what happened?"

"Things became more complicated," Hackett said.

52

They sat quietly for a moment while the housekeeper cleared away their lunch dishes. When she had finished, Stone asked, "Complicated? How?"

"Part of what I have to tell you was not directly known by Whitestone; he figured it out later."

"Tell me."

"Palmer's daughter—Penelope—told Whitestone she wanted to have the child, that she would wait for him to get a divorce and marry her."

"And how did Whitestone feel about that?"

"He was very willing, and he told her so in no uncertain terms."

"Is that what happened?"

"Alas, no. Penelope was terribly frightened of what her father would do if he found out about her pregnancy, and, of course, she could hardly conceal it for long."

"So she had an abortion?"

"Abortion was legal at the time, but she was afraid to go to a clinic, for fear that the gutter press would find out. She knew her father was planning a political career, and she was afraid the news would ruin his chances. He was going to run for a Conservative seat in the district where his country home was. It was a *very* conservative district—with a small C—you see."

"So, what did she do?"

"She had a friend who was a medical student, and she confided in him. He had seen a D & C performed, and even though he had not performed one himself, he agreed to do the procedure. A bank holiday weekend was coming up, and they borrowed a country cottage outside Cambridge. He brought the necessary instruments and performed the abortion on Friday evening, then stayed with her through the night to be sure she was all right.

"The following morning, after she assured him that she was fine, he left her and went back to London to see his boyfriend—he was gay. As it turned out, he had perforated her uterus, and an infection ensued. She grew very ill, and he had not left her with an antibiotic—a stupid omission on his part.

"The boy returned on Sunday evening to find her in extremis. He took her to a casualty ward at the nearest hospital and told the physician there what had happened, but she died later that night. That incident is what informed Palmer's hatred of Whitestone."

"I can understand that," Stone said, "but why is Prior involved?"

"The boy was thrown out of medical school and arrested and tried for manslaughter. He received a light sentence—two years—but, of course, his future as a physician was ruined. Then he was raped and murdered in prison."

"Jesus."

"Yes. I don't believe I mentioned that the boy was Prior's son."

Stone hardly knew what to say.

"So," Hackett added, "there were two bereaved and aggrieved fathers who blamed Whitestone for the loss of their children."

"But he had no part in the girl's decision to seek an abortion?"

"None whatever. He was as stricken as the two fathers. Palmer was his senior at MI-6, and influential. Whitestone left, unceremoniously, and disappeared."

"Is that when Lord Wight came into the story?"

"Yes. Whitestone was a friend of Wight's daughter, a painter, and had previously impressed Wight, who took him in, so to speak. Whitestone took to business very quickly, and the relationship turned out to be very profitable for both of them."

"So why has all this come up twelve years later?"

"Because both Palmer and Prior were later elected to Parliament, and two years ago, with a Conservative victory in the election, both received cabinet posts, Foreign Office and Home Office. They have become the two most powerful cabinet secretaries in this government and, one might say, drunk with power. They were now able to use their positions to avenge the loss of those two young people."

"But first," Stone said, "they had to find Stanley Whitestone, and they enlisted Felicity Devonshire."

"Yes," Hackett said, "but it's uncertain if she ever knew why."

"She knew how serious they were, though," Stone said, "and she did everything she could to stop them."

"How did she, at last, stop it?" Hackett asked.

"I believe she threatened to give someone in the press the story, if it wasn't stopped."

"God, that was brave of her," Hackett said.

"She risked being removed from her post," Stone agreed.

"No, not that; if they'd sacked her she could still have talked to a reporter," Hackett said. "My guess is, had they managed to kill Whitestone, they would have killed her, too."

Hackett picked up the half-empty bottle of wine and his glass. "Come on, let's finish this on the porch; it's such a lovely day."

Stone picked up his glass and followed him outside.

"Oh," Hackett said, "given the favorable course of events, we can return to New York tomorrow morning. I'll fly back with you."

"Fine with me," Stone said, taking a rocker and sipping his wine.

Hackett walked to the porch railing and leaned against it, facing Stone.

Stone looked past him out over the water. It was a perfectly windless day, so much so that the towering cumulus clouds were reflected on the water. The boats in the harbor floated with their mooring lines slack.

Hackett took a sip of his wine. "Something I'd like you to know, Stone: except for that business about the Whitestone grave in the Somersville churchyard, I never lied to you about anything."

Stone was about to reply when there was a noise, a thud, and Hackett made a peculiar jerking motion. He looked down at his chest, surprised, where a hole the size of a golf ball had appeared, then he sank to his knees, dropping his wineglass, and fell forward onto his face. There was another hole, smaller and neater, in his back.

Stone hit the deck, which was splattered with Hackett's blood. He waited for more shots, but none came. He felt Hackett's neck for a pulse, but there was nothing.

With no wind, it was deathly quiet for a moment—then Stone heard an engine start in the distance and raised his head from the floor long enough to see a boat leaving the harbor, seemingly in no particular hurry.

Stone clawed at his cell phone.

53

Felicity was working in her temporary office on Sutton Place when her cell phone went off. "Excuse me," she said to her agent, Smith, who sat across her desk with some files. "Yes?"

"It's Stone. Are you alone?"

"No."

"Get away from whomever you're with, right now," he said.

She took the phone away from her ear. "Smith, will you excuse me for a few minutes? I have a personal call to take." She watched him until he had closed the door behind him and then went back to the phone. "What's going on?" she asked.

"I'm in Maine. Hackett is dead."

She was alarmed. "How?"

"Bullet through the chest—sniper."

"Good God."

"Hackett told me that if they got Whitestone, they'd go after you, too."

"They?"

"Palmer and Prior. Now listen to me very carefully."

"All right, I'm listening."

"Can you get out of your building without being seen?"

"Probably," she said.

"Do you have any cash?"

"A few hundred dollars and some pounds and euros."

"I want you to do exactly as I say," he said.

"Well, maybe. What do you want me to do?"

"I want you to leave your building without being seen, find a cab and go directly to my house. Make sure you're not being followed. You can't trust your own people, so be careful."

"Why do you think I will be safe at your house?"

"You probably won't be for long. I want you to pack a bag and leave the house by the rear door. Walk across the common garden; you'll find a corner exit to the street, one block over. Take a cab to Teterboro, to Jet Aviation, and take a seat in the pilot's lounge, not the passenger lounge. I'll have a man named Dan Phelan meet you there and bring you to me."

"Bring me where?"

"To the place we went where you worried about landing."

"All right."

"Are you armed?"

"I can be."

"Good. Also, go into my dressing room and find my safe, behind a picture." He gave her the combination. "Bring me the little .45, an extra magazine and a box of cartridges."

"All right."

"Any questions?"

"How long will we be there?"

"Not long, I hope."

"I'm on my way," she said. She hung up and buzzed her secretary. "Send Smith back in," she said.

Smith returned and took his seat. She spent ten minutes going through the remainder of the files and then sent him back to his own office with a task to perform. As soon as the door closed she got her coat, took a pistol from her desk drawer, put it into her handbag and left her office by a rear door that opened into a stairway. Moments later, she was in a cab, looking over her shoulder.

STONE LOOKED FOR Dan Phelan's number in his cell phone and then dialed it.

"Phelan."

"Dan, it's Stone Barrington. Where are you?"

"Hi, Stone. I'm at Teterboro. I just finished with a student."

"I have a serious emergency, and there's something I hope you can do for me."

"Shoot."

"Have you flown a JetProp?"

"A couple of times."

"There's a woman on her way to Jet Aviation now. Her name is Felicity Devonshire. She's a tall redhead. Wait for her in the pilot's lounge. While you're waiting, file a flight plan for a little airport in Maine called Islesboro, identifier five-seven-bravo."

"Yes."

"The desk at Jet Aviation has a key. I'll tell them to give it to you. While you're waiting for Felicity, see that it's refueled. Call me just before you start your engine. You have my cell number?"

"Yes."

"I'll meet her at the runway in Islesboro. You'll have enough fuel for the round-trip."

"Okay, got it."

"Send me a bill."

"Don't worry."

Stone hung up and called about the key, then he found the number for the Maine State Police in Augusta and called his old acquaintance, Captain Scott Smith.

"Hello, Stone. How are you?"

"Not well, Scott," Stone said. "I've just witnessed a murder on Islesboro, the house next door to mine. Can you get a team out here?"

"Of course. Tell me about the murder."

"Sniper, firing from a boat in the harbor, I'm pretty sure. Immediately after the shot, the boat motored slowly away."

"Description?"

"Thirty, thirty-five feet, blue or black hull, white superstructure."

"That describes hundreds if not thousands of boats in Maine."

"It seemed to be headed east, but it could have gone anywhere. My guess is there's an airplane waiting for the shooter somewhere, Rockland, maybe, or wherever else is close."

"I'll get an airplane over Penobscot Bay now to look for the boat, and we'll cover the nearby airports. I'm going to chopper over there with my people. I have two men and a car on the island now on another case, so no need to meet us. I'll be there in, say, an hour. Who's the victim?"

"James Hackett, head of Strategic Services. Know the name?"

"Of course. I've heard him lecture on protection operations. How do you know him?"

"He was my client. I'll meet you at the house. At some point I'll have to go to the airport to meet a friend who's flying up in my airplane."

"How did you get there?"

"In Hackett's airplane, a Cessna Mustang."

"I'll see you soon." Smith hung up.

Stone got up off the porch floor for the first time. There was blood on his clothes. He called Felicity.

"Yes?"

"Where are you?"

"Just getting to your house. The coast seems to be clear."

"Phelan is waiting for you at Teterboro. You'll be here in two, maybe three hours. Don't forget my weapon."

"That's the last thing I would forget," she said. "I'm inside the house now and hurrying."

"Keep hurrying." He hung up and called Strategic Services and asked for Mike Freeman.

"Stone?"

"Mike, you know where Jim is, don't you?"

"I can't say."

"I'm with him, and he's dead. A sniper got him no more than ten minutes ago, and I've already called the state police. Can you get into a cab without being seen?"

"I'll try."

"My airplane is at Teterboro, where Jim kept his. Felicity Devonshire is being flown up here. If you get there in a hurry, you can come with her. She'll be in the crew lounge with the pilot, whose name is Dan Phelan."

"Will do."

"Watch your ass—these people may not be finished."

"Will certainly do."

Stone called Felicity and told her to wait for Freeman; then he hung up and looked at Jim Hackett's corpse. It shouldn't have ended this way, he thought.

54

The state police had been there for an hour when Captain Scott Smith came out of the house and onto the porch, where Stone was waiting. Hackett's body was being removed.

Smith held up a small, plastic bag with a slug in it. "This went through Hackett's body, right past your head as you were rocking"—he pointed at the hole next to Stone's chair—"through the exterior wall of the house and ended up imbedded in a plaster wall in the living room."

"Wow."

"It's a 30-06, probably a special load, given the velocity and penetration. A pro's weapon. Who do you think did this?"

"I don't know," Stone said. "Hackett had just begun to talk to me about his situation when he was hit. He was up here because he feared for his life."

"Did he tell you whom he feared?"

"He didn't have time," Stone lied. His cell phone rang. "Excuse me. Yes?"

"It's Dan Phelan. We're rolling with two passengers."

"Thanks, Dan." He hung up. "I have a couple of guests arriving here by airplane in an hour or so; I'll need to meet them at the airfield."

Captain Smith nodded. "Might these people have anything to do with Hackett?"

"One of them, Mike Freeman, works with him, but I don't think he knows anything about this. I talked with him before he got here."

"Be sure you come back here; I'm not finished with you yet."

"All right. We'll go to my house, next door."

"I'll come over there when I'm finished here." He looked Stone up and down. "You might want to change those clothes."

"I'll do that now," Stone said, and then went upstairs. After he showered and changed, he called his caretaker and informed him of guests to come. He put his bloody clothes in the liner of the room's wastebasket and then took it downstairs. "You want these clothes?" he asked Captain Smith.

"Thanks," Smith said, taking the bag and handing it to a subordinate. "Log this," he said. "Mark it 'clothing of the witness.'"

"Have you had any luck finding the boat?" Stone asked.

"No, and no luck with an airplane out of place at any local airfield. If I were the killer, I'd have dumped the rifle in the bay, motored to a cove nearby and anchored for the night, maybe longer. We're not going to find him, unless we get very, very lucky."

Stone packed his bag and put it into Hackett's car, then drove to the airfield. He preferred waiting there to waiting at the house, where he was only in the way. He sat in the car, numb, wondering how this had happened and if the fault somehow lay with him. He didn't see his airplane until it whooshed in over the trees and settled onto the runway. Phelan taxied over to where he was parked and shut down the engine.

Stone opened the airplane's door and helped Felicity down the air stair. Mike Freeman was right behind her, and he shook Stone's hand. Stone went to the luggage compartment and began removing their bags, and Freeman followed him.

"Where's Jim's body?" he asked.

"The police removed it from the house more than an hour ago. It will be on the mainland and on the way to the morgue in Augusta by now."

"Any sign of the perpetrator?"

"I think he was in a boat moored in the harbor, maybe two fifty, three hundred yards away. Not a difficult shot in no wind and with the right weapon, scope and ammo."

Freeman nodded. "Where are we going now?"

"To my house, next door to where Jim was staying."

"I've got a hundred phone calls to make to clients before they hear about this on the news," Freeman said.

"You can use my phone," Stone said.

He shook Phelan's hand and thanked him. Phelan got back into the airplane and started the engine. Driving down the road toward his house, he saw his airplane take off and turn to the southwest.

Stone drove to the house, which Seth, the caretaker, had already opened and where he had made rooms ready. Stone showed Freeman where he was sleeping, then led Felicity to the master suite, her second visit there.

"I gather this Mike Freeman worked for Hackett," she said.

"His number two."

"He hardly said a word from the time we met."

"He has a lot on his mind. I expect he's already phoning clients around the world to tell them what's happened. He has to protect the business now."

She nodded and sat down on the bed. "Tell me what you and Hackett talked about."

Stone laid it all out for her. When he had finished, he asked, "Did you know about the two kids?"

"Yes," she replied. "I remember when it happened, but I didn't know the full story until recently. That's when I threatened Palmer with exposure."

"Hackett predicted that, if they killed him, they'd go after you, too," Stone said, "because they'd be afraid you'd talk."

"I'm about to do that now," she said. "Can I use this phone?" One line was already lit up.

"Yes, use the next line. You're sure you want to do this?"

"The only way I'll know I'm safe is if everybody else knows what I know."

"You may have a hard time proving it," Stone said.

"I don't have to prove it," she replied. "They'll probably never go to prison, but I want it hung around their necks."

"Are you going to resign?"

"No, but I'll bloody well see that Palmer and Prior do. I'll go to the prime minister if I have to."

"I'll be downstairs." He turned to go, but she stopped him.

"Stone, did Hackett admit that he was Whitestone?"

"He wouldn't confirm or deny it," Stone said. "He kept referring to Whitestone in the third person. Still . . ."

"I think he was Whitestone. That's what I'm going to put out. I want an end to all this."

"You would know better than I how to handle it in London," he said. The light went out on the phone. Downstairs, Stone found Mike Freeman talking to Captain Scott Smith, and he joined them.

"You can't think of any business reason why anyone would want to do this?" Smith was asking Freeman.

Freeman shook his head. "I've been going over this in my mind since Stone called me, and I can't see how it could be business-related," he said.

"Surely, yours is the kind of business where a man could make enemies," Smith said, sounding skeptical.

"You'd have to understand Jim," Freeman replied. "He was a

charming man, and he went out of his way to treat people decently, even those who didn't like him. He worked hard not to make enemies."

"How about a competitor? Surely, he would be resented by people who had lost contracts to him."

Freeman thought about it. "I think that, in his early days, he went after business pretty hard, but for the ten years I've been with him, he pretty much sat back and let the business come to him. He was a very popular man."

"Was he married?"

"Divorced, many years ago, in England."

"Has he been seeing someone else's wife?"

Freeman shook his head. "That wouldn't be Jim. He loved beautiful and accomplished women, but they were all single."

"Jealous boyfriend of one of his women?"

Freeman shrugged. "If so, he never mentioned it."

Stone spoke up. "He would have to be a jealous boyfriend who was a pro at this sort of thing."

"Agreed," Smith said. "Should I talk to the lady upstairs about this?" he asked.

Stone shook his head. "She's a friend visiting from London. She wouldn't contribute anything to your investigation." God knows, he thought, that's true.

55

The three of them sat at dinner, prepared by Seth's wife, Mary, eating quietly. Mike Freeman's reticence seemed to affect them all.

"Did you call all your clients?" Stone asked him, in an effort at conversation.

"Just about," Freeman replied.

"How are they taking it?"

"Shock, mostly."

"Did you tell them he was murdered?"

"I didn't have a choice," Freeman replied. "It's probably already on the evening news."

Stone polished off his wine and set down the glass. "Let's go find out," he said, looking at his watch. "It's almost six-thirty."

He led Freeman and Felicity into the living room and switched on the lights and the big flat-screen TV.

"Earlier today," the anchorman was saying, "James Hackett, the head of the worldwide security firm Strategic Services, was shot to death by a sniper at a friend's home on an island in Maine."

There followed an interview with Captain Scott Smith. "We have no suspects at this time," he said, "but the case bears the earmarks of a professional killing."

They watched as various experts were interviewed. All suggested a contract murder. The news show moved on to other stories.

Freeman turned to Felicity. "What about you?" he asked. "Any idea who might be responsible for this?"

"Listen," Stone said, pointing at the TV.

"This breaking news just in," the anchorman said. "A London newspaper is reporting that the director of MI6, the British foreign intelligence service, is charging that Foreign Minister Douglas Palmer and Home Secretary Eric Prior are jointly complicit in the murder of James Hackett. The paper goes on to say that Palmer and Prior believed that Hackett was a former MI6 agent named Stanley Whitestone, who disappeared twelve years ago, and that the two cabinet ministers held him responsible for the deaths of Palmer's daughter and Prior's son at that time. We hope to have more on this before the program's end."

Felicity turned toward Stone. "Can I get to your fax machine in Dick's office?" she asked. "It's late in London; I may have something by now."

Stone unlocked his cousin's little office. Felicity went to the fax machine and came back with a couple of sheets of paper. The head-line screamed:

FOREIGN MINISTER AND HOME SECRETARY
BLAMED BY MI6 IN MURDER OF U.S. SECURITY
FIRM CHIEF

Felicity handed the other sheet to Freeman.

Freeman read it. "And I thought Jim was being paranoid," he said. "He predicted what would happen."

Stone spoke up. "You mean, when he told you about this you didn't believe him?"

"Jim had a way of drawing worst-case implications from any problem," Freeman said. "It worked for him in business a lot of the time, but I'll admit, this sounded a bit far-fetched to me. Obviously, I was wrong."

"You can take some comfort in the fact that he acted on his instincts by coming up here," Stone said. "Have you any idea how the assassin might have located him?"

"I've been thinking about that," Freeman said. "How did he contact you and ask you to come up here?"

"He gave me a prototype of a phone scrambler your people are working on," Stone replied. "I got a call from him last night."

"Then that has to be it," Freeman said.

"You mean a scrambled message was intercepted? Didn't the thing work?"

"It worked between landlines and landlines," Freeman replied, "but I just learned this morning that some cell towers have not yet been equipped with the requisite electronics to scramble every call when one end of the conversation is from a cell phone."

"But how could they intercept a cell phone call from up here? They wouldn't have known where it was."

"They could intercept it from your phone," Freeman said.

"Remember," Felicity interjected, "the foreign secretary knew you were in touch with Hackett."

Freeman looked at Stone. "I don't understand," he said.

Felicity spoke up. "I hired Stone to help find Stanley Whitestone," she said.

"Was Jim Whitestone?" Stone asked.

Freeman shook his head. "I don't know. If he was, he never confirmed it to me."

"Tell me," Stone said, "if Jim were Whitestone, would he have had the resources to establish an identity as Hackett twelve years ago?"

"Yes, but he would have had to establish that identity longer ago than that. Still, he could have done it."

Felicity went to the bar and poured herself a brandy, then went and stood at the window, looking out on the harbor. A big moon was rising as the sun set, illuminating the boats at their moorings.

There was a slapping noise, and Felicity emitted an involuntary shout and fell to the floor.

Stone dove for the light switch, and the room went dark. He crawled across the floor past Freeman to where Felicity lay and turned her over.

"I'm all right," she said. "What was that? There was this noise right in front of me."

Freeman spoke up. "I can see from here," he said. "The window is broken, but it didn't shatter."

Stone crawled out of the living room and found a flashlight in a kitchen drawer. He got down and crawled back to Felicity, then played the light on the broken window. "Good God!" he exclaimed. "There's a bullet stuck in the glass."

"Impossible," Freeman said.

"No, all the glass in this house is armored. The CIA installed it when Dick was building the house." He held the light steady, so Freeman and Felicity could see.

"Well, thank God for the CIA!" Felicity said.

Stone got out his cell phone and called Captain Scott Smith's office and was transferred to his cell.

"Captain Scott Smith," he said.

"Captain, it's Stone Barrington. Our assassin is still out there; he just took a shot at my house. Fortunately, the armored glass stopped the bullet."

"I'll get a chopper over there right away," Smith said.

"Hang on," Stone said. He crawled to the back door and opened it. The sound of a boat's engine could be heard leaving the harbor. He looked outside. "Captain, there's a boat leaving the harbor right now. It's just turning the point, headed south. It's not wearing any nav lights."

"We're on it," the captain said. "I'll call you if we have any luck." He hung up.

Stone stood up. "I think we're all right now," he said, helping up Felicity, who was still clutching her glass of brandy. "You didn't spill a drop," he said.

"Well," she replied, "it's awfully good brandy."

56

It was past midnight by the time the state police had cleared the house. "You folks had better get some sleep," Captain Scott Smith said as he left.

Stone shook his hand and closed the door behind him. "How is everyone?" he asked.

"Wide awake," Felicity replied.

"I'm wired," said Freeman.

"I'm not sure this is over," Stone said. "Why don't we get out of here right now and fly to Teterboro?"

"I'll pack," Felicity said.

"I'll arrange a car to meet us," Freeman said. "And I think you two should stay again at our company suite at the Plaza."

"That's good for me," Stone said.

LESS THAN AN hour later Stone taxied to the end of the short Islesboro runway. He switched on the pitot heat, centered the heading bug and turned on the landing light and strobes.

"Want me to call the speeds for you?" Freeman asked. He was in the copilot's seat, while Felicity sat in the rear of the airplane.

"Please do," Stone replied. He set the takeoff speeds so that they would appear next to the airspeed tape on the primary flight display, then he stood on the brakes and shoved the throttles all the way forward to the takeoff detent. The ribbons on the power display rose and stopped at full power. Stone released the brakes, and the airplane leapt forward.

"Airspeed's alive," Freeman said. "Seventy knots. V1, rotate!"

Stone put both hands on the yoke and pulled it sharply back, and the Mustang began to climb.

"That is a very short runway," Freeman breathed.

At 700 feet Stone pulled the throttles back to the climb detent, switched on the autopilot and turned the heading bug to the southwest. Then he went into the flight plan and tuned in ENE—Kennebunk—their first waypoint, pressed direct, enter, enter and NAV on the autopilot. The airplane picked up the GPS heading for Kennebunk, and they climbed at 3,000 feet per minute into the cool Maine night.

At flight level 330, 33,000 feet, Stone let the airplane gain some airspeed, then pulled the throttles back to the cruise detent. There was nothing more to do until they picked up the Automated Traffic Advisory Service, ATIS, at Teterboro.

"Are you enjoying flying the Mustang?" Freeman asked.

"I am," Stone said.

"Then continue to use it whenever you like," Freeman replied.

"Did Jim plan for a succession?" Stone asked.

"He did. The documents are signed and in the safe in his office. I'll present them to the board in a few days, but as of right now, I'm CEO, and it will stay that way."

"What about you?" Stone asked. "Do you have a succession plan?"

Freeman chuckled. "So soon?"

"As I said, I don't think we're out of this yet."

"There are a couple of younger men, one in London, the other in Johannesburg, who'll be competing for the COO slot."

"How long have you been with Strategic Services?" Stone asked.

"Just passed the ten-year mark," Freeman replied.

"How did you happen to come aboard?"

"Jim hired me to work out of Riyadh, Saudi Arabia. I had spent some time out there, and I had the language."

A little bell went off in Stone's brain, and he remembered the last thing Jim Hackett had said to him before he was shot. "Except for that business about the Somersville churchyard," Hackett had said, "I never lied to you about anything."

Stone looked over his shoulder. The moonlight that was coming through a window illuminated Felicity, fast asleep in her comfortable seat, a cashmere blanket over her. He took a deep breath. "I remember now," he said. "Jim told me about how Lord Wight recommended a man to him, someone with experience in North Africa and the Middle East."

"Yes, that's how I found my way to Jim," Freeman said.

Stone turned and looked at Freeman. "And he told me the man's name." He saw Freeman wince. "Stanley Whitestone, I presume."

Freeman's shoulders sagged. "Can Felicity hear us on the intercom?" he asked.

"No, she's not wearing a headset," Stone replied, "and she's asleep."

Freeman sighed. "I thought that, with Jim's death, I'd be safe. I should have known that someone would figure it out. I'm sorry it was you, Stone."

"So you arranged Jim's death?"

Freeman turned to face him. "I most certainly did not! My, God, I loved the man!"

Stone shrugged. "I had to ask."

"Does Felicity believe that Jim was Whitestone?"

"Pretty much," Stone said.

"Are you under some ethical obligation to tell her the truth?"

"I'm no longer employed by her service," Stone said. "She paid me off and fired me the day before yesterday."

"I think it might be best for everyone if she continued to believe what she believes," Freeman said.

Stone thought about that for a few minutes as they moved through the night at 400 miles an hour. Finally, he spoke. "I concur," he said.

They flew along for another ten minutes without talking. Stone wondered if Freeman had fallen asleep, but then he stirred.

"Since we don't know what's waiting for us in New York," Freeman said, "I think we have to get Felicity back to London, and quietly."

Stone thought about it. "Once again, I concur. How are we going to get her home quietly?"

"Leave that to me," Freeman said. "I think it would be best if you accompanied her."

"I can do that," Stone said.

"Have her ready to go tomorrow night. You'll be picked up at nine at the Plaza. Someone will call your suite and ask if the package is ready for pickup. You reply, 'Not until tomorrow at noon.' He'll give you instructions."

Eighty miles out of Teterboro, Stone tuned in the ATIS and jotted down the information. He loaded the Instrument Landing System for runway 19, and as soon as he was handed off from Boston Center to New York Approach and got his first vector, he activated the approach. He got graduated instructions to descend to 3,000 feet and was cleared for the approach. His was the only airplane on the air at that time of night.

The Mustang's autopilot flew the airplane down the ILS, and Stone made one of his better landings. Shortly, they were in a Mercedes headed for Manhattan and the Plaza.

57

Stone woke a little after nine and ordered breakfast sent to the suite's living room, leaving Felicity to sleep. He showered, shaved and dressed, then went downstairs and got a taxi.

He was dropped off in the block behind his house and entered the Turtle Bay Gardens through the rear entrance, then walked to his own back door and let himself into the kitchen. Helene was surprised to see him. "I think Miss Joan has someone waiting to see you," she said.

Stone grabbed a mug of coffee and went into his office. Joan buzzed him immediately. She always seemed to know when he was there. He pressed the button.

"Yes, ma'am?"

"There's a Mr. Smith to see you," she said.

"Send him in." Stone wondered what Captain Scott Smith was doing in New York.

"I'm going to the bank," Joan said. "Be back in a few minutes."

Stone was about to reply when his office door opened, and to his surprise, the little gray man from Felicity's office walked into the room, closed the door behind him and leaned on it. "Oh, you're *that* Mr. Smith," Stone said.

"Where is she?" he asked.

"Where is who?" Stone asked back.

"Dame Felicity. Where is she?"

"She checked out of here the day before yesterday," Stone replied, "and she didn't leave a forwarding address. I assumed she'd gone back to London."

Smith unbuttoned his jacket and introduced a Walther .380 to the conversation. It was equipped with a silencer. "I'll ask you just once more," Smith said quietly, "and if I don't get a satisfactory answer I will shoot you in the head."

Stone rather believed him. "I will give you the only answer I have," he said, "and hope it will be satisfactory. She is back in London at her office, her home or her country house."

"That is entirely unsatisfactory," Smith said, raising the pistol and pointing it at Stone's head.

"Would you like to have a look upstairs?" Stone asked. "I suppose she could be hiding in a guest room."

"Never mind," Smith said, and thumbed back the hammer on the pistol.

As he did, Stone heard the doorknob turn, and the door struck Smith hard in the back, knocking Smith to his knees. Herbie Fisher walked into the office, rubbing a shoulder, and held Joan's .45 to Smith's head, while he relieved the man of his pistol. "Joan wasn't at her desk," he said, "and you left your intercom on, so I heard what this guy had to say to you. Do you want me to shoot him?"

"Not yet, Herbie," Stone said. "Before you do, I'd like to ask him some questions. Mr. Smith?"

"May I get up, please?" Smith asked.

"You may not," Stone replied. "I like you on your knees. Now, why have you come here looking for your boss with a gun?"

"She is no longer my boss," Smith replied. "She has been sacked by the foreign minister."

"Which foreign minister is that?" Stone asked.

"The British foreign minister, you twit!" Smith said.

"Name?"

"Palmer!"

"You don't watch TV or read the papers, do you, Smith?"

"Sometimes."

"Well, when you get out of jail, you might read up on what's been happening at home," Stone said. "Herbie, do you think you can render Mr. Smith unconscious without fracturing his skull?"

"Sure," Herbie said, and he swung the barrel of the .45 at the back of Smith's neck. Smith collapsed in a heap.

"Thank you, Herbie," Stone said.

"Any time, Stone. Who the fuck is this guy?"

"I've no idea," Stone said. "See if he has a wallet or a passport."

Herbie went through Smith's pockets, came up with both and handed them to Stone, who put them in a desk drawer. Then Stone picked up a phone and called Dino.

"Bacchetti," Dino said.

"Morning, Dino. A strange man just walked into my office with a silenced pistol and threatened my life."

"Okay, what's the punch line?"

"No joke. Fortunately, Herbie Fisher happened in and made him go to sleep. Do you think you could haul him away and let him stew in your very excellent drunk tank for two or three days?"

"I don't see why not," Dino replied. "I'll be right over." He hung up.

Stone hung up, too. "Herbie, did I mention how very glad I am to see you?"

"No, you didn't."

"I am very glad to see you. That little man was about to put a round in my head."

"I'd better put Joan's .45 back in her drawer; she's fussy about it." Herbie walked down the hall toward Joan's office, then returned.

Stone's phone rang, and since Joan was out of the office, he answered it. "Stone Barrington."

"Mr. Barrington?" a woman's voice said. "I was expecting Joan."

"She's out at the moment."

"I have Mr. Bianchi for you." There was a click on the line.

"Hello, Stone?" Eduardo said.

"Yes, Eduardo. How are you?"

"I am greatly relieved," Eduardo replied. "Yesterday, Dolce landed in Palermo and was recognized by some acquaintances of mine who happened to be at the airport."

"Happened to be at the airport?"

"At my request," Eduardo replied. "In any case, she is now sequestered in a safe and comfortable place, and is no longer a threat to you or anyone else."

"I'm very happy to hear that, Eduardo," Stone said.

"I wish to apologize for any inconvenience she may have caused you. I saw to the hospital bill of the gentleman she, ah, perforated and reached an immediate settlement with him, so he will not be a bother to you."

"Thank you again, Eduardo."

"If you will forgive me, I am rushing off to a board meeting."

"Of course, Eduardo."

"Come and have lunch in a couple of weeks. I'll call." He hung up.

Stone hung up, too, relieved.

Dino walked into his office, followed by two burly detectives. "This the guy?" he asked, indicating Smith, who was awake now and trying to get up. The two detectives helped him, and one of them introduced him to handcuffs.

"That's the guy," Stone said. "I've no idea who he is or what he wants, but he did point that gun at me."

Dino took the Walther from Herbie with two fingers. "This Walther?"

"The very one."

"Check him for ID," Dino said to the detectives.

"Nothing on him, Lieutenant," one replied.

"My name is Smith," Smith said.

"Sure it is," Dino replied. "I'm Jones."

"I have a British diplomatic passport," Smith said.

"Well, just show it to me and we'll forget this ugly little incident," Dino replied.

"It's in my inside coat pocket," Smith said.

"No it ain't," a detective replied.

"I had it when I came here."

"You had this gun when you came here," Dino said, "and we frown on that in New York, unless you've got a permit."

"He ain't got a permit on him," the detective said.

"And we don't issue permits for silencers," Dino pointed out.

"I protest!" Smith said.

"You go right ahead, but do it quietly," Dino said, "or somebody will put you to sleep." Dino made a motion with his head, and the two detectives dragged Smith, still protesting, out of the office.

"Okay," Dino said to Stone, "who is he?"

Stone took Smith's wallet and passport from his desk drawer and handed them to Dino. "One of Felicity's," he said, "who has turned unfriendly. Can you lose him for a couple of days?"

"Sure," Dino said. "Elaine's tonight?"

"I have to leave town, but I'll be back soon. I'll call."

Dino left, and Stone turned to Herbie. "What's up?"

"I wanted to invite you to my wedding."

"When is it?"

"The day after tomorrow, at the Pierre. It just reopened after a big renovation. Stephanie's parents live there."

"I'm sure it's very elegant, Herbie, but I'll be out of the country tomorrow."

"Maybe next time?" Herbie asked.

"Sure, next time. Put me down for it."

58

Later that day Stone packed Felicity's remaining bag and one for himself, then walked through the garden to the street and found a cab.

He walked into the Plaza suite to find Felicity parked in front of the TV, watching MSNBC. "Hey, there," he said, kissing her on the neck.

"Good afternoon," she said tonelessly. Her eyes never left the TV.

"I had an encounter with your minion, Smith, this morning."

She turned and looked at him for the first time. "What sort of encounter?"

"One reinforced with a silenced pistol. I believe he intended to use it on me, because I wouldn't tell him your whereabouts, but Herbie Fisher interrupted him. God bless the boy."

"Where is Smith now?"

"In the drunk tank at the Nineteenth Precinct."

"Dino?"

"You betcha."

"How long will he be incarcerated?"

"Since he doesn't have any identification, probably two or three days. Has Smith gone off the reservation?"

"Either that, or I have."

"He seemed to be laboring under the misapprehension that Palmer has sacked you."

"At least one of your television networks seems to be laboring under the same misapprehension," Felicity replied. "Something has gone horribly wrong, and I don't know what it is."

"Don't make any phone calls," Stone said.

"Do you think I'm mad?"

"Certainly not."

"I may be able to fix this once we're back in the UK," she said.

"*May* be able to?"

"I don't know what's going on," she said. "The afternoon papers in London didn't carry the story. I'm beginning to think that the Official Secrets Act may have been imposed."

"The one I signed?"

"One and the same. The PM can impose it, and nobody can report the story."

"What about the American afternoon papers?"

"Nothing there, either. There was a piece in *The New York Times* this morning reporting Hackett's murder but few details."

"You hungry?" Stone asked. "They're not coming for us until nine; we have time to order some room service."

"Please. I'd like a steak, medium rare, and a baked potato laden with whatever they have to offer. Wine, too."

Stone ordered the same for both of them and a bottle.

Felicity turned down the volume on the TV but left it on. "I believe I'm being sought on both sides of the Atlantic," she said, "and I won't survive being found."

"Why do you think that?" Stone asked.

"Your Smith story, for one thing," she said. "He's a fairly timid man, and he wouldn't be pointing guns at you, unless he'd been so instructed. I think that, if I'd been there, he'd have shot me."

"Then your government has turned on you," Stone observed.

"Some of my government, at least: that part of it who are afraid of Palmer and Prior."

"And where is the PM in all this?"

"That remains to be seen."

"Are you going to be safe in London?"

"As long as no one knows I'm there," Felicity replied. "Or everyone."

DINNER ARRIVED, AND they dined in front of the TV, but the only new story was one saying that a morning London paper had gotten the story wrong, that Palmer and Prior—or the two P's, as the press called them—were still in their offices. Stone, not understanding all the ins and outs of current British politics, was baffled, but Felicity didn't seem inclined to explain things to him. She was obviously thinking hard.

At a quarter to nine the phone rang, and Stone picked it up. "Yes?"

"Is the package ready for pickup?" an unfamiliar voice asked.

"Not until tomorrow at twelve."

"A bellman will come for the luggage first, then someone will come for the two of you."

"All right." The line went dead. Five minutes later the doorbell rang, and Stone saw a uniformed bellman through the peephole. He opened the door, allowed the man to retrieve their luggage from the bedroom, tipped him and closed the door.

At nine o'clock the bell rang again, and a check of the peephole revealed a man in what appeared to be an airline uniform with a raincoat over his arm and a large bouquet of flowers in his other hand. Stone opened the door.

"Mr. Barrington?"

"Yes."

"I'm Don Quint, the first officer for your flight." The man handed him the raincoat. "There's a folded hat in the pocket. Please put them both on."

He turned toward Felicity. "Dame Felicity?"

"Yes."

He walked over and handed her the flowers. "If we encounter anyone, anyone at all, on the way out, please hide behind these."

She accepted the flowers, and the two of them followed the man down the hallway, away from the main elevators. They took a service elevator to the ground floor, which opened into a kitchen, then followed the man through a scullery and out into East Fifty-eighth Street, where a black stretch Mercedes with darkened windows awaited.

The man in the airline uniform opened the rear door for them and relieved Felicity of the flowers. Then he got into the front passenger seat.

Mike Freeman was already in the car, sitting in a jump seat. "Good evening," he said, and the car drove away. "Take the tunnel," he said to the driver.

"Thanks for your help, Mike," Stone said.

"I'm happy to be of service," he replied. "I think you should both know that something odd has happened in the reporting of this story in London."

"We noticed," Felicity replied.

"Then you'll know that it seems to be quashed and that the government has resumed the appearance of normalcy."

"Quite."

"What are your intentions on arrival?" he asked her.

"I haven't entirely decided," she replied. "I assume we're going to an airplane."

"Yes, at Teterboro. It's our company jet, a Gulfstream 550."

"May I assume it has a satellite phone aboard?"

"Yes, and a high-speed Internet connection. Both numbers are blocked, so no one you call or e-mail will know where the transmissions are coming from."

"Very good. I'll make my arrangements in the air, then."

"As you wish. You'll be landing at a general aviation field southwest of London, called Blackbush."

"I know it," she replied. "Good choice."

"A car will be waiting to take you wherever you wish to go. Stone, the airplane will wait for you at Blackbush to return you to New York. If you find you'll be in London for more than forty-eight hours, please call me at this number, and I'll make arrangements for your return whenever you wish." He handed Stone a card.

"Thank you, Mike."

They were through the tunnel now and on the way to Teterboro. When they arrived at the airport, they were driven through an opened gate to the airplane, which sat on the tarmac, its engines already running.

"Your baggage is aboard," Freeman said, getting out of the car and having a look around. "Let's do this quickly."

Stone and Felicity were out of the car in a second, and in another, up the stairs with the door closed behind them. They were greeted by a uniformed flight attendant, and the man they had traveled with was in the copilot's seat. In a matter of half a minute, they were taxiing.

The flight attendant showed them to their seats. "My name is Nancy White," she said. "Please take your seats and fasten your seat belts. The captain would prefer it if you kept them loosely fastened after takeoff." As they taxied, she showed them the controls for television and music, and indicated a laptop, which could be used for e-mail. "There is a private cabin aft with twin beds," she said, then went forward and buckled herself into her own seat.

A moment later the engines spooled up, and they were rolling, then flying. Half an hour later, when the screen on the bulkhead showed that they were well east of Long Island and at flight level 510, another uniformed woman left the cockpit and walked back to where Stone and Felicity sat.

"Good evening," she said, "I'm your captain, Suzanne Alley." She was tall and quite beautiful. "We'll have a nice tailwind tonight and clear weather. We should arrive at Blackbush at nine a.m., local time. Is there anything I can do for you?"

Stone resisted an affirmative reply. "Thank you, Suzanne. I don't think so."

"Nancy will take good care of you," she replied. "Let her know if you'd like some dinner." She returned to the cockpit and closed the door behind her.

Nancy returned. "Can I get you anything?" she asked.

"I'd like a glass of Champagne," Felicity said, "and a telephone."

"Certainly," Nancy said, and she brought both.

Felicity was still on the phone when Stone went aft to the private cabin, removed his jacket, loosened his tie and quickly fell asleep on one of the compact beds.

59

As soon as the airplane rolled to a full stop and the engines were cut off, Nancy had the door open. Stone and Felicity, freshly showered and dressed, came forward to where Captain Suzanne Alley awaited them at the stairs. She handed Stone a card.

"Please call me when you know your return plans, and we'll be ready," she said.

Stone thanked her, and slipped the card into his pocket. He and Felicity descended to a waiting Bentley Arnage and were driven away.

"Do you want to tell me what you're going to do?" Stone asked.

"No," Felicity replied. "If I recount my plan to you, just hearing it might cause me to . . . What's the American expression? Chicken out?"

"That's it," Stone said. "Come to think of it, I'd rather not know."

As they approached the airport gate, Stone saw a television van with an antenna on top and two other cars waiting there, and they fell in behind the Bentley.

The driver lowered the glass partition and asked, "Excuse me, madam, to what address would you like to be driven?"

"To Number Ten Downing Street, please," Felicity replied.

Stone looked at her askance, but she said nothing.

AT NUMBER TEN the prime minister's secretary knocked on the door of the Cabinet Room.

"Come!" a voice growled.

The man opened the door and stepped in. "Please excuse me, Prime Minister," he said, "but we've had rather an odd report from Blackbush Airport."

"What is it?"

"A Treasury officer, who was arriving there by aeroplane, called to say that he is certain that he saw Dame Felicity Devonshire alight from a jet and get into a chauffeured car."

The PM's eyebrows shot up. "And where did she go?"

"The man is following in his own car, and he says her car was met at the gate by several members of the media, and she seems to be headed for Whitehall, should arrive in about twenty minutes."

"Call the foreign minister and the home secretary and tell them I want them here *now* and to use the rear entrance, through the garden."

"Yes, Prime Minister."

THE BENTLEY DROVE past Buckingham Palace and down the Mall, through Admiralty Arch and past Trafalgar Square to Whitehall, where it came to a barrier at the entrance to Downing Street. Felicity put down her window and offered her identification to the policeman on guard there. "They're with me," she said, hooking a thumb in the direction of her media escort.

They pulled up in front of Number Ten, and another police officer opened the rear door.

"Just a moment," Felicity said to Stone. "Let's let our friends get into position."

Half a minute later, cameras were pointed at the Bentley, and Felicity got out, signaling to Stone to follow. Lights were switched on.

"Dame Felicity," a woman with a microphone said, "what is the occasion of your visit to Number Ten today?"

"I'm here at the invitation of the prime minister," Felicity said, "and I'm sure he'll tell me when I am inside." She brushed past the cameras with Stone in tow and flashed her identification to the policeman guarding the front door. "The gentleman is with me," she said. He rapped sharply on the door, and it was opened wide. The PM's private secretary was waiting in the foyer.

"Good morning, Dame Felicity," he said. "The prime minister is expecting you in the Cabinet Room."

Felicity didn't even slow down, and another minion barely got the door open for her in time. She swept into the Cabinet Room with Stone close behind. Three men sat at the long table, and they stood as she entered.

"Good morning, Prime Minister," she said, ignoring the other two. "May I present Mr. Stone Barrington, of the New York law firm of Woodman and Weld, who is present as my legal adviser. And as my witness."

The three faces fell a bit as Stone pulled out a chair for Felicity, then took one for himself.

"Prime Minister," Felicity said, "would you prefer the foreign minister and the home secretary to be arrested in the garden, away from cameras, or here in the Cabinet Room?"

"Arrested?" the man on the left asked.

"Those are the alternatives," she replied.

"Prime Minister," the man said, "the home secretary and I insist on being present for this . . . conference."

"All right," the prime minister said, "what is the purpose of this meeting?"

Felicity managed a tight smile. "The purpose is for you to accept the resignations of these two . . . *gentlemen*," she said.

"On what charge?" the foreign minister demanded.

Felicity ignored him. "These two persons, having failed to press me into their service, have taken it upon themselves to directly order the assassination of an American citizen, Mr. James Hackett, formerly a British subject and a member of the Paratroop Regiment, in the belief that he was responsible, some years ago, for the deaths of, respectively, their daughter and son."

"Can you substantiate that?" the prime minister asked.

"Mr. Barrington, here, was in the company of Mr. Hackett at the moment of his death from a sniper's bullet, having heard the whole story from Mr. Hackett. I am advised by the police of the state of Maine that, late last night, they arrested the assassin aboard a boat in the environs of Penobscot Bay and that he is helping them with their inquiries."

The prime minister went pale. "I knew nothing of this!" he stammered. "Palmer? Prior? What have you to say?"

Prior was speechless, but Palmer didn't miss a beat. "Prime Minister, Mr. Prior and I will have nothing to say until we have had an opportunity to avail ourselves of counsel."

"Very well," the PM said. "I want both your resignations on this table within the hour, and your resignations from Parliament to the speaker of the House before the day is out. Get out, both of you, and through the garden."

The two men rose and left.

"Well, now, Felicity," the PM said, "was it absolutely necessary to deal with this matter in this manner?"

"I'm sorry, Prime Minister," she replied, "but since those two had also ordered my death, I thought it best to go to the top before they were successful. Would you like my resignation now?"

The PM threw his hands up. "No, no, of course not," the man replied. "You are invaluable to me."

"Then, if you will excuse me, Prime Minister, I will return to my offices. I've clearly been absent for too long." She stood, and the prime minister leapt to his feet.

"Do you really expect me to have them arrested?" he asked.

"That has already been seen to, Prime Minister," Felicity replied. "The director of the Metropolitan Police and his officers met them in the garden."

The prime minister seemed to sag. "Good day to you, Dame Felicity, Mr. Barrington."

Stone followed Felicity out of Number Ten and into the Bentley. She paused for a moment to advise the media to look to the PM for a statement, then got into the car and gave the driver another address.

Stone heaved a sigh of relief and mopped his brow.

A FEW MINUTES later, with Felicity still on her phone, the car was waved through a pair of discreet iron gates and into a small turn-around and then stopped before a pair of large black doors. A man in a severely cut suit waited under a portico.

"Pop the boot, please," Felicity said to the driver. Then she turned toward Stone. "Thank you so very much, Stone."

"Are you going to be safe now?"

"Never safer," she said. She kissed him and got out of the car while the man in the suit held the door. He closed it firmly behind her.

"Where to, Mr. Barrington?"

"The Connaught Hotel," he said, digging out his cell phone and calling for a reservation. What the hell, he thought. He might as well visit his tailor and see some friends while he was here. Then he had another thought. He fished Captain Suzanne Alley's card from his pocket and dialed the number. He didn't see why he should spend his evening in London alone.

Anyway, if he went straight back to New York, he'd have to attend Herbie Fisher's wedding.

ABOUT THE TITLE

I have cheerfully stolen the title of this book from a friend, the distinguished Atlanta attorney Robert Steed. Bob has published several collections of short humor, one of them called *Lucid Intervals*. After reading it, I told him I admired his title and would, one day, steal it.

"Feel free," Bob replied. (As an attorney, he knew that a title cannot be copyrighted.)

The day has come. Just to confirm things, I called him at his law office, as I had heard that he might have died; his secretary told me he was on vacation in Mexico. Since this did not sound like a euphemism for dead, I left a message for him.

On his return from Mexico, Bob called, and I declared my intentions with regard to his title. "Send me a copy," he said.

I have done so.

AUTHOR'S NOTE

I am happy to hear from readers, but you should know that if you write to me in care of my publisher, three to six months will pass before I receive your letter, and when it finally arrives it will be one among many, and I will not be able to reply.

However, if you have access to the Internet, you may visit my website, at www.stuartwoods.com, where there is a button for sending me e-mail. So far, I have been able to reply to all my e-mail, and I will continue to try to do so.

If you send me an e-mail and do not receive a reply, it is probably because you are among an alarming number of people who have entered their e-mail address incorrectly in their mail software. I have many of my replies returned as undeliverable.

Remember: e-mail, reply; snail mail, no reply.

When you e-mail, please do not send attachments, as I never open these. They can take twenty minutes to download, and they often contain viruses.

Please do not place me on your mailing lists for funny stories, prayers, political causes, charitable fund-raising, petitions or sentimental claptrap. I get enough of that from people I already know. Generally speaking, when I get e-mail addressed to a large number of people, I immediately delete it without reading it.

Please do not send me your ideas for a book, as I have a policy of writing only what I myself invent. If you send me story ideas, I will immediately delete them without reading them. If you have a good idea for a book, write it yourself, but I will not be able to advise you on how to get it published. Buy a copy of *Writer's Market* at any bookstore; that will tell you how.

Anyone with a request concerning events or appearances may e-mail it to me or send it to: Publicity Department, Penguin Group (USA) Inc., 375 Hudson Street, New York, NY 10014.

Those ambitious folks who wish to buy film, dramatic, or television rights to my books should contact Matthew Snyder, Creative Artists Agency, 9830 Wilshire Boulevard, Beverly Hills, CA 98212-1825.

Those who wish to make offers for rights of a literary nature should contact Anne Sibbald, Janklow & Nesbit, 445 Park Avenue, New York, NY 10022. (Note: This is not an invitation for you to send her your manuscript or to solicit her to be your agent.)

If you want to know if I will be signing books in your city, please visit my website, www.stuartwoods.com, where the tour schedule will be published a month or so in advance. If you wish me to do a book signing in your locality, ask your favorite bookseller to contact his Penguin representative or the Penguin publicity department with the request.

If you find typographical or editorial errors in my book and feel an irresistible urge to tell someone, please write to Rachel Kahan at Penguin's address above. Do not e-mail your discoveries to me, as I will already have learned about them from others.

A list of my published works appears in the front of this book and on my website. All the novels are still in print in paperback and can be found at or ordered from any bookstore. If you wish to obtain hardcover copies of earlier novels or of the two nonfiction books, a good used-book store or one of the online bookstores can help you find them. Otherwise, you will have to go to a great many garage sales.